Trace Their Shadows

Trace Their Shadows

Ann Turner Cook

Mystery and Suspense Press
San Jose New York Lincoln Shanghai

Trace Their Shadows

Mystery Writers of America Presents
an imprint of iUniverse, Inc.

For information address:
iUniverse, Inc.
5220 S. 16th St., Suite 200
Lincoln, NE 68512
www.iuniverse.com

ISBN: 0-595-20410-4

Printed in the United States of America

To my husband, Jim,
who always believed I was a writer

To my friend Marie Claire Anspaugh
for her valuable editing assistance

To Dr. Edgar W. Hirshberg,
professor emeritus of the University of South Florida,
and his Life Enrichment Center Creative Writing class,
and to the Tampa Writers Alliance
for their help and encouragement

ONE

1^{990}

Brandy O'Bannon looked up at the dormer windows, shrouded in Spanish moss, not because she believed in ghosts ——she was open minded on the question——but because a good ghost story could save her job on the paper.

"People say a woman's face appears on the top floor," she said from her seat in the pontoon boat. "At night they see a figure gliding along the shore."

John Able stepped to the bow and picked up the end of a precisely coiled line. "You talk like you believe such stuff."

With an effort she kept her tone light. "The origin of the story interests me. Isn't it true a woman disappeared here almost fifty years ago?"

"Something like that may have happened." John glanced back at her, frowning. "You must be a romantic. Think all old houses are haunted. In your interview, don't mention that notion. My great–aunt's a sensible woman." He reached with a boat hook for a piling. Brown water slapped the metal pontoons. "It upsets her. Starts gossip. I certainly don't want to annoy her now."

Brandy fell silent. The ghost story was the main reason she had come. If the old lady would talk, Brandy could write about a mystery in an historic house facing demolition—a story to prove her talent.

Able knelt and looped a clove hitch around the weathered post. At the motion a cormorant lifted from the water, flew to the roof of the ruined boat house, and spread its black wings in the dying sunlight.

She remembered her editor's words. No initiative, Mr. Tyler said. Not aggressive enough. When she helped on the county news beat, he said her stories lacked spark. Next week when the regular county reporter advanced to the Leesburg daily, Mr. Tyler would ask someone to replace him. He wouldn't choose Brandy——unless she hooked him with this feature.

She steadied herself on the small table behind the captain's chair and smoothed down the skirt of her modest sun dress, an apricot print that set off her blue eyes and blended with her amber bob, a dress suitable for a summer call on a seventy–year old great–aunt. "I have to show my editor I have a nose for news," she said.

John Able helped her through the boat's aluminum gate and onto the splintering planks of the pier. "I invited you here for one reason, O'Bannon. To explain to the public why we need to save the house."

They started across the pock–marked lawn beside a chain link fence that separated the house from a new development. "Don't be such a skeptic. After all, a woman vanished here. Maybe her spirit didn't."

He gave her a withering look. "In architecture we deal with certainties. Spatial relationships. Geometry. Not some vague something no one can verify. There's plenty of history here. You don't need to fall back on the haunted house cliché. I didn't invite the *National Inquirer*."

Mathematics suited him, she thought, noting the sharp planes of his young face, his creased pants, his neatly trimmed mustache. A tin soldier really. No spontaneity. And no curiosity.

Above them the gray frame house loomed like a neglected monument, its copper roof tarnished, its walls almost bare of paint. It rose a full four stories, a long narrow box, taller than the dark heads of the cypress and cabbage palms, a solitary shape against the late afternoon sky.

Together they climbed a curving stone staircase and halted on the porch before a pair of ornate doors with peeling paint. Over the spikes of saw palmettos in the next lot, Brandy could see a bulldozer among the piles of upturned earth, could smell the rotting Florida water lilies uprooted on the bank. John punched the bell. "I only hope I'm not too late."

She would help John Able if she could, Brandy told herself, but she would also dig for facts, even disagreeable ones. She had angled for this interview, dreamed of a journalism career through high school and college. She would not be intimidated now.

She looked up at John. "Are all architects so interested in old houses?"

"In the first place, I haven't qualified as an architect yet. But I am interested in Florida vernacular——early homes like this one. It's a hundred years old."

"Your great–aunt must hate the thought of losing it," Brandy said as the door opened.

Sylvania Langdon was, like her house, surprisingly tall. All of her growth must have gone into that remarkable upward thrust, leaving little extra flesh for her arms and legs. She peered down through silver–rimmed glasses with eyes that were gray and piercing.

"I came right after work," John began. "Like I told you on the phone, I brought a reporter who's interested in writing about the

house. Brandy O'Bannon, with the *Tavares Beacon*." Brandy
squeezed out a smile. Sylvania would know her paper was a free
weekly, picked up in most Tavares stores, and she felt skewered by
that dour gaze. John did not seem to notice. His attention was
focused on his great–aunt. "I'd like to talk to you about your
plans to sell the house."

Brandy edged over the threshold, while the older woman gave
her a thin–lipped nod.

Although John had mentioned his great–aunt's age, Brandy
would not have guessed seventy. With straight back and brisk
step, Sylvania led them into a wide hallway, past the staircase, and
toward a window capped with a crescent of blue and red glass.
Here they turned under an archway into a long, dim room that
once would have been called a parlor. The heat was oppressive. A
floor fan stirred the stale air around a fireplace, two faded uphol-
stered chairs, a mahogany secretary, and a shabby couch flanked
by piecrust end tables.

Brandy thought of the ghostly shape that was supposed to
brood at the fourth floor window, then sweep down the long
stairs.

Sylvania stopped at a fireplace below the portrait of a stern
faced man and looked directly at John. "I hear you got your
degree last month in architecture. I suppose you're one of those
preservationists. Want me to restore the old place."

Brandy looked up in surprise. There was no regret in the older
woman's voice. "No one says where the money would come from
for a new roof or plumbing. Not to mention air conditioning."
She pulled a handkerchief from a sagging pocket and wiped perspiration from her forehead. "My friend Mr. Blackthorne offered
to rid me of this burden, and I'm grateful. He's due here directly."

John moved toward her, his dark eyes earnest. "The house qual-
ifies for the National Register. Someone's got to start preserving

Lake County's heritage, or it will all be gone. Your buddy Blackthorne's throwing up manufactured homes cheek to jowl. There won't be any natural shoreline left." He lifted his arms in a sweeping gesture. "Yours is the only house around here built in the last century."

Sylvania drew herself up. "And what do I use for money after I move? How do I buy into a retirement home?"

"Let me look for another buyer, Aunt Sylvania." His hands came down, palms up. "Let me see if I can't find someone——a group, maybe——that would buy the house and restore it. You can still get rid of it. Just don't sell to someone who's going to knock it down."

Brandy reached into her shoulder strap bag for her note pad and pen, her eyes on Sylvania. Yesterday afternoon she had heard John Able mention the house at a county commissioner's reception. She'd approached him then, said she'd like to write a story about the history of the house, maybe dredge up a sympathetic buyer among Lake County preservationists. Surely that showed initiative.

Sylvania was not wavering. "I know you're quite the scholar, young man," she said, "but you don't get top marks in understanding. I'm old enough to do as I like, and I've already taken the best offer. The matter's settled." She lowered her long body into one of the chairs and followed Brandy's glance to the portrait above the fireplace. "My brother, Brookfield Able," she said. "I inherited the place from him."

The effect of the portrait was hypnotic. Sylvania's brother, a powerfully built man with a heavy black mustache, stood with a shotgun in one hand, the other on the head of a black and white bird dog, and stared out over the room with an imperial gaze. Brandy compared Brookfield Able's portrait with his grand-nephew. The high cheekbones were similar, but the younger man had a slimmer build and his eyes were not as harsh. Pity he had no imagination.

"I'm not giving up," John said. "Please don't sign anything until I've made some calls."

Brandy sank down next to John. "Would your brother have wanted the house torn down, Mrs. Langdon?"

The old lady had a regal look, in spite of her unkempt white hair, shapeless smock, and black oxfords. She turned to Brandy. "Brookfield was not a sentimentalist. He lived here only a short time in the nineteen–forties, when he was first married. Long enough to build a hideous boat house and do some remodeling. But Grace didn't like being this far out of town. The house made her——"she hesitated "——squeamish. After they moved out, my husband and I stayed here to take care of the place, though Elton never liked the house either."

She looked down at Brandy's jottings and clasped long, thin fingers together in her lap. "Elton and Brookfield worked together in the family citrus business. After Brookfield's death two years ago, I inherited the house." She paused for a fraction of a second. "I wound up living out here alone. I don't plan to any longer. And that's an end of it."

People in Tavares said no one could live in the house for long, no one but Aunt Sylvania. Something about the atmosphere. Now she was throwing in the towel. "Aren't there any heirs who care about the house?"

She shook her head. "None of us except John's daddy and granddaddy had children." For a split second she paused again. "I talked to Brookfield about the house before he passed away. I know what he valued, and it wasn't this property. I've always followed his wishes."

Outside the summer sky was growing darker. Brandy leaned forward, fingers tight around her pen. John had made his fruitless pitch. Now she wanted her story. "Mrs. Langdon, I plan to write a history of the house."

Sylvania's expression softened. "Family history is my special interest."

Brandy glanced at John. He touched his mustache and raised his eyebrows, but she remembered that reporters must be forceful and plunged ahead. "I want to ask a few questions about the tragedy that happened here. I'm sure you know people think this house is haunted. There must be a reason."

Tilting her head back, Sylvania clenched her fingers and briefly closed her eyes.

"The ghost is supposed to be the figure of a woman," Brandy said. "What really happened here almost fifty years ago?"

Sylvania stiffened as Brandy dated the interview on her note pad——June 7, 1990.

John stood, strode to one of the small side windows, his hands in his pockets, and looked out at the gathering dusk, plainly irritated. But to Brandy, her story was more important.

Two

"I need facts," Brandy said, pen poised. "If the house is going to be torn down, we ought to set the record straight."

Sylvania gestured with one big hand toward a bookshelf with two periodicals, *The Florida Genealogist and The Journal of the Florida Genealogical Society.* "Check with the Lake County Historical Museum in Tavares about the house. It was built out in the country for safety, after a fire burned half the town in '88. Later on, the family used it mainly as a hunting and fishing lodge. You'll find a book at the museum about Tavares pioneers. My granddaddy was also named John Able. A Director of the Tavares Citrus Growers' Association."

Her voice hardened. "But as for those other stories ...Some silly people started tales after the war. World War II, of course. A girl drowned in the lake here. She was foolish and went in alone." Sylvania looked down at her fingers, now locked in her lap. "We've never done much swimming here. There are 'gators, of course, and heavy weeds. But the young people *would* go in sometimes. We had a house party here that weekend. We were all celebrating the end of the war and Brookfield's homecoming. It happened at the end of the second day, when everyone was leaving." She shifted in the chair. "A hired girl saw the young woman wade into the lake. She drowned before anyone could reach her."

Brandy scribbled a few lines in the tattered notebook. "How sad! Is she buried in a local cemetery?"

Sylvania arched her long neck. "That's probably what caused the stories. Everyone searched for days but they didn't recover the body. The sheriff's office didn't have the expert divers they have now." She rose suddenly and crossed to a window, her voice lower. "The water is very dark around the cypress, you know. It was late in the day when she went in, rather like it is now. And of course, 'gators very rarely *kill* people, but, I'm sorry to say, they *are* scavengers."

John moved toward his great–aunt. "You don't have to answer any questions you don't want to. I didn't mean the subject to come up."

"When the party was over," Brandy interrupted, why would this woman go into the lake by herself?"

Lines around the older woman's mouth tightened. "No one knows. She simply disappeared into the water." Downstairs the door bell jangled. Her face brightened. "Lands, that must be Axel now."

As Sylvania hurried into the hall, John turned on Brandy, furious. "Now she's in a hostile mood. She'll think I put you up to this."

Brandy bit her lower lip. Her ploy had been a tad questionable but productive, and she had never really promised not to ask about the missing woman. "Sorry, but I am a reporter."

A shaft of light slid across his face. The muscles in his jaw tightened. "You're quite the little manipulator, aren't you?" He sat down on the couch again, arms folded. "So you just wanted to see the house. Maybe put a nice story in the paper, maybe interest a buyer?"

Brandy shrugged. Reporters had to be callous. "Also I need a human interest angle. The *Beacon* comes out four times a month. Who's to care about a little ghost story?"

"Two families," he said between his teeth.

Brandy ignored his remark and scribbled a few more notes. "Are Sylvania and her husband separated?"

John rubbed his forehead and looked away. "Sounds like it," he said. "Uncle Ace always spent a lot of time in town. Now he's finally pulled up stakes. I can't blame Aunt Sylvania for wanting to move. It's lonely out here."

Below, the door opened and Brandy heard a heavy tread in the hall. In a few minutes Sylvania swept back into the room with the developer, a stocky figure in an open-necked sport shirt, a brief-case in one large hand.

"My old friend, Axel Blackthorne," Sylvania said, seating herself beside the fireplace. "He bought the land to the west. He wants this lot, too."

Blackthorne extended a hand to John, a sapphire and gold ring glinting on one chubby finger. Across his bald head several strands of grey hair lay in moist arcs.

"I'm a grand-nephew," John said. "I came to talk to Aunt Sylvania about a national register plaque for the house. It'd be a shame to see it torn down."

Blackthorne sat with a thump in the remaining easy chair and mopped his ample forehead. He spoke softly through widely spaced front teeth. "Sorry, young man. But Mrs. Langdon agreed to a deal last week. The lake front development is well started. After all, the house is falling apart, and we've offered your aunt a very fair price." He smiled.

His great-aunt turned from Blackthorne to Brandy. "This is a friend of John's. A Miss O'Bannon." Her voice took on an edge. "A reporter for the Tavares weekly."

The developer bobbed his head in Brandy's direction, then leaned purposefully toward Sylvania. "I came by, Syl, to drop off some papers." He took a folder from his brief case and laid it on the nearest end table. "I'll see you again next Saturday, and we'll get the contract for the house out of the way."

He heaved himself out of the chair and hesitated in front of Sylvania. "Before I forget, we've had some pilfering on the building site next to your lot. At night mostly. We've put up a chain link fence, but I've got guard dogs to patrol after working hours. We'll keep the gate between your place and our property locked and give you an extra key." He set a padlock key down with the papers.

Sylvania stood to see him out, her tone firm. "I don't go out at night, Axel."

Before the builder followed her, Brandy saw him take a furtive glance up the darkened stairway. Brandy and John sat in frigid silence, listening to the older couple's voices recede.

When Sylvania strode back into the room, John rose. "There's not much time, but maybe by next weekend I can find someone who'll make a better offer. Someone who'll restore the house. I know a couple of architects who care about the county's historic buildings."

Sylvania remained standing, her back rigid. "I greatly doubt you can. I've told Axel I'd sign the contract when it's ready next Saturday. And that'll be the end of it."

Brandy followed John and his great–aunt into the hall. "I'll be in touch again, too," she said, dropping her card on a side table. "I'll probably have some more questions after I check out the historical museum. And I'm still interested in the woman who disappeared."

Outside a light wind rustled the cypress and cabbage palms. On the porch Brandy turned again to Sylvania. "Do you ever see or hear anything unusual yourself? The sightings are supposed to appear in the top floor window and then down by the boat house."

"I don't use the top floor," Sylvania said sharply. "And you heard me tell Mr. Blackthorne I don't go outside at night. I especially don't go near that old boat house. I don't allow anyone else near it, either. And not just because it's about to fall down. I worry more about cottonmouth moccasins than I do about spirits."

She stared down at Brandy. "I should add, young lady, that I don't want to see any publicity about what I've told you today. Dredging that story up again would be unpleasant for the drowned girl's family and for ours. Stick to the building of the house and its early history. The death of that poor girl is something everyone has tried to forget."

That's just the trouble, Brandy thought. Sylvania stood for a few seconds, her angular figure silhouetted in the doorway, and then closed the door. Without looking at Brandy, John thrust his hands in his pockets and started toward the pier.

Brandy followed across the sandy grass. "I pity the dead girl. No one cares what happened to her."

"For God's sake, it was a long time ago."

Blackthorne's two black Dobermans trotted beside the chain link fence, watching them. Beyond the dock the lake stretched for a mile and a half until it vanished into shadowy trees on the opposite shore.

John stamped across the broken planks. "My objective isn't to irritate Sylvania. Don't expect me to bring you out here again."

Unfortunately, Brandy thought, she probably would need to come. "As soon as Mrs. Langdon sells the house, some reporter is going to ask about the ghost. It might as well be me."

Grudgingly, John offered his hand when she stepped onto the boat. "It's already Monday. Damn!"

Brandy moved past the polished console before the captain's chair and slumped down on the rear seat. All the usual gear on the eighteen foot Lowe had been neatly stowed away. This guy was orderly and rational, probably why they had started out, ghost–wise, on opposite sides.

John settled behind the wheel, turned the key, and runnning lights winked on at the bow and stern. "Whenever I can, I come out and just drift," he said, backing the hull away from the old boat house and the smell of rotting water lilies in the next lot. "Watch the cormorants and herons and egrets. Maybe do a little fishing."

Brandy stared into the tannic stained water around the knotted cypress roots. Her lit degree often surfaced at odd moments. "That missing girl, pulled down to muddy death, like Hamlet's Ophelia." John nodded from the captain's chair. At least he understood the reference, even if he had the curiosity of a department store mannequin. Her current boyfriend would have thought Ophelia was a yellow–flowering ground cover.

Briefly Brandy wondered if Mack would help investigate the ghost story. She had known him since high school, an iron–pumping jock with an Atlas build and a daddy who owned a Buick agency near Leesburg. Mack got his thrills from his two hundred horse outboard, not from fishing and bird–watching. He'd rather crouch on water skis behind his Bowrider with Brandy at the wheel and a wide open throttle. Not exactly the skills he would need to stake–out a ghost. Still, she couldn't expect any more help from Sylvania's grand–nephew. She would have to ask Mack.

Sighing, she tucked her bulging bag, the only untidy object on the deck, under the table. "Was your great–uncle very rich?"

John glanced back and lifted one eyebrow. "Very. Citrus. Brookfield and his wife. Both families had miles of groves south of here. He was the big success of his generation."

"It's strange about the house. Not keeping it up, I mean. I still want to see if anything funny goes on around there at night."

A blue heron flapped down and roosted on the sagging boat house roof. From one side came the hoarse grunt of an alligator. The animals were settling down for the night. Brandy looked back at the tall, silent house. A solitary light burned on in the crescent window. "I wonder who the missing girl was," she said, "and what happened to her body? The 'gator theory sounds pretty thin to me. Surely someone would find something eventually."

As they drew away from the fringe of cypress knees, a bone–white sliver of moon rose in the east. Brandy leaned back against the vinyl seat for the dark, two mile ride to the dock in Tavares. At least, she had made a beginning. Showed some initiative. Maybe been a bit aggressive. The first thing a real reporter would do, she said to herself, is look up the old newspaper reports.

THREE

At eight the next morning Brandy nodded to the advertising clerk at a cluttered desk in the Tavares Beacon's reception area and paused before the secretary's desk. "Did you find the clipping I wanted?"

The fifty–year–old woman bobbed a wavering pile of lacquered hair. Customers and staff often judged her by her coiffure and one inch fingernails, a mistake. She knew more about the paper than anyone except the editor himself. "Got it right here, sugar." She opened a drawer, laid a column of newsprint on the desk top, and tapped it with a crimson nail. "*Leesburg Commercial.* Ran about a year ago."

Brandy put the story from the larger county town in her notebook, crossed to the editorial room, and set her bag next to a laptop computer, gathering her courage. Six weeks ago she had graduated from the University of Florida, ambition at full tilt. The let–down came when she had to launch her career at a weekly that shared a building with a strip shopping center, a shoe repair shop, a recycled clothing store, and a unisex hair salon. In mostly rural Lake County, journalism jobs were scarce.

Would her critical new boss buy the Able mansion story? Brandy's main task was to help cover courthouse and city hall. But

the fight between developer and preservationists and its background ghost story should jog Mr. Tyler's interest, even catapult
her into one of the full time reporter positions, the county news
beat.

When the article actually appeared the house would surely be
sold. Then John Able shouldn't care. Brandy stiffened her back
and rapped on the editor's door.

Irritable Mr. Tyler, who had retired from a respectable northern
newspaper, barely tolerated his job on a throw–away weekly. At
least once a month he threatened to resign, but the extra income
had become addictive, and he didn't want another stressful job on
a big daily.

As soon as Brandy stepped into the room, he sat forward,
clasped his forehead with one thin hand as though exasperated
beyond endurance, and with the other stabbed out the butt of a
cigarette. "Have you forgotten to cover the Chamber of
Commerce referendum meeting? It starts in thirty minutes. I suppose you want to ask a favor."

He cocked his narrow head to one side. "The new city council
candidate interview is at 1:00 P.M. And you haven't forgotten the
cookie fund–raiser at the library, I hope? You ought to be able to
handle that one."

Brandy ignored his tirade. "Not to worry, Mr. Tyler. Every story
is on my calendar. I'm out of here in five minutes." She gave him
her most beguiling smile. "But you *are* perceptive. I do need a
favor. I've stumbled onto a great human interest feature." Show
initiative, she thought. He ought to like that.

He straightened up, eyes wide in mock astonishment. "Miss
O'Bannon, you were hired to help out with county stories. We're
not the *Leesburg Commercial*. Readers pick up our rag to clip
coupons and see what's listed in the yard sales. And maybe to read
about local events the *Commercial* skips.

Like a partner in a conspiracy, she lowered her voice. "But it's a ghost story, Mr. Tyler. A story about a grand old Lake Dora home, the old Able mansion. It's about to be demolished in the interest of progress. Or maybe in the interest of profits. A ghost of almost fifty years is about to be evicted. Now isn't that a story?"

Behind his glum expression Brandy caught a flicker. She handed him the column. "I remembered reading this when I was home last summer. High school kids out in a boat spotted the ghost on the Able property. According to this, there have been rumors for years. The *Commercial* column gives a name. A witness."

He wagged his head. "Some columnist hard up for an idea used a bunch of impressionable youngsters."

"But wouldn't it be fun to scoop the *Commercial*? Everybody loves a ghost story, and everybody will hate to see the old home go. People would pick up more papers. Surely that would make our advertisers happy."

He raised his eyebrows and drummed the desk with one finger. "I'll make a deal," he said at last. "I don't want to throw cold water on your first story idea. But your other assignments have to be nailed down and copy–ready before you tackle anything else." He shoved a manila folder of notes toward her. "And you have, let's see…" He consulted his desk calendar. "This is Tuesday. You only have until next Monday. Sorry. Then someone's got to take over the county news beat." He leaned back. "Let's see what you can do." She had won, but she felt a tightness in her chest. He would consider her——if she didn't fail.

Mr. Tyler's pale eyes locked with hers. "Do this mansion story with interviews and observations, well–documented. No mystical baloney, just facts. I want to know who, what, when, where, and how. And check with me every morning. We'll need you on other stories, too. Our clients are mainly interested in county business."

"You got it." She picked up the bulging folder. "I bet you'd love to one–up the *Commercial.*"

He looked down at the papers on his desk, but she could see his tiny smile.

Seymour Hammond was the name the *Commercial* columnist gave for the witness. A half hour on the phone to nearby Mount Dora located his mother. "Seymour's home from college for the summer," the woman said. Her voice rose and sharpened. "Why would a reporter want an interview?"

More manipulation needed, Brandy thought. The boy's mother mustn't be apprehensive. "We're considering a story about summer jobs for college students," she said, and told herself Mr. Tyler might okay one.

The woman's voice warmed. "That would be great. Seymour works nights at the Burger King on Route 441. He'd love to find something, well, more genteel." Brandy left her name.

Mid–morning at the Chamber of Commerce meeting she heard architect Curt Greene argue for a lands acquisition and protection program. Most Lake County developers like Blackthorne would fight a voter referendum. John Able had his job cut out for him. The only citizen to speak up for preservation was a lakeside restaurant owner. His Irish pub in Tavares benefited from the view.

A nervous city council candidate backed off the environmental issue, but Brandy raised her own morale with chocolate chip cookies at the library bake–off contest, and returned to the office to type her stories. A telecom system would transmit them to Mr. Tyler's screen for his often caustic editing.

At four she nosed her '84 Chevrolet hatchback——the major purchase of her young life——west on her missing woman mission, through heavy traffic along the narrow arm of land that separates three large lakes. Here Florida's native live oaks and cypress had been replaced by eight miles of billboards, gas stations, strip shopping centers, and the Buick and General Motors dealership where Mack Lynch worked for his father.

When Brandy spotted Mack's big Sierra pickup in the rear, she pulled into a parking space. Through the plate glass window she could see his muscular form in a chest–hugging polo shirt, tipping back a coke can in the air– conditioned display room. It was a sight that excited most of the female population of Tavares. When he saw her, his square face broke into a wide grin and he waved. Now's as good a time as any, she decided.

As soon as she stepped though the door, he threw an arm round her shoulders. "What can I do for you, kid?"

She knew exactly what she wanted him to do, but she wanted to spring her plan in a more seductive setting. Twisting free, she glanced at the open office door. "Your dad's probably watching. But, yeah, there is something. How about meeting me at the Pub on the Lake tonight about six–thirty? I have a favor to ask."

His thick blond eyebrows contracted. "Like what?"

Moving closer, she beamed up at him. "Like you remember the movie Ghostbusters? You can help me on a stake–out."

It took a minute for the words to register. Then he threw back his head and let out a yelp of laughter. "You're kidding!" He gave her arm a nudge. "I can think of something more fun than that."

No need to scare him off. She patted his hand. "At six–thirty. We'll talk then." He was still chuckling when she trotted back down the steps.

＊   ＊   ＊

At the Leesburg Public Library Brandy asked for the 1945 microfiche files of the *Commercial.* When the missing girl vanished into Lake Dora, Brandy judged the news would be covered by the county's largest newspaper. Perched in a carrel before a viewer, she began to check the editions after September 2, the day World War II ended.

In a November edition, she finally found the story of the drowning, the heading prominently displayed on page 2 of the first section: **Tavares Girl Dead in Tragic Accident** and beside it, her photograph. The picture, undoubtedly an earlier high school yearbook pose, took Brandy by surprise. It showed a stunning face——great, dark eyes, delicate features, dark hair caught up in a pompadour and then allowed to fall in a shining sheath to her shoulders. Beneath it ran a two–column story:

> *A combination welcome home and engagement party at the home of Mr. and Mrs. J. D. Able on Shirley Shores Drive, Lake Dora, turned tragic Sunday afternoon with the apparent death by drowning of a guest, Eva Stone, 23, daughter of Mr. and Mrs. Richard Stone, 210 St. Abrams Street, Tavares.*
>
> *The weekend celebration was drawing to a close about 5 P.M. when a maid cleaning on the top floor looked out a window and saw Miss Stone enter the lake. The witness, Lily Mae Brown, 20, of 55 Lincoln Street, Tavares, said the young woman was in street clothes. Alarmed, Miss Brown called for help. By the time the gardener, Henry Washington, could launch a row boat and summon assistance, Eva Stone had disappeared beneath the surface.*
>
> *Mr. Able, Sr. and the male guests returned from quail hunting in time to join Sheriff's Office deputies in a search of the area and in dragging the lake. According to Mr. Able, the lake bottom takes a sudden drop several yards from shore.*

Earlier, water activities had included boating but not swimming. The other women guests had departed earlier and did not see Miss Stone leave the house.

Both family members and guests were unable to explain Miss Stone's actions. Her parents were not available for comment. The search for the body continues.

The evening before the tragedy the engagement of Grace Southerland, daughter of Mr. and Mrs. C. D. Southerland of Leesburg, and Captain Brookfield Able, son of hosts Mr. and Mrs. J. D. Able of Tavares, had been announced at a gala dinner–dance on the property.

An inquest will be held on Friday at 2:00 P.M. at the county courthouse in Tavares.

Brandy carried the story to a microfiche copier, then flipped quickly through the next week's file to find the report of the inquest. The verdict, she learned, had been an apparent suicide by drowning. The girl's parents remained uncommunicative in their grief. No suicide note was found. Since authorities couldn't recover the body, a memorial service took place with little publicity two days after the inquest in the historic Tavares Congregational Church.

Sitting back in her chair in front of the viewer, Brandy drew in her breath. Sylvania Langdon had said nothing about her brother Brookfield's engagement party that weekend. Nor did this newspaper account sound like the accidental drowning Sylvania described. Yet for what reason besides suicide would Eva Stone have walked into the lake that November afternoon fully clothed? Was there a scandal that Sylvania did not want resurrected? A good reporter, she decided, would go to the original source. But where was Lily Mae Brown now, the witness to the drowning? A task for another day.

At six Brandy parked in front of her mother's white clapboard cottage on the outskirts of Tavares, next to a vacant lot of pines, saw palmettos, and wax myrtle. Brandy and her mother shared the house conveniently——if not very congenially——until Brandy could afford her own apartment. Until then, this isolated back street was handy to the court house and the city hall for Brandy, and to the high school for her mother, an English teacher there.

Mrs. O'Bannon's Ford was already in the driveway in front of the small frame garage at the rear of the lot. From the back yard Brandy heard a familiar happy bark. Inside the gate she knelt beside a ligustrum hedge, glanced at the border of petunias, and put her arms around the frantic golden retriever to whisper, "No digging today. Good. C'mon, Meg. Let's chance it."

As soon as she opened the kitchen door she could see her mother at the dining room table. Mrs. O'Bannon, an imposing widow of fifty–two with a tight permanent and a square no–non-sense face, sat with her lesson plan book open. She turned level gray eyes toward Brandy. "Have you forgotten our war with fleas? The dog stays out."

"She'll be in my room just a few minutes. I see little enough of her now." Dropping her feathery tail, Meg slunk, head down, toward the hall.

"Fleas migrate. And the way that animal sheds! It's a wonder she isn't bald. Don't think I don't know you sneak that dog in at night."

Before Brandy could reply, her mother tacked in another direc-tion. She had a more important warning flag to hoist. "Summer school began today." She gave Brandy the look that turned her students' knees to jelly. "You ought to be going with me to talk to the principal. I could probably still arrange for an internship at school next fall." Twenty years of teaching had lent her voice authority.

"Let's not hash that over again," Brandy said. "I'm a reporter, not an English teacher."

Her mother slapped her pencil down. "What kind of job security do you have? Reporters shuffle from paper to paper. What kind of pension can you count on?" She thumped the heavy textbook closed. "An honor graduate! You could so easily have a steady, reliable position teaching English and journalism."

Brandy started for her bedroom. "I got certified in English as a back–up, but you know I've always wanted to be a reporter. I'm onto a really good feature. A mystery about a girl who drowned years ago at the old Able mansion."

Distracted, Mrs. O'Bannon nodded. "I remember my dad talking about it. A lot of folks thought she didn't really drown." Brandy looked up quickly, but her mother was back on track. "You'll never be able to make your car payments."

Brandy rolled her eyes upward. The pathetic thing was, unless Brandy got the promotion next week, her mother was probably right. From the dining room came her mother's parting shot. "Marry Mack Lynch and you won't have to worry. He'll inherit his father's business."

Brandy spun through door after Meg and called back. "I'm not ready yet." Mack was, however, in spite of his playboy reputation. He'd asked her, but she had stalled, said she wanted to focus on journalism first. She poked her head back around the door jamb. "But you'll be pleased to know I'm having supper with him tonight."

In the bedroom Brandy could hear claws scrabbling on the floor under her bed——Meg seeking safety. "Some watch–dog," Brandy murmured. "Before you'd bark at a prowler, he'd have to find you." The red–gold head with its curious, cream–colored mask peeped out, then scrambled across the rug, nosed under a pile of Brandy's cast–off jeans for a favorite chew–rag, and disappeared again among the dust balls.

Brandy admitted that her mother had a point about the way she kept her room. Because she saw it as a way station between college and her own apartment, she had unpacked only her well–marked Folger Shakespeare paperbacks, a current mystery novel, a tape player and a stack of classical tapes she seldom had time to hear.

But she was now a professional. Soon she must hang all the clothes, straighten the shoe rack, re–order the clutter on her desk and vanity. But tonight there wasn't time. Maybe if her dad had been better organized... For a quiet moment she looked at his silver framed photograph beside her jewelry case. He had been her model, and his study had been littered with books and papers.

Ever since Brandy's dad died of a heart attack three years ago, Mrs. O'Bannon had been hung up on the question of her daughter's livelihood, probably because of her own financial struggle. She had met Brandy's dad after his tour in Viet Nam, while they were both taking education courses. Both landed jobs at the high school in her mother's home town, where her dad became its most popular social studies teacher. Seniors dedicated the yearbook to him twice.

Unlike her mother, Brandy's dad didn't urge her to follow his example. She'd been the English department's Pride Award winner, but she'd also been the editor of the school newspaper. Her dad always said, "You're a good writer, Bran. You've got curiosity and you've got heart. Do your own thing." And she had.

It hadn't been easy after his death. She had paid most of her way through college, working in Gainesville department stores and restaurants, sometimes staying out whole semesters until she could save enough for the next one. She didn't want to accumulate debts. She had graduated older than her classmates at age twenty–four.

Peering into the mirror above the tissue box, make–up kit, and magazines, she flipped back her hair at the temples with a curling iron, and applied a muted pink lipstick. Tonight she'd test her dad's faith and her own investigative talent. She would interview the latest witness to a haunting, maybe become a witness herself.

She whistled for Meg. On her dad's last Christmas, the puppy had been his gift to her, a legacy of love. He had not consulted her mother. Obediently, the copper–colored retriever slithered out, deposited her chew rag on the pile of jeans, and followed at Brandy's heels past the hazard of Mrs. O'Bannon and into the back yard.

As Brandy closed the gate, she thought of her mother's recollection. If Eva Stone didn't drown, what happened to her? But first, the ghost. She'd try to persuade Mack to watch the mansion with her. It would be friendlier with two. But before they staked out the Able mansion, she'd interview the student witness.

FOUR

At six–thirty that evening Brandy drove past the police department and city hall toward the lake and parked before a squat building with green shutters and a shamrock over the door. Mack's giant pick–up was already there. Beyond the Wooten Park tennis courts a light burned at the end of the pier.

Inside the darkened pub a melancholy Irish ballad floated around Celtic tapestries on the walls. An O'Bannon could feel at home here. Mack was leaning over the bar in the lounge, eyes on the television screen, one big hand around a beer mug, ignoring the moist smile of a blonde with teased hair on the next stool.

Brandy steered him to a table under a green fringed shade beside a window. Across the water she could see the ragged shapes of pond pine and cypress, the view the pub owner wanted to preserve. Two miles to the southeast the ninety year old Able homestead and its specter were lost in the distance and darkness.

After Brandy had a glass of burgundy in hand and placed an order for her favorite shrimp–stuffed mushrooms, she brought up the subject of the Able mansion.

"The Ables!" Mack took a generous swig of beer. "Bunch of crazies, kid——especially the women. The old scarecrow lives there now——nutty as a fruitcake. Husband's a boozer. He checked out of the place years ago. The owner before them let it go to pot."

"Brookfield Able?"

Mack attacked his large T–bone. "Yeah. His wife's as wacky as his sister, only more lady–like. Since Brookfield kicked off, she lives in a fancy condo with a keeper." His voice emerged through a mouthful of baked potato. "That's how crazy the Ables are."

Brandy stared into her glass. "I met John Able. He seems sane enough."

"That branch got it together a little better. Old man went into law enforcement and retired a captain. He's got a son who's a county cop now. But the guy you're talking about——a flake. Some kinda tree–hugger. Lives like a monk in a trailer somewhere on the Dora Canal, trying to be a hot shot builder."

Out the window Brandy could hear an engine and see a pontoon boat maneuvering into a slip. She tried not to watch the young boatman walk alone up the pier toward the restaurant.

"Architect," Brandy said in spite of herself. "He wants to be an architect."

"Whatever."

When the pub door opened, she lifted her gaze above Mack's thick shoulder. No mistaking the slender young man stepping into the only pub in Tavares.

Mack warmed to the topic. "You mentioned staking out some ghost at the old Able mansion. I don't know any more than you do about a chick drowning at the Ables almost fifty years ago. And I don't want to know. Now Axel Blackthorne, the guy who's buying up the land——he's good for business, good for the whole county. He'll bring in more customers."

Brandy gave him a wry smile. Blackthorne would, indeed, bring in the customers. There were all those manufactured homes, all those shopping strips to fill. She shifted subjects. Like Lady

Macbeth, she would appeal to his manhood. "Of course, it would take courage to get the camera shots I want. If there's nothing there to see, that's part of the story, and there's not much time left." She nodded for emphasis. "The weather's good. We'd better try tonight. First I'll do some interviewing, get more details."

Mack laid down his fork and bent across his ravaged plate. "I'll put this flat–out, because I care about you. I'm not going out there, and you're not going out there, either. You're sure not going out there at night. No telling what varmints are loose in those woods. And old lady Langdon's got a lug nut loose." He sat back. "That's settled. C'mon." He reached one large hand across the table for hers. "Let's take a little spin."

Brandy could see John Able saunter from the lounge into the dining area, cradling a highball. She thought he spotted her. Maybe now he was her only chance for help. Maybe his attitude had softened.

When the waitress brought the check, she gently shook her head and pocketed it herself. "My treat. I asked you to meet me. And sorry, I've got to be up early. I've still got copy to write."

He stood, stretched, glanced behind him at John's table, and hovered for a moment above her. "Suit yourself, kid. I'll go work out at the gym before it closes, but take my advice. Don't get tangled up with that Able bunch." He flexed biceps that made her girlfriends swoon and grinned. "If you gotta late date, remember——I could make spaghetti outta that guy."

"My acquaintance with John Able," Brandy said, "is strictly professional."

When she stopped a few minutes later at John's booth, he looked up, eyes wary. She slid into the opposite seat. "May I? Please——go ahead with your patty melt." She took a sip of the remaining burgundy. "I found the name of the girl who drowned at your Aunt Sylvania's house. Maybe you knew it. Eva Stone."

She could visualize the yearbook picture——the high forehead, the large eyes, the shining sheath of dark hair.

In the background hung the thin, clear tones of an Irish harp, and then a wistful voice—— *"O you are not lying in the wet clay..."*

John touched his trim mustache and hesitated before he spoke. "The Stone family still lives here. At least I believe her mother does." A fact to store away, Brandy thought.

"... for it is a harvest evening now," the Irish voice sang, *"and we are piling up ricks against the moonlight..."*

"Eva Stone was a beauty," Brandy said. "I looked up the news story."

The harp faded and the Irish singer breathed the final lyric *"...And you smile upon us eternally."* Was Eva Stone "smiling eternally?"

John's brown eyes went grave. "Some interesting information came my way today. Aunt Sylvania's buddy Blackthorne called me at my job. Wanted to give me some advice about the house. He said to leave well enough alone. Doesn't want me looking for another buyer. He even hinted he'd make it worth my while. Said he has connections who would help me find an apprenticeship."

"Is that important?"

He sighed. When he was troubled, she noticed, he rubbed his forehead. "I spent six years studying to become an architect. Now I've got to do a three year internship with a firm. They're not easy to find. After that, I get to take the four day exam. Right now I'm working as a draftsman at a civil engineering company." He shrugged. "Blackthorne builds shopping malls, business properties, housing developments. He's a power in Lake County."

Brandy stared into her empty glass. She wasn't the only one under pressure. "What are you going to do?"

He carved decisively into the ground beef, jaw set. "I'm not going to back down. I made an appointment tomorrow afternoon to take three architects through the house. They're all from the Lake County Historical Society. Aunt Sylvania's a member, so she can't very well object. They could nominate the house to the National Register of Historic Places. With luck, I can still find a buyer who sees its potential."

Privately, Brandy thought his plan was a long shot. "I heard Curt Greene today," she said. "He's the architect who's trying to save woodlands and lake front. I think he has his eye on the property east of Sylvania's house. That might help." Leaning forward, she met his eyes. "I'm going to level with you this time. I still plan to investigate the legend that's grown up around the house. Maybe the publicity about the missing woman will actually help."

Once more she was conscious of a quiet Irish vocal, "...*it was a moment when I sensed a miss in the beat of time...*"

She tested him with another Shakespearean reference. "I feel like Owen Glendower. I plan to 'call forth her spirit from the vasty deep.'"

For the first time she saw his rare smile. "But will she come?" He remembered his *Henry IV*. Maybe he wasn't all angles and algebra.

Outside on the lake Brandy could see only the flicker of a fisherman's light. "I'm going to watch at the house tonight. I hoped you'd help me."

John pushed his plate away and reached into his pocket for the tip, his tone once again frigid. "Get my family involved, right? I can't help you there."

"...*On a frosty night a bashful star... stood frozen in the sky...*" sang the gentle voice.

A frosty night indeed. Brandy had never spent this much time with a man without arousing his interest. Meet the ice–man, she thought. Not a hint of a thaw. Not even the offer of a drink. Maybe he didn't like the look of Mack Lynch. Maybe Mack was right. He was a wimp.

She shoved her chair back, her own voice suddenly business–like. "I also have the name of a witness to the supposed ghost. I plan to interview him before I case the place myself."

*   *   *

About eight–thirty Brandy swung from Tavares onto busy Route 441 and followed it to a strip shopping center near Mount Dora. When she spotted a telephone booth beside a supermarket, she put in a call to her mother. "Don't expect me until quite late," she said when Mrs. O'Bannon answered. "I've got a hot lead on the story I mentioned last night."

She expected her mother's flinty reaction. "My Lord, you act as if you worked for the *Washington Post*! A girl your age shouldn't be out alone at night."

Brandy made a face into the receiver. "Mount Dora's hardly Tombstone. No lecture, please. Just feed Meg."

Farther east she pulled into the Burger King parking area. Seymour Hammond turning out to be an underfed youth with a mop of hair over one eye. Brandy ordered coffee and ice cream, introduced herself, and favored young Hammond with her most winning smile.

He peered back with his one visible eye. "My mom told me you were coming. Said you want to talk about summer job opening for teens. Find a seat. I'll take a break in half a shake."

Brandy settled into an empty booth in front of the plate glass window, spooned her ice cream, and watched while the lines dwindled. After Seymour served the last customer, he signaled a female companion at the counter, then slid into a seat across the table. Brandy reached for her note pad. For a few minutes she asked questions about his job needs and search, his qualifications, his career goals. Then she eased into the major subject.

"There's something else. I'm also working on a story about the old Able mansion on Lake Dora. Last June another paper reported you and some friends saw something unusual out there."

The question clearly made Hammond uncomfortable. With a paper napkin he scrubbed a faint stain on the table. "So that's the real reason you're here. I can't tell you much."

Or doesn't want to, Brandy thought.

He stopped rubbing, clasped his fingers together on the table and looked up. "I really didn't see anything myself." Judging by the forelock dangling over one eye, she found that fact predictable.

"We were planning a late cook–out on my buddy's pontoon party boat, okay? I was fixing some hot–dogs on a grill at the bow. We'd been cruising around and it was getting dark. My buddy had just put on the running lights. We were idling along a few yards off shore, a couple of miles from town, across the lake, you know. It's awful isolated out there."

He paused. Obviously, he did not relish the memory. "First thing I knew, some of the girls started pointing and whispering and pretty soon getting pretty hysterical." Seymour's gaze shifted outside to the dark parking lot. Then he faced her again. "My buddy, he gunned the engine and took off like a bat out of hell. I was hanging onto the butane stove."

"What exactly did the girls see?"

His bony fingers twisted a class ring, and he glanced at Brandy's note paid. She put it back into her bag. "Let me call a girl who was there," he said. "She's the only one who'll talk at all. She's taken a lot of kidding. But maybe she'll be willing to talk to you."

He disappeared into a back room to use the phone. A few minutes later he emerged to say his friend Charlotte would meet Brandy at the Burger King, but the girl had to drive there from south of town. Charlotte didn't want to see Brandy at her parents' home. With that cryptic comment, Seymour hurried back to the counter and did not look her way again. Twenty minutes later Brandy saw a car driven by a lone girl turn into the parking lot. When the driver sat another five minutes, hands still on the wheel, peering through the windshield into the fast–food restaurant, Brandy realized her witness might not want to come where she could be overheard.

She dropped her empty paper cup and plate into a trash can and slipped outside. Her intuition proved correct. When Brandy rapped on the driver's window, Charlotte motioned for her to come around to the passenger seat. As Brandy ducked in beside her, Charlotte faced her, blue eyes seeking Brandy's, face pale under a smooth cap of blonde hair.

"I know what I saw," she said defensively. "We'd stopped the boat near the shore. Kind of in front of that old house. Then one of my girl friends goes, 'Look over there. Isn't that the house that's supposed to be haunted?' That's when I looked. I go, 'Oh, you must be joking.'" Her eyes grew rounder, remembering. "First I just looked at how big the house was, like it was so high, right near the edge of the water. And then I saw something that looked like a figure at one of top windows. I couldn't make out much about it, but it moved. Looked like someone's head and shoulders. That was spooky enough."

When she removed her fingers from the steering wheel, Brandy could see they left damp streaks. "I was still trying to figure out what I'd seen at the window when something moved down on the lawn. Lights were on downstairs, so I could see. The shape of a woman was coming around from behind the house. But it didn't look like a *real* woman, you know what I'm saying? It's hard to explain.

"You couldn't see through it or anything, like in the movies. But it didn't seem to walk. It kind of glided, like its feet weren't touching the ground. It kept moving toward the lake and when it got to the boat house, it went right into the wall. It was there one minute and most of us saw it, and then it was gone." The girl's eyes pled with Brandy to believe her.

"Do you mean it went through a door?"

Charlotte shook her head. "No, Ma'am. That was what was so scary. The figure just disappeared into the wall. I didn't see any opening."

"Could you tell me what the figure was wearing?

"Well, it was pretty dark, but there was light from the house and our boat. Whatever, the thing was wearing, it didn't reach to the ground. Seemed like it had something white around its neck."

Brandy hoped she could get some details to connect the figure with Eva Stone. She framed her next question carefully. "Try to describe what was at the neckline."

"It wasn't white like a mist or a fog, or like that. It looked like it had sharp edges. It wasn't very long. Below that I saw something like reddish cloth. Well, we didn't wait to examine anything carefully, Miss O' Bannon. I wasn't the only one who saw it. Some of the girls started screaming, and we just took off."

"I appreciate your telling me about this," Brandy said.

"None of the other girls will talk about it. The guy driving the boat says it must've been a trick of light, or the shadow of a cloud passing over. Our folks want everyone to forget what happened. They say it was all in our imaginations. They think we were drinking——but it happens we weren't."

Charlotte stared through the windshield, chin up and defiant. Then the blonde head dropped, and she gripped the wheel. "Still,

I don't want you to use my name. I don't care if you write what I told you, but to get my parents off my back, I told my parents I'd shut up about it. If they see I've talked again to a reporter, they'll ground me for a year."

Well–documented interviews, Brandy thought grimly. Those were Mr. Tyler's instructions. She thanked Charlotte, nevertheless. Even though she wouldn't be quoted, the girl's description might later give Brandy's account credibility.

She pulled out of the parking lot, aware that she faced her moment of truth. Who could she use as a witness? None of the other students were even willing to speak to her. Only one possible witness came to mind——herself. She would have to follow her plan, even if she followed it alone.

FIVE

After Brandy checked her county map, she took 441, turned south, passed over a canal, and finally cut right on the small road near Lake Dora's south rim. Mentally she took inventory. Her mother didn't expect her until very late. She had a pen flashlight——its beam would be hard to see from the house——and her note pad and a flash camera. To look professional, unfortunately, she had worn a shirt waist dress and pumps, not entirely suitable for a stake–out in the woods.

As she made the final turn into Sylvania's lane, she faced the inky blackness of woods. Overhead, branches arched in a thick, dark canopy. She felt a sudden tightness in her chest and lectured herself severely: nothing was here at night that was not here in the day time. Besides, no one had ever claimed this alleged haunting hurt anyone. What danger could there be in simply watching?

Before she came to the parking area, she pulled off the road under a live oak draped in Spanish moss. Then tucking her purse under the front seat, she locked her car, pocketed the pen light and her car keys, and hung her camera on a strap around her neck. As she slogged through the sand toward the uneven side lawn, she cursed her high heels. Skirting a ragged fringe of cherry laurel, she inched around the back side of the house and crouched behind shrubbery several yards from the lake. She had a good view of the boat house where Charlotte claimed she saw the figure. Because the lake side of the house and its dormer windows faced the shoreline, they were not in her direct line of vision. No light came from the two side windows.

Time passed slowly. Her legs began to cramp, her eyes to ache from sheer concentration. Far across the dark expanse of water glimmered the tiny lights of Tavares. For an hour the only sound was a throaty chorus of frogs. Then behind her on Blackthorne's lot something creaked. She caught her breath, heard small thuddings, raspy panting. A metallic clank, the rattle of a lock.

And then she knew, knew with absolute certainty, what was coming. Someone had opened Blackthorne's gate. Even while she stumbled to her feet, she could hear claws raking the ground. She screamed a panicky "Help!" her voice lost in the oaks and the cypress, and looked toward her distant car. No way could she reach it. No way could she reach Sylvania's door, either, even if it were unlocked. The house loomed tall and silent. At the same instant the Dobermans leapt through the gate, she scrambled toward the boat house, then spotted the padlock rusted on its side door. In front of her lay the black waters of the lake.

Frantic, she glanced over one shoulder. Both dogs were loping toward her, their strides long and confident, their teeth flashes of white. Kicking off her pumps, she flung the camera on the ground and dashed, gasping, toward the water's edge. Again she heard herself call out, but she was not conscious of making those strange, high sounds. If she turned around, if she tried to go back, the dogs would fall upon her.

"Oh, God!" she thought when she felt the cold wetness over her feet. Would they follow? She'd never been around attack dogs. Her feet slipped and she caught herself, one hand plunging under the surface to steady herself. The muck of the lake bottom rose over her ankles. Groaning, she pulled free, threw herself forward, dragged one foot after another.

Behind her the Dobermans had paused at the water's edge. One whined and trotted back and forth, undecided. The other, bolder, tried the water daintily with both paws, then waded out a little, stretching his neck, baying. In a nightmare corner of Brandy's brain lurked the sound she had heard the night before——an alligator's grunt.

Like a thunderbolt it came to her. She was re–enacting Eva Stone's walk——only not deliberately, not with dignity, but with a frenzied desire to live. The news story had mentioned a drop off, but where? Behind her the second Doberman had now lunged into the water and was striking out toward her, his neck and head extended, ears flat. She lurched on.

Suddenly near the boat house she felt the water tremble. Something large was moving toward her, something churning under the surface. Her mind exploded with the paralyzing image of a huge 'gator. Her heart gave a giant leap, and her foot stepped into nothing.

She forgot every rule about saving herself. Floundering blindly, she tangled her arms in weeds, strangled on a mouthful of fetid water, was dragged down by wet clothes, and went under.

*   *   *

She was only half conscious when she felt herself lifted, water swirling around her, felt her lungs fill with air, felt her head forced into a collar, and then the cool night on her face. Hands pulled her through an opening above the lake and she found herself lying on her back on a hard, vibrating surface, eyes shut, head to one side, water dribbling from her lips——cold and wet and sick at her stomach.

Shivering, she opened one eye and looked into a canopy of stars. Next to her a thin band of light fell across a man's sodden tennis shoe. Mack, she thought groggily and murmured his name. He came, after all, hauled her to safety. But there wasn't a deck this broad in his speed boat. She opened the other eye, stared up at the base of a console and a captain's chair.

"Better?" A man knelt beside her and gently removed the life jacket. Brandy could not hear an engine, yet the craft was steadily moving. His next words answered her question. "Glad I got a trolling motor. Gets me in closer and quieter. We're pulling out now."

The churning in the water——the blades of an electric motor? A face came into focus——a wet lock of dark hair, sharp cheekbones, a damp mustache. When she looked into the concerned brown eyes, she tried to speak and instead moaned.

"Gotta guard against shock," he said. "You're white as a ghost. No sick joke intended." He began tucking his jacket around her. "Better move you to the back seat, get your feet up a little."

"John Able," she said faintly. "But how?"

He sat back on his heels. "Now's not the time to argue. You said you were coming back to ghost hunt. Everyone warned you, even the delightful Mr. Blackthorne. But I worried, so I phoned your mother after dinner. She told me you were working on some mysterious story and wouldn't be home until late. That cinched it. I cruised up behind the boat house about the time you hit the lake."

"I thought..."

"I know. You thought I was the overfed hunk you were with at the pub. You said his name. Sorry." She felt arms under her knees and around her back, knew her tattered dress clung to her body, felt rivulets of water drain onto the deck. His own jeans and tee shirt were soaked. He must have jumped in himself.

He carried her across the deck and laid her on the cold vinyl. Then he forced a seat cushion under her knees and peered once again at her face. "Hard to tell about shock in this light. Your skin's a little bluish, but you didn't inhale much water. You were just scared to death."

Below the white running light, Brandy could see ripples glisten along the shore where the Dobermans had retreated. Then her eyes widened, and she drew in her breath. Under a cypress tree several yards away a long, corrugated shape slid from the bank. About twelve feet of thick, smoke–green hide stretched forward on the surface and drifted through the bar of light, nostrils and eye ridges elevated, pointed tail raking the water. Brandy's teeth chattered, her whole body shook. The 'gator had been there, close by, after all.

Once more John knelt beside her, leaned against her, tried to quiet her tremor while the huge back gradually submerged and was gone. "With all that ruckus going on," he murmured, "the old boy probably thinks the neighborhood's gone to pot."

A smile trembled on her lips. She buried her face in his chest and knew the tingle she felt was not from trauma.

After wrapping his jacket more tightly around her, he held his fingers on her pulse. "Still rapid and not strong enough. We got to get you warm and dry. Get some hot tea down you." He lifted a water hyacinth from her soggy hair. "Tonight you're not exactly Cleopatra on her barge, but hang in there. This is the best I can do until I get you to the trailer."

His trailer, she thought. She did not protest. Even shuddering with cold, she admired the grace with which he stepped to the bow, cut off the silent trolling motor, and switched on the gasoline engine. How could she have ever called him unimaginative? Mack would not see her as a bedraggled Cleopatra. He never read anything but the sports pages.

Yet as John guided the boat away from shore, he gave no sign that he felt the same electricity. In the distance a thin whistle shrilled and then faded. At the sound, the Dobermans whirled and tore back around the house out of sight.

Weakly Brandy raised herself on one elbow. "Someone opened the gate. There were only two keys——Blackthorne's and your Aunt Sylvania's."

"Probably thought you were a burglar. The dogs are lucky the 'gator didn't go for them." He looked back at her and shook his head. "But Aunt Sylvania's right about one thing. The lake can be dangerous. Especially if you run across a cottonmouth moccasin."

Brandy watched the high, gray front of the house recede, its curved window on the second floor lit like a giant eye. But the figure emerging from the rear was not ghostly. Brandy recognized Sylvania's tall silhouette. She walked across the grass, and stood beside the boat house, looking out over the saw palmettos.

John nodded in her direction. "The keeper of her brother's flame. Must've heard me and the dogs. She's probably the ghost people think they see."

Brandy dropped her head back on the hard seat while John set a northwest course and shoved the throttle forward. My nice white pumps, she thought, and my camera——on the lawn somewhere. My car with my bag and driver's licence and all my cards——in the lane. My keys at the bottom of the lake. Sylvania would have no trouble identifying her prowler. She winced at the thought of facing John's great–aunt again.

When the running lights of a motorboat flickered on west of the Able mansion and roared past, Brandy wondered if Blackthorne already kept a boat at his new property. "Sometimes we get a few night fishermen," John said. His own boat bucked solidly on, the drone of its engine the only other sound on the moonlit surface.

Brandy closed her eyes, strangely warmed in spite of her chill, and faded in and out of awareness.

Once she was jolted by the other boat's engines close behind them and turned her head to watch it swerve north toward the Wooten Park pier. The Dora Canal would be at least another mile and a half. She awoke at last when she felt herself lifted again, then heard John's footsteps beneath her on the wooden dock. He was shaking with cold, too, and almost as wet. Halting under a porch light, he worked awkwardly on the lock, and then swung her, feet first, into his small, tidy living room.

SIX

Brandy had a rapid impression of colorful wall prints, a bookcase, a tiny kitchen area. Mack had said John lived like a monk. She glimpsed no feminine touches as he whirled her down a short hall.

"Can you stand?"

His voice so close to her ear rattled her. "I think so." Tenderly he set her down in the tiny bathroom beside the stall shower, but as her bare feet touched the floor, her knees buckled. He caught her again, close, and held her with one arm while he reached into the shower and turned on the tap. "Soap's on the shelf," he said, his voice unsteady.

Her head felt woozy. With fingers stiff as ice, she fumbled with the zipper in the back of her dress. "I can't seem to…" Suddenly she felt the zipper pulled down, felt the sodden fabric tugged over her head, felt hooks unhooked, and knew that she was naked——and that she did not care. John's own waterlogged jeans fell to the floor. Then they were both standing under the warm stream, John still holding her. She threw her arms around his neck and pressed her body to his. Unresisting, she felt herself being carefully lathered, rinsed, gently toweled dry, then picked up once more and carried into the darkened bedroom.

*   *   *

Brandy woke from a light, refreshing sleep, rolled on her side, and reached out to touch John's bare chest. Once she had thought him a tin soldier. Big mistake.

Leaning on one elbow, he peered into her eyes. "Revived?"

She nodded, smiling. Softly, with one hand he traced her body from hip to breast. "I've got to get home, you know," she said, "or my mother will send out the gendarmes. She's a worrier."

"I wish you'd stay." When she shook her head, John swung his legs over the side of the bed, sat up, and rubbed his forehead. "A long time ago I believe I promised you some hot tea." He stepped to a closet, pulled on a pair of jeans, and handed her a man's lounging robe. "A Christmas present. I never wear it. In a few minutes I'll look for something you can wear home." He gave her a long, warm look. "Of course, I prefer what you're wearing now." At the door he paused. "There's a hair dryer in the upper dresser drawer."

Brandy stretched and lay for a few minutes, gazing around the small bedroom, listening to him move about in the kitchen. On one wall hung a Miro print cut from a magazine, wine colored drapes, a dresser clear of everything except a clothes brush, a manicure set, and a framed photograph she could not see well in the dim light. Finally she rose, slipped her arms into the robe, found a pair of men's flip–flops and shuffled into the living room where John was dropping tea bags into two mugs. The muted strains of a Mozart concerto came from a tape player on a corner cabinet.

"I didn't know you like classical music," she said.

She plumped down on the couch before a small coffee table and pushed her still damp, stringy hair behind her ears.

"Music is mathematics with emotion."

She glanced approvingly around the tidy room and thought of her own cluttered bedroom. "I'm impressed by your housekeeping skills, too."

John set the tea box back in the cabinet, came over and kissed her. "My dad left his mark on all of us. The guys in the department called him Old Spit and Polish." He stepped back to the counter, poured hot water into the mugs from an aluminum tea kettle, and rummaged again in the cabinet. "A few saltines is all I've got to go with the tea."

On the opposite wall beside the drawn drapes hung a color photograph of an unpainted house with tin roof and wrap–around porch. John arranged crackers in a bowl and followed her glance. "Some day I'll use what I learned at the university. While the other students were designing new forms, I was figuring out how to resurrect the old ones, the ones before air conditioning. Those guys built practical houses. Cracker houses. I'm glad the Ables were among them."

She looked from the framed photograph to the bookcase beside it. He had a library, too. She knelt to read the titles——not the latest potboilers, either——Dickens, Melville, Conrad, Mark Twain. "Your place tells a lot about you," she said. "Things I like." On the lowest shelf she could see what looked like a high school yearbook with a worn cover and below it an old photo album. Maybe Able family history, the kind that wouldn't be in the historical museum.

John set the steaming mugs and the bowl on the coffee table, and drew her down beside him. "Lots I like about you, too." He pulled her against him with one arm, his lips brushing her ear. "I'm not so sure about Brenda Starr, Girl Reporter, though. A bit brittle. Not the real you."

She patted his hand and wished he had not started to sound like Mack, who was always asking her to give up reporting and take care of him. Apparently being assertive wasn't attractive. Where was her editor when she needed him?

She lifted the tea bag, studied the cup, and let it soak further. "I do get paid to do a job."

John rubbed his forehead. "I heard something about my own job today. From Blackthorne again, this time indirectly. I had a call from the CEO who promised me an apprenticeship. Blackthorne's one of his firm's important clients. Blackthorne's upset that I ignored his warning. Word gets around. Blackthorne insists he needs Sylvania's lot for his development. The CEO politely told me not to interfere with Blackthorne's deal if I wanted to intern there."

Brandy frowned and nibbled a dry cracker. "What do you plan to do?"

For a moment John studied the contents of his mug. "Somebody's got to try to save the county's heritage. It's too late to turn back now. I might as well find out what kind of folks I was planning to work for." He gave her a half grin. "I'm taking the committee from the historical society to see the house tomorrow."

She set down her tea and gave him a kiss on the cheek. "Backbone. I like that." Then she paused, eyebrows contracted. "About tonight——us. I wouldn't want you to think that I sleep around."

He squeezed her hand. "You were vulnerable. Maybe I took advantage. I'll try to make it up to you."

"If you really want to help me…" She stood, knelt before the bookcase, and pulled out the yearbook and the album. After all, Mr. Tyler said a reporter had to keep pushing. He would also say a reporter shouldn't become emotionally involved. Too late for that now.

"Just quickly, you might show me these, tell me more about the family." She glanced up, eager, her mind again on her story. She had to retrieve her car, and while she was at the house, to plumb Sylvania's memory and try to talk to her husband.

She set the volumes on the coffee table and cuddled next to him. As she tilted up her face, she was scarely aware that he had withdrawn his arm. "You could take me along tomorrow with the architects. Sylvania won't talk to me if I go back alone." She glanced down at the two large books. "I've done research about Eva Stone's disappearance. I think Sylvania knows more about that girl than she lets on. Maybe Blackthorne was a guest at the weekend party, too. I need to ask her some more questions." She patted his arm. "I've got to get my car and things, anyway."

Later Brandy would remember how John's face darkened as she babbled on. He stared at her, one eyebrow raised, then carried his mug to the sink and spun around to face her. "I ought to have guessed what you were up to. Here I was blaming myself for taking advantage. I see now it was the other way around."

Stunned, Brandy pulled the robe tighter around her. "What are you talking about?"

"Manipulation. Tonight was just like the last time. You're good at getting what you want from a guy. Latching on to my album and yearbook. Enticing me to take you out there again after I said I wouldn't." He leaned against the counter and folded his arms. "You've got a big lug of a boyfriend who could buy and sell half the town. You even thought he'd come tonight instead of me. I hear he's the town catch. What do you want with me?"

He turned to rinse his mug, the muscles in his jaw twitching. "What you want is your damned story, and you think I can help you get it. You don't care if you hurt me and two families."

Brandy shoved the volumes under the coffee table, blind–sided and confused. There was an element of truth in what he said, but until a few minutes ago he had swept the story completely from her mind. "No, I just thought…"

But John was not listening. He strode back into the bedroom, returned and held out a pair of women's jeans and a woman's shirt. "These ought to see you home. Take the damn books, too. That's what you really want. This wasn't the beginning of a relationship. You were softening me up."

Hurt and indignant, Brandy reached for the clothes. In the bedroom, as she plugged in the hair dryer above his dresser, she peered at the photograph she'd noticed earlier. A young woman with windblown hair smiled saucily back at her. How had John suddenly come up with a woman's pants and a fashionable name brand shirt? A woman's brand of shampoo? Why would he have a hair dryer?

He lives here like a monk, Mack had said. Indeed. She gritted her teeth and stifled an impulse to run to him, to make excuses, to try to recapture the earlier mood. How many other women had he entertained in his little trailer on the canal? Savagely she slammed down the dryer. Now he was looking for an excuse to get rid of her. She was the one who had been used.

In the bath room she rolled her wet clothing into a ball and stalked into the kitchen where John silently handed her a plastic bag. The Mozart concerto was coming to its vibrant conclusion. Lips trembling, she snatched the damp bag and stood at the door, head high.

Within fifteen minutes John was driving her home. The ice man returneth, she thought. Not until he turned down her isolated block and pulled up before her mother's house did he face her. "Like you said at the trailer, you have to get your car. You certainly owe Aunt Sylvania an apology. I'm going out there at ten in the morning. I can pick you up in front of the *Beacon*, but only if we have an understanding. I'm not involved in your so–called research, and you'll not embarrass Sylvania or anyone else with your questions."

Brandy longed to fling herself out of the car without a word, but she had to be practical. If she asked her mother to drive her, she would have to explain tonight. She couldn't very well tell Mack what happened, either. Fortunately, the only light on in the house was at the kitchen door. Her mother had not yet raised an alarm about her absence.

She bit her lip. "All right. No favors. I'll just see Sylvania and get my car." She wanted to thank him again for pulling her to safety, to say she hadn't meant to use him to get a story. But then she thought of the girl's picture, looked at the grim set of his jaw, and shoved open the car door.

At the back gate Brandy checked her watch. After four. She rushed up the driveway toward the garage, unfastened the gate into the yard, and knelt to muffle Meg's bark. Then she retrieved the extra house key from under a flower pot on the back porch and sneaked into the kitchen with Meg at her heels. Not until then did she hear John's car pull away. At least he had waited until she was safely inside.

Meg slid under the bed, tail thumping in gratitude. As for Brandy, she undressed, crawled into bed, and imagined John chalking up one more conquest on his score card. She was conscious of her father's portrait on the dresser and felt ashamed. She would not allow herself to become so vulnerable again, nearly drowned or not. Mr. Tyler and the textbooks were right: never become emotionally involved in your story.

But when she tried to stay angry, she thought of those hot brown eyes and her own grew wet. Maybe John was right. Maybe she was too bull-headed. Maybe she did allow her schemes to hurt others. Maybe she should tell Mr. Tyler tomorrow that there wasn't a story.

SEVEN

In the morning Mr. Tyler leaned back at his desk, listened to Brandy's account of her investigation, and flicked his cigarette into an ashtray with a sour look. He'd failed in his effort to give up the habit, and that failure contributed to his crankiness. "So you found this witness to the ghost, but she won't be quoted. All you learned is already a matter of record. There's a weekend party. Then the girl walks out in the lake and drowns. Where's your alleged ghost story?"

Brandy fingered her spiral note pad. Now was the time to toss in the sponge. Even so, she had been up early and recorded in her usual unsightly scrawl all the night's events except one. She dropped her gaze. "I staked out the grounds myself, but I didn't get a chance to see anything. The developer next door has Dobermans. Someone turned them loose on me. I had some very unpleasant moments." She tried not to think of the pleasant ones that followed and looked up again.

"Maybe you were right. Maybe there isn't a story. Not if no one will talk."

Mr. Tyler studied the end of his cigarette. "Too tough for you, Miss O'Bannon? I figured you needed your spine stiffened, but I didn't figure you for a quitter."

Brandy closed the pad with a snap. "I do think there's a story——if I can only find it."

"First thing you've got to find is your focus. Is this about a ghost or the loss of an historic house? Maybe about a lost woman?" He glanced at her note pad. "One thing I'll give you. You take complete notes." He leaned forward and caught her in his sharp blue gaze. "Get out there. Use your eyes. Talk to people." He flipped a page of his desk calendar. "It's now Wednesday. You have until next Monday to come up with a story." He sat back again, blew two perfect smoke rings, and watched them rise. "Don't take those rings as models. Be sure you get facts." His tone hardened. "And remember, there are laws about people's property. I'd rather you didn't get the paper sued for trespassing."

A few minutes later Brandy stepped out on the sidewalk to wait for her awkward meeting with John. She'd have to learn more family history, get more physical details about the house, probe Eva Stone's disappearance——all in a couple of days. Without a concrete ghost, the missing girl was the best angle. She'd make her the focus, then line up supporting facts.

At ten John's '85 Mustang drew up in front of the *Beacon* office, followed by an impressive Chrysler and a Ford LTD bringing the committee. A boat ride across the lake would be quicker, but not suitable for the group. After Brandy climbed into the passenger seat beside John, he avoided her eyes. He's embarrassed about last night, she thought bitterly, and so am I. She tried to imagine Mack sitting between them. Good old dependable Mack.

"I told the architects you're writing a news story about the house," John said as he pulled away from the curb, his eyes on the road. "Design and age make it eligible for historic preservation, even without the local family history."

He glanced at Brandy, who had dutifully begun taking notes. "A nomination would put pressure on Aunt Sylvania, maybe make her delay the sale. It takes a few months to hear from the Review Board. The owner can still disapprove the nomination, but by then I hope to have a buyer."

Brandy's fingers clenched around her pen. Could John really pretend that nothing had happened between them? Not even the argument? She closed her note pad and spoke in an even tone. "I never meant to manipulate you or anyone else."

The lines of his face tensed. "We called a truce last night. Let's not talk about it. You can get your data without upsetting the family——or yourself." That remark stung. Did he think she'd sleep with him to get a story? Her fingers trembled, while he stared ahead and went on talking. "You need to know that Curt Greene's one of the architects. Blackthorne bought up the land west of Sylvania's property, but Greene might be able to save wetlands to the east."

If John was going back to square one, she could, too. She bit her lip and tried to concentrate on the facts John was giving her. He might have another reason for cultivating Greene. He headed the county's most prestigious architectural firm, one with offices in more than one central Florida town.

"I saw Mr. Greene at the last Chamber of Commerce meeting," Brandy said. "He ought to impress your great-aunt." They rode in silence until he swung onto the dirt road leading to Sylvania's house. As they passed Brandy's abandoned hatchback, she tucked her note pad into her canvas bag, felt inside to be sure she had the extra key to her car, and snapped the bag shut.

The three cars parked in a lot covered with pine needles, John between a shabby sedan and a sleek white Mercedes. Probably, she thought, Sylvania's car and an earlier caller's. John led the way toward the lake for a front view of the soaring height of the house, its gray siding, its buff brick first floor bays, its dormer windows and high–pitched copper roof.

"Unique," said Greene, lifting his camera and focusing on each feature. Brandy scanned the grass for her own camera. Gone. So were her white pumps. Across the padlocked gate to the west, she looked in vain for the dogs. Beyond the saw palmettos, a crew of workmen were sinking tall posts into the ground, nailing the planks across them about a foot above the grassy soil, and every few yards, interspersing wooden benches that faced the lake. A barge waited off shore. Along the water's edge a board walk was advancing toward the boat house. She couldn't see the developer's black Cadillac, but near the first portion of the walkway a motor-boat rocked at Blackthorne's dock.

John walked the group back to the curved stair of the front entrance. When Sylvania opened the door, Brandy saw that she had dressed herself with more care than usual. Her snowy hair was pulled back in a severe but tidy bun, her face dusted with powder, her cheeks lightly tinged with rouge. Her lips were still a pale line. Over that awkward frame she had dropped a gray linen sheath, fashionable perhaps two decades ago. She had not aban-doned her black oxfords. She bore down the stairs toward them, face thrust forward like a proud ship's figurehead leaning into a storm.

Curt Greene, middle–aged, affable, neatly groomed in suit and tie, assumed the lead. "Mrs. Langdon, this is indeed a pleasure," he said, and shook her hand.

Sylvania remained crusty. "We'll see, gentlemen."

After they stood in the broad second floor hallway, Greene spoke again. "For years we've admired this impressive house from a distance. We're looking forward to really seeing it for the first time."

While he introduced the others in his party, John and Brandy stayed discreetly in the rear. More than once Sylvania cast a sharp, knowing eye in Brandy's direction, but for the moment her attention centered on the trio of architects. In the living room she introduced the earlier visitor, a frail woman with silver–blonde hair, lounging by the fireplace in an ivory crepe pants suit as stylish as Sylvania's sheath was drab.

"My sister–in–law, Grace Able," Sylvania said briskly, turning her eyes toward the mantelpiece portrait. "Brookfield's widow. She asked to look for a little table of theirs before I sell the extra furniture."

Mrs. Able rose with a shy smile. "Goodness, don't let me interfere with these gentlemen. I was curious when I heard the old place was being destroyed, but Sylvania's explained. I'm leaving as soon as my companion checks upstairs for a Duncan Phyfe end table we used to own. It's the only piece I have room for now."

Brandy stepped forward, ignoring Sylvania's scowl. "Brandy O'Bannon from the *Beacon*, Mrs. Able. I'm doing a story on the house. How do you feel about seeing it sold and perhaps torn down?"

Grace pressed a dainty hand to her cheek. "Goodness, it's no secret that Brookfield and I didn't enjoy living here." She looked around with a perceptible shiver. "It's not what I would call a friendly house. No, I really shan't care what happens to it." She favored Brandy and the others with another genteel smile. "Goodness, perhaps that isn't what you expected to hear." She shrugged thin shoulders. "Talk to Sylvania. She's the family historian."

At that moment a stout, tweedy looking woman came struggling down the stairs, carrying a scarred mahogany end table.

Grace rose, waved a hand in her direction, and moved toward the hallway. "Here's my companion, Mrs. Mabel Boxley. Like a dear, she drove me over this morning. Not that I couldn't drive myself, of course. I've got to go now. It's time for my morning swim. The pool at my condo won't be crowded yet."

"She's still a marvelous swimmer," said the loyal Mrs. Boxley.

Grace turned back with a patrician smile. "Thank you, Sylvania dear, for allowing me to come."

While the committee members produced yellow pads from their briefcases and began examining the blue glazed tile on each side of the fireplace, the tile mantel, and the cast iron insert and wrought iron grate, Brandy slipped into the hall and caught up with Grace and Mrs. Boxley at the door.

"I'd very much appreciate talking again with you, Mrs. Able," she said. "Is there a time I could see you?" In the newspaper account of Eva Stone's drowning Grace had been the party's guest of honor.

Grace Able held her fingers to her shapely lips, considering. "Well, of course, there's the flower show tomorrow afternoon. I'm exhibiting. Mabel, would you give Miss O'Bannon the address? About four o'clock. The judging should be finished by then."

The indispensable Mrs. Boxley dug a small card from her purse and handed it to Brandy. This woman must be the "keeper" Mack had mentioned, Brandy thought. But Grace Able seemed quite able to keep herself.

In the living room the trio were admiring the wide, irregular cypress floorboards. Brandy scribbled notes about the cornices and the chair rails in the hallway. When one man started up the steps, Sylvania watched with arms folded. "I don't use the upper floors any more myself," she said. "I don't know what you'll find there."

Indeed, when Brandy followed him into the first two bedrooms on the third floor, she saw only tarnished brass headboards, a broken rocker, and a plain oak highboy. But through the half–open door of the last room, she was startled to spot an unmade bed, a closet with a man's shirts and trousers on hangers, and a dresser drawer with a brown sock dangling over the side. Although the examiner did not continue up to the fourth floor, Brandy noticed an accumulation of dust on the steps above. Apparently the top floor with the dormer windows was unused. If John was correct and Sylvania herself was the reported "ghost," how could she appear as a shadowy figure in the dormer window without making footprints on the stairs?

Downstairs Brandy overheard Greene marvel over the faded dining room wallpaper, blue flowers and egrets by a water fountain. "Turn of the century," he said. "You really cannot let someone demolish this house, Mrs. Langdon."

Sylvania appeared torn between pride and irritation. She sat looking out the window toward the lake, as if none of them were there, her eyes fixed on something distant. "It's not been a happy house, Mr. Greene," she said at last. "And that's an end of it. There's been tragedy here, and loneliness." Again she gave a lift to her chin. "In any case, I can't afford to put it back in good condition, and I don't know anyone else who can. I don't intend to spend the rest of my days protecting..." she hesitated for a split second... "protecting the house."

Brandy wondered what——or who——else she had shielded.

"Will you let us try to find a buyer. Perhaps a group?" Greene answered quietly. "There would be no problem in having the house registered as an historic building, like the Congregational Church in Tavares."

Sylvania rose from her chair and surveyed them all. "You have until Saturday afternoon. I've given my word to sign the contract then with my friend, Mr. Blackthorne." Polite but unshaken, she showed the committee down the hall to the front door while John stood across the room from Brandy, staring out the window, his hands in his pockets.

"She thinks no one but Blackthorne will want it," he said.

Brandy sensed his reluctance to leave. Perhaps he thought this was the last time he would see the house. Perhaps for the moment he had forgotten his anger. "Both Sylvania and Grace Able say they don't care about the house," she said, moving closer. "But I think there's more to this sale than that. After all, who wants to live with a ghost? Or," she added, seeing John's lips tighten, "with something folks *think* is a ghost? Actually, someone does live on the third floor."

The outside door closed, and in a few minutes Sylvania clumped back into the room, swinging Brandy's white pumps in one hand and her camera case in the other. She advanced across the worn carpet. "And now, you two——what explanation do you have for your disgraceful activities last night?"

Shocked, Brandy turned to John. Surely Sylvania owed her an explanation for the attack dogs. Instead, Sylvania thrust the shoes into Brandy's hands. "You do not deny, I'm sure, that it's also your car out in the lane, young lady?" She faced Brandy, arms crossed. "You can't deny you were trespassing last night?" She rounded on John. "I recognized your boat. Apparently you're involved, too. A family member!"

Heatedly, Brandy spoke up. "John had nothing to do with my coming here last night. I told you I wanted to investigate the tale about the house. I was trying to verify what people claim they've seen."

"Surely you could have asked me first."

"You made it plain you wouldn't agree."

John moved toward his great aunt. "It's true Miss O'Bannon didn't follow your instructions, and I'm sorry about that. I asked her not to come. But whatever she did as a reporter, she shouldn't have been attacked by those vicious dogs. If I hadn't been worried and checked on her, there would've been a second tragedy here."

Sylvania looked more calmly out the window toward the boat house and the new board walk. "Axel——Mr. Blackthorne——is anxious because I'm alone. He's told the watchman to keep an eye on the house. If that man saw a prowler come into my yard, he would've tried to scare the person away." She looked at Brandy squarely. "Mr. Blackthorne knows I don't go out on these grounds at night myself."

"But you did last night," John said. "We saw you." In spite of herself, Brandy felt a tiny thrill. For the moment she and John were united.

Sylvania remained unruffled. "Of course. I heard the dogs and then someone call out. I had to see what was happening." Her voice rose. "By the time I got outside, what I saw was your boat leaving."

Brandy was ready to let the matter of the dogs drop. While Sylvania was on the defensive, she had questions. "We know Axel Blackthorne's been a friend for a long time. Was he also at the party when Eva Stone disappeared?"

John thrust both hands deeper into his pockets and turned his back. Brandy knew she'd blown their solidarity. Sylvania rolled her eyes as if imploring the deity for patience. "Yes, as a matter of fact——since you will not let this unpleasant matter alone—— Axel was there. A lot of young people were there that weekend, including Brookfield's friend from the Air Forces. He became my husband shortly afterward. I suppose you'll want to know about him, too."

"I haven't seen Uncle Ace in years," John said, steering the conversation away from the disastrous party.

Sylvania's face hardened. "Married me for my money. Drinks. The family all know that. But, in my time…" She sat down at last on a chair before the fireplace and spread her hands out before her, as if trying to explain something they could not understand. "In our time, we made the best of things. In the early years we got on well enough, most of the time. At least, I wasn't the Old Maid Aunt. These days you wouldn't know about that stigma." She raised steel gray eyes. "But the two of us have finally come to the parting of the ways, and that's that."

John looked away, embarrassed, but Sylvania plowed on. "His real name's Elton, of course. Always likes to be called 'Ace.' A nickname from the war years. Always had an eye for the girls, too. He did at that party you're so interested in, and at all the parties that followed." She turned those sharp eyes again on Brandy. "But that weekend didn't cause Eva Stone's death. Her tragedy has nothing to do with this house." She stood and moved again toward the window. "I'm doing now what Brookfield would've wanted. I owe him that."

Brandy ached to pull out her note pad, but she didn't dare. "You mean, by selling the land and seeing the house pulled down?"

"I talked to him in the hospital before he died. He asked for me. He told me how he felt about this place. He'd be glad to have it gone. Tomorrow Axel's men will take down the walls of that awful boat house. They'll build the boardwalk over the old flooring. It will certainly improve the view. I'll be glad to see that eyesore go. And the house, too."

John rubbed his forehead. "Isn't the boat house in your yard?"

"I sold that spit of land with the property on the other side."

"Mrs. Langdon," Brandy said, "I wanted to ask about Brookfield's heir, his wife Grace. She seemed fine this morning, but——forgive me——I'd heard she wasn't mentally very strong."

Sylvania looked down at her hands, as though studying her response. "I never got on well with Grace. Very different interests. Except for our mutual concern for Brookfield, of course. Grace was always a nervous little thing, and her nerves have been worse since his death. Lives in a fancy condominium in Leesburg. Fortunately, money is no problem. He left her very comfortable. She still even has her own small flower garden." And to his sister, Brandy thought, Brookfield left this disintegrating house.

At the end of the hallway a door opened and closed, followed by a quick step on the stairs. Sylvania jerked her head up, alert, like a horse who detects an alarming scent in the air.

EIGHT

"Came to get the rest of my things," called a voice from the hall. A man with thick, gray hair and a wide grin peered around the doorway, as if testing the waters. Seeing John and Brandy, he gained assurance, stepped into the living room, and saluted the three by lifting a paper cup in their direction. "Face is familiar," he said to John. "S'been a long time. You one of Cousin Jake's boys?"

Sylvania stood. "This is John Able," she said, "as you'd know if your memory weren't impaired. And a reporter, Miss O'Bannon." She turned to Brandy. "My husband, at least for the moment——Elton Langdon. He can't stay."

"Oh, no.'Course not, Syl." The old gentleman wavered forward. "Long time no see." He winked at John and stuck out his hand. Then he faced Brandy. "Name's Ace, little lady," he added with a mock bow. "Ace Langdon."

Brandy had hung the camera around her neck, but she held the dirty white pumps in one hand behind her, not caring to explain them, and shook hands with the other. Langdon was of medium build, trim for his age, and light on his feet in spite of the clear liquid in the paper cup. Vodka, Brandy surmised. Probably thinks it doesn't have an odor.

He looked up and hoisted the cup toward the portrait of Brookfield Able. "Damn fine pilot," he said and focused bright blue eyes on Sylvania. "But I liked him better as a buddy than a boss."

"Elton." Sylvania advanced a few paces, menace in her voice. "Your room is untouched. Get your things. John and Miss O'Bannon are just leaving, and so am I. I'm on my way into town this afternoon and I won't be back tonight. I'm completing arrangements for my new apartment. Saturday the house goes. Now is the time for you to pack anything you left."

Her husband shrugged. "No problem. You'll have to excuse me then. I have a carry–all bag in the hall." He backed out of the room, the cocky smile still on his face.

Brandy rose suddenly. "I'm sure you'd like a few minutes alone with your aunt," she said to John and followed Ace Langdon out of the room. She had not forgotten that he was at Brookfield's welcome home–engagement party. In the hall Ace retrieved a blue canvas bag and went briskly into the kitchen. From the pantry he lifted down two bottles. Then, seeing Brandy behind him, his grin widened. The dimples must have been devastating combined with a flyer's rakish cap. "First things first," he explained. "Got to pack my gin and vermouth."

Brandy leaned against the linoleum covered kitchen counter. "I'm researching the history of this house for the *Tavares Beacon*. I'm especially interested in the drowning of Eva Stone. I thought you might be able to tell me something useful. Maybe help me reconstruct the event."

His smile faded. He set the bottles heavily down on the counter top, pulled two dish towels from a drawer, rolled them around the bottles, and thrust them into the bottom of his bag. "S'not a good time to talk. I mean with the Moose—— excuse me——with Syl in the next room. But don't go dredging up that stuff about Eva

Stone now. The house and everything around it will be gone soon. And good riddance. No matter what happened to Eva Stone, she's ancient history now." Langdon looked toward the hall stairs. "I've got to pack before the Moose throws me out."

Brandy handed him her card. "Can I see you again?"

His former grin and the dimples returned. He slipped the card into his carry–all and looked her up and down. "Little lady, if I was thirty or forty years younger, you'd see a *whole* lot more of me." On the stairs he paused at the carved newel post, looked back, and winked. "I'm staying at the Comfort Inn. If you don't reach me there, try A & S Citrus. I still stop into the office now and then."

As he vanished up the stairs, Brandy joined John and followed Sylvania's tall form down the hall. The older woman opened the outside door, her back rigid as a totem pole. "When I get home tomorrow," she said, "that old boat house will be gone at last." She stood for a few minutes looking over the ragged hedge and the weeds along the driveway, then fixed her stony gaze on John. "I'm looking forward to my nice new air conditioned apartment."

From the porch Brandy spoke up quickly. "I noticed the boat house is locked. Doesn't look like it's been opened for a long time. Could there be anything in there you'd want to keep? Maybe something of your brother's?"

Sylvania's lips turned down. "Lands, all Brookfield kept there was fishing tackle and gear for his boat. He hadn't used the boat house for years before he died. And Elton—— " She gave a little snort. "He didn't care for any sports. Didn't hunt or fish. He certainly wouldn't have put anything in the boat house. Good riddance of bad rubbish, I say. I'm glad Axel will tear it down and haul off the trash."

Head down, John led the way toward his Mustang. Beyond it, half–concealed under the trees, Brandy could see the fender of her own hatchback. "John," she said, stopping and turning toward the spit of land and the boat house, "I don't think you should let Blackthorne throw everything away, not until you've seen what's there. Sylvania obviously doesn't know."

John made a wry face. "Aunt Sylvania's probably right. People don't usually keep the family jewels in a boat house." But his long strides had halted and he sounded uncertain.

"Could be gear from the 1940's. Even war time stuff. Sylvania said he built it right after he came home and didn't use it long. You really ought to check it out. Memorabilia's valuable now. Sylvania wouldn't even think about that. It would add detail to my story."

Again Brandy felt a twinge of guilt. Her main interest in the boat house was not family mementos. It was how the figure Charlotte described was able to walk right through the closed back door.

In a few minutes they stood before the sagging plank structure. Its boat slip faced the lake with a sizable storage shed covering the ground at the rear. The yard entrance fastened with the rusty pad-lock Brandy had seen the night before. On the lake side a pair of weathered doors swung outward, allowing boaters to step onto a narrow platform and enter the shed through a front door, now also padlocked.

The purr of a car engine interrupted their inspection. Across the chain link fence Blackthorne's Cadillac eased along the grass and stopped beside the new board walk. The developer clambered out. "I need a word with you two," he called, placing plump hands on the bars of the gate.

Brandy prepared to be bawled out again for being attacked, but John took the initiative. "Did you turn the Dobermans loose last night?" he asked.

Blackthorne's heavy face remained unperturbed. "My watch-man may have. He has orders to look out for Mrs. Langdon. If he saw somebody on her property, he might turn the dogs on them. He'd think it was a burglar."

Brandy was sure he knew about the attack——knew and did not repent. Blackthorne passed his hand over his balding head and went on in a milder tone. "I wanted to ask you to go easier on your great–aunt, Mr. Able. She doesn't deserve more trouble dumped on her now. Just leave her alone. She's got enough headaches dealing with that lush she's married to. Let her finally get rid of this place. She wants to sell it."

John's voice was level, but firm. "I got your message at work, but if I find a buyer with the same offer, someone who'll preserve it, what's the harm to her?"

The developer turned toward the crew still working on the walkway. "No harm, I suppose," he said. "But you won't find a buyer by Saturday." He waved toward the workers behind him. "The development's well underway. We'll put a board walk and benches all along the water front. Take down some cypress to improve the view." He smiled. "You know the old Florida saying: You can make more money from Yankees than oranges. We can get three homes on Sylvania's one lot."

As Blackthorne stumped over to talk to his foreman, John frowned and shook his head.

Brandy put a hand on the blistered boat house wall. "Your Aunt Sylvania won't be home tonight," she murmured. "Tonight's your only chance to see what's inside."

John shook his head. "You want to court the Dobermans again?"

"I'd help you. We could come across the lake in the boat and tie up in the slip. The dogs couldn't get to us there. I'll be the lookout. Besides, Sylvania wouldn't care. She wants it all destroyed anyway." Brandy ran her fingers over the corroded lock. It hadn't been opened for years.

Above the clatter of a cement mixer, workmen were pounding posts into the damp soil. John glanced at the new boardwalk. "Well," he said, pausing at the spindly pier, "I guess Aunt Sylvania really wouldn't care. Tomorrow a crew will pull down the walls. Haul everything away." He frowned. "We'll take a quick look. I'll bring my bolt cutter." He gave a decisive nod. "Come over a little before eight."

Mr. Tyler had cautioned Brandy not to trespass. She didn't mention the warning to John, already striding across the lawn toward his car. "Come on," he said. "I've got to check out a stress problem at work."

She trotted after him, still swinging the muddy white pumps in one hand. It was almost as if he had forgotten last night's anger. "About seven–forty–five tonight, then? It's not as though we'll disturb anything."

He halted under the live oak beside her car, the planes of his face half in sunlight, half in shadow. Her heart gave a sudden lurch. Another evening together. Maybe he hadn't lost interest, maybe that wasn't a girlfriend leering from his dresser top.

But he responded in his ice–man voice. "I'm doing this for the family. Maybe I'll turn up something related to the history of the house." A wary look came into his brown eyes. "I'd better not find you've got another agenda."

Still hostile and suspicious, she thought. Not, she had to admit, without reason.

*   *   *

That afternoon Brandy covered a legislative hearing and left a story for Mr. Tyler on the laptop. By six–thirty she was driving home under her street's overhanging oaks. As she passed the sole neighbor's corner house, she was glad to see Mack's pick–up wasn't waiting in front of her mother's. No need to tell him she planned to search a deserted boat house with John. He'd either be jealous or vow again that the Able family was all crazy. Likely both.

In the kitchen she turned down her mother's offer of fish broiled on the hibachi, slapped together a tuna sandwich, and was careful not to explain her plans for the evening. After a quick shower she changed into pair of jeans, pulled on a light–weight jacket, and made a few passes through her tousled hair with the curling iron.

From a desk drawer she took a page of notes and stuffed them along with her note pad and pen into a her canvas bag. "My research on ghosts," she muttered. "Just in case."

When she pulled up beside John's Mustang, the sun had already dropped below the fringe of cabbage palms at the rear of the park. She tried not to look at his trailer, tried not to remember his arms around her. When she stepped aboard the pontoon boat and reached for his Styrofoam cooler of ice and cold drinks, their fingers touched. She felt the former electricity and moved her hand quickly away,

"Investigators are entitled to a little refreshment, I guess," he said, apparently impervious.

Brandy seated herself at the stern while he coiled the line at the bow, took his seat behind the wheel, and backed smoothly into the channel. After switching on the green and red running lights at the bow, he adjusted the tall, white one above the canvas top at the stern, and noted the compass heading for the three mile cruise.

Before them floated a white, misshapen moon. The mansion's distant cypress trees lifted like spires against the evening sky. Behind them thin clouds were still stained with crimson. The water rose and fell in a black chop. When a late–flying osprey glided overhead, a fish struggling in his claws, John's eyes followed. "If Blackthorne has his way, there won't be any birds of prey. No habitat left."

Brandy moved onto the bench across from the captain's chair, pulled a billed cap out of her canvas bag, and settled it on her head. She was thinking of another possible prey. "What if we see some kind of a specter tonight?" Her shiver was caused only partly by the wind.

He gave her a fleeting smile. "I've watched you work. I imagine you'll take notes." Then his smile disappeared and he raised his eyebrows. "Your real agenda, right?"

She ignored the dig. "I'm interested in whatever we find in the boat house, natural or supernatural. People see something unusual around the boat house. When I started to work on this story, I read an article by a parapsychologist. He says what we call "ghosts" are really electromagnetic..." she reached into her bag, retrieved her notes, and read "biochemical multidimensional organisms. He says they're the remainders of a person's aura, which he says are alpha, beta, delta, gamma brain waves. These waves are supposed to make the electromagnetic energy that surrounds all life forms."

She glanced up, her voice steady. "He says these special impressions in the atmosphere can form at moments of extreme trauma."

He shook his head, plainly amused. "Not very convincing proofs for a student of mathematics. If you spot one of these multidimensional whatevers, ask if the theory's right."

"Not possible." Brandy sighed. "He says you can't really communicate with one. It just sort of drifts around. He also says they're more likely to be seen when the moon is full." She looked up at the three–quarters moon hanging in the eastern sky. "They're more frequent around a body of water."

The stern light cast a sharp band across John's high cheekbones and left his dark eyes in shadow. "Then conditions are favorable for a sighting. You should be pleased."

When they passed the Wooten Park pier, she had noticed two night fishermen in a small boat, a yellow lantern glowing at the stern. "Maybe there'll be other witnesses tonight." There was no other activity on the silent lake.

"The guys out for catfish are too far away," John said, "so forget them."

They had reminded her of her father. For a moment the old sadness returned. "My dad taught me to fish here. How to run a boat, too."

He leaned forward, scanning the dark water for buoys. "Both useful skills." As they neared Sylvania's property, they lowered the canvas top, and he cut off the running lights. John surveyed the shore line. "No use alerting the watchman next door. It's bright enough to see what I'm doing." He pulled back on the throttle and turned off the gasoline engine. "When I start the trolling motor, switch on the depth finder."

At the bow he started the silent electric motor and guided the boat quietly around the spit of land that curved out from the lawn, nudging it along the bank toward the darkened boat house.

Brandy called softly, "Four feet, three feet, two…"

The square hulk now loomed before them, its boat slip clear, a heavy beam spanning the open structure above it. In the past boats would have been suspended from it for dry dock. They glided between weathered posts and a narrow deck that lined the outer walls. As the bow bumped against the side of the slip, John stepped up onto the pier, pulled the prow against a post, and threw a clove–hitch around it. Beside him the deck widened before the padlocked door that led into the storage shed.

"Watch your step," he said. "The platform's rotten. Could be termites. Maybe that's why Sylvania and Blackthorne are so eager to get rid of it."

"But the house is all cypress." Brandy stood and steadied herself by reaching up to hold the beam above her head. "It's termite–proof. Maybe the boat house is inferior wood. Sylvania says Brookfield built it in a hurry when he first moved in."

After she lifted the heavy bolt cutter up to John, he held his hand out for her. No romance in that, she thought as she scrambled onto the rickety platform. He just doesn't want to pull me out of the lake again.

"I saw lights on the Blackthorne site," he said, dropping her hand. "We can assume the watchman's on duty."

The high shape of the house itself rose to their left, in the dim light the dormer windows of its fourth floor blank, its lawn in shadow. As she stepped forward, a plank cracked. She grabbed for John's hand just as her foot disappeared into the ragged opening. Carefully she pulled free.

"This place is hard on shoes," she said, her voice shaking. "I almost lost one pair already."

John scowled at the uneven boards and the large, rusty nails protruding from the pier and the shed. "This wasn't built by the same craftsmen who built the house. I guess old Brookfield really did it himself."

Leaning the bolt cutter against the door, he produced a pen light from his pocket. "Hold the light on the lock. Here goes my first criminal act. Breaking and entering. If we're caught, an arrest will look great on my resumé. My father and my brother would never understand."

Brandy trained the beam on the encrusted metal loop. "It may be useful to have a sheriff's deputy and a retired captain in your family."

"As soon as we've seen inside the storage shed, we're out of here."

Gripping one side of the padlock shackle with the bolt cutter, he pressed hard, his lips contorted. "People think metal lasts, but it doesn't. Natural things like leather and shell and bone far outlast a lock." There was a loud snap. He rotated the body of the lock and then slipped it off. "I hope we can get the door open."

Together they lifted the sagging door until they could pry it forward, creaking and scraping against the floor boards. No way, Brandy thought, could anyone have entered either door a year ago. When they had forced it wide enough to see inside, John turned the flashlight beam into the moldering interior. The musty odor of decay and mildew struck them in a wave. From a rear corner came a flurry of movement, and then quiet.

"There'll be spiders and rats," he said. "Wait here." While John inched into the small room, Brandy shivered and halted outside. The flashlight beam played across shelves along the back wall. Above his shoulders she could distinguish dusty cans of paint, a few rotting boat cushions, and scattered among them, hundreds of white, diaphanous insect wings. In one corner sat a rusted tackle box, laced with cobwebs, several bent fishing rods, and a broken bench. There were no windows.

"Fortunately no one can see our light from next door," Brandy said.

John glanced back at her, frowning. "Looks like nothing of interest, just like Aunt Syl said. You'll have a hard time making copy out of this stuff." The flashlight swept over an old battery. "I hope no one notices tomorrow that the lock's been cut off." He stepped toward the door. Boards groaned and sagged.

"I don't see the ghost, either," Brandy said.

His iceman voice returned. "Of course not. I'm not hanging around while you wait for some figment of your imagination. Instead you'd better be looking for the watchman."

Brandy was picking her way toward the boat for a view from the stern, when she heard loud splintering behind her. John muttered, "Damn!"

She turned to see him teeter on the edge of a plank that had cracked in two under his weight, trapping his right foot in the gap. He knelt on his left knee, yanked his foot and leg out, and squatting at the edge of the hole, swiveled his flashlight downward. With the other hand he ripped off more of the rotted wood and shone the light underneath, rotating the beam in all directions.

"The storage shed was built over the ground," he said, "but I don't suppose there's any buried treasure."

Brandy moved back into the doorway while he leaned forward, swore under his breath, and then sat back on his heels.

"There's something under here," he said finally. "I'm not sure what."

Brandy edged into the darkened shed. "What do you mean?"

"I don't know how to tell you this," he said, "but I think I'm looking down at a skull."

NINE

"What do you mean, a skull?" Brandy knelt by the opening in the floor. "Maybe they buried cats or dogs here."

"I'm no paleontologist, but I do know a human skull when I see one." John handed Brandy the flashlight.

The beam played over a brown, dirt encrusted portion of bone, rounded like a cranium, protruding from the damp earth. Brandy could make out the hollow of one eye socket and the open triangle of the nose. The rest was sunk beneath ground.

She murmured, "Oh, my God! It's not only a skull. Look to the left. You can see the tips of other bones——maybe a rib cage. Looks like a skeleton was buried, but over the years water leached out the soil around it."

Feeling faint and nauseated, Brandy straightened up. "We've got to call the law."

"Immediately. We can't touch anything. We'll have to call the Sheriff's Office. They'll keep Blackthorne's crew from starting tomorrow." John stood and took Brandy's elbow. "Maybe there's some perfectly innocent explanation."

"Sure. Someone crawled up under the boat house to die. And then conveniently buried himself. Or herself."

"The criminal division can sort this out." He guided her across the creaking planks toward the door. "There's only one thing to do. I'll have to stay on guard while you get help." Beside the boat's aluminum gate they paused. "I'm glad you know boats. You're going to back out of here as quietly as you can and make a beeline across the lake for help. If the water's not too rough, you can make it to the Wooten Park pier in maybe twenty minutes."

"John," Brandy said, her voice hushed. "I've a terrible suspicion about who that skeleton is."

He pulled the hull closer to the dock. "Don't stop and think now. There are places I'd rather be, so for God's sake, hurry. If you tie up at the pier, it's only two blocks to the police department. This place is in the county, but the police will call the Sheriff's Office. You'll probably have to go there and make a report. Give them my brother's name. Tell them we've found a human skeleton, and be sure they know the boat house is going to be torn down tomorrow. They'll get somebody out here to secure the site."

In the boat Brandy moved toward the trolling motor at the bow. "Why can't you come, too? With luck we wouldn't be gone more than an hour."

"Because we don't know whether anyone's heard us or not. I don't trust Blackthorne or his guy next door. The skeleton will throw a monkey wrench into his plans, for sure. We might get back and find it gone."

He lifted the line from around the post and threw it back onto the boat deck. With nervous fingers she switched on the electric motor, grasped its lever, shifted into reverse, and began backing soundlessly out of the slip.

He sat down on the end of the pier. "So much for getting away with the break–in."

And I'm responsible, she thought, maneuvering around cypress knees that reached, claw–like, out of the water. The motion of the bow startled an anhinga, and she gasped as it flapped suddenly up from a tree limb, its black snake–neck extended. As she glided further out from the bank, she looked up at the tall, silent house along the water's edge. From the branch of a fifty foot cypress, a web of Spanish moss brushed against the east dormer.

The cold bright moon, now high above the lake, cast a pale light on the pane. Her heart gave a thud. A fragmentary shape wavered in the narrow window, a momentary dark figure like a head and shoulders drifted behind the glass. For perhaps half a second she stared and held her breath, but once again there was no time for her ghost watch. She thought of John, and her glance shifted to the pier where he waited, looking progressively smaller and more alone in the shadow of the boat house. She must hurry.

About twenty yards out from the Able boat slip, she cut off the trolling motor, stepped back to the helm to start the gasoline engine, switched on the running lights, and threw the throttle forward. The engine thundered on and the boat gave a great leap toward Tavares, now a rim of lights to the northwest between the blackness of the water and the sky.

The wind had risen, kicking up a heavier chop, and the boat dipped and climbed in the troughs. She gripped the wheel, and reminded herself that a pontoon boat couldn't actually sink. Of course, she knew, it *could* turn over.

At the half–way point, while she strained to recognize the street lights of Wooten Park a mile and a half away, she heard the start–up roar of an engine from the shore behind her. Turning her head quickly, she saw Blackthorne's motorboat leap away from the boardwalk. With quickening pulse she watched as its running lights flicked on, and its nose turned in an arc toward her stern. A pontoon boat is not built for speed. It is built for leisure, for nature–watching, for fishing, for people who are not in a hurry. Now she pushed the throttle as far forward as she could and felt the crashing bounce as she turned into the highest waves. Even at that distance, she also knew, the other boat with its powerful engine could easily overtake her.

The throb of the larger engine rocketed across the lake, the boat's green and red bow lights locked in a direct line with her own rudder. Plainly someone was aiming straight for her. She knew without looking that the distance between them was rapidly closing. Under the pressure of her engine's thrust and the heave of the waves, her boat lurched to one side, spray cascaded onto her starboard bow, and drenched her at the helm. She wrenched the wheel to the left, rode heavily into the next swell. The boat rocked violently, then righted itself. Without question, if the motorboat kept up its pace and swept around her, she would be swamped by its giant wake. She had not the strength to keep it upright. No one would have to do her any physical violence. The faster boat could just disappear into the darkness. If she was not struck by the motorboat itself, she would be left clinging to the pontoons on a black night in waters rough enough to wash her away. She could almost feel the bite of the metal into her fingers, the pounding of the waves. She could never swim the distance to the shore. And there would be no witnesses. Then she remembered the night fishermen.

Brandy peered frantically ahead. To the left shone the dim glow of their lantern. Soon she could make out the dark shape of the little Jon boat, rocking at anchor in the calmer water off shore. As she drew nearer she saw two hunched figures. She twisted the wheel to port, the boat tilted deeply into the water, once again righted itself, and she aimed just to the left of the small boat. According to the rules of the road, she should cut her engine as she drew near, but she did not dare. Behind her the motorboat was so close that she could almost see the features of the shadowed figure at the helm. One of the fishermen stood up in the small boat, already pitching from side to side as she bore down on them. She could see his angry face, white and sharp in the stern light, see the fishing pole still in his hand. In spite of what John had said, they were both witnesses after all.

As Blackthorne's motorboat shot past, she throttled back her engine at last. The faster boat slowed, curved west along the shoreline of Tavares past the tall, round tower of the old courthouse toward the Dora Canal, and disappeared. Trembling now, she cruised by the Jon boat and raised a hand in an apologetic salute. The man on his feet shook his fist. Although she had frightened away his catfish, they had saved her from far worse than a fishhook.

If the person in the other boat was looking for John's trailer, he would find no one there. Would he come back? Now she turned, picked up speed again, and raced toward the shelter of the Wooten Park dock. By the time she had pulled into a boat slip, cut off the engine, and thrown a line around the capstan, she saw that it was ten, later than she had hoped. She secured the stern and the bow, snatched her canvas bag off a seat, scrambled up onto the pier, and began to run across the grass and the asphalt parking lot toward Rockingham Avenue.

She could hear an engine churning along the shore toward the park. Had they already found that John was gone? She stumbled over the railroad tracks, glanced with longing at the bright windows of the Pub on the Lake——safety and a telephone would be there——but tore on, unsure where the person in Blackthorne's boat might have gone, and rounded the corner onto Rockingham.

A couple walked out of the restaurant and climbed into a sedan. Behind her another car started up, and she could hear it backing around. She sprinted past the bank, across a deserted

Main Street, along the sidewalk beside the city hall building, and sides aching, rounded the last corner and dashed into the police station behind it just as the car raced past her down the empty street.

An officer at a counter looked up from a computer monitor, startled. In a glass screen she saw her reflection—hair blown into peaks, shirt tail hanging, eyes wide and panicky. He had a kind young face and he rose, came around the counter toward her, and politely asked her to sit in a chair by his desk. Soon she was pouring out her story——the skeleton, John waiting at the abandoned boat house, the race with another boat across the lake. The officer held up his hand.

"Whoa," he said. "Let me call the Sheriff's Office. This is county business. I'll get someone to take you over there." He peered at her anxiously. "You're sure you're all right now, M'am?" She nodded and looked at her watch while he dialed. Time was passing too quickly.

In a few minutes she was sitting in the white concrete Sheriff's Office across from the courthouse, and re–telling her story to a thin, dark–complexioned sergeant with sharp eyes and a crisp green uniform. He turned a pencil reflectively in his fingers, then opened a narrow spiral notebook. "You're sure this is a human skeleton?"

"We're sure of it. Of course, we can't tell about its age. We haven't touched anything."

He rubbed his chin. "Doesn't sound recent. If the boat house hasn't been used in years, it's hard to see how it got buried under the floor. Floor hadn't been disturbed?"

"Only by termites, officer." She looked again at her watch—— ten thirty. "Look, it's urgent. The boat house is going to be torn down tomorrow. The whole site will be destroyed. That's why the owner's grand nephew stayed behind ——John Able. He's there now. We want the site secured."

The bright eyes were grave. "And what were the two of you doing there at night yourselves?"

Brandy squirmed. "I'm writing an article about the house for the *Beacon*. We were looking around before it's all gone. You can check us out with Deputy Steve Able. He's John Able's brother."

The sergeant nodded when she mentioned Steve and she felt relieved. "And the owner wasn't there? Had she given permission?"

Again Brandy shifted in her chair. "This morning she told us she'd be away. She knows about the newspaper story. We didn't think she'd mind. A spur of the moment impulse. We were out on the lake in John's boat." She smiled weakly. "The important thing is the skeleton."

The sergeant scratched a few notes on the pad. "There's a patrol car not too far from that area now," he said. "I'll call the officer. It shouldn't be long before he finishes his assignment. He can get over there."

She rose. "Mr. Able's pontoon boat is tied up at the public pier. I've got to go back there for him, and I can't leave the boat at the park overnight." She twisted the strap on her canvas bag. "Only I'm a little nervous about the lake. I told you, I'm sure I was chased coming over here."

"Probably kids out on the lake for a lark. Thought they'd give you a scare. Kids around here will do that." The sergeant reached into his desk and pulled out a flashlight. "Still, if someone did try to keep you from reporting this, they'll know it's too late now. But I'll ask someone to watch. You signal with this if you have any trouble. We can get a patrol boat there pretty fast." He turned and called to a corporal who was walking in through a rear door. "Give this lady a ride down to Wooten Park and see that she gets

off in her boat all right. Get on the horn like a shot if anyone gives
her a problem——and check her gas tanks first."

He picked up the phone and she heard him ask for the patrol
car. Taking the heavy flashlight, she followed the other deputy
outside. When they pulled up in the parking lot in front of the
pier, she was relieved to see John's boat still rocking, undisturbed,
in the boat slip.

The deputy leaned over the stern and inspected the tanks.
"Looks okay for a round trip, m'am." He lifted the lines off capstan and cleat. "I'm to wait here until you signal you're safe on the
other side. Just give one long wave with the flashlight."

The water had quieted, the moon sunk low in the west. Brandy
peered again at her watch——eleven. John would be restless. The
deputy scanned the lake with a pair of binoculars. Nothing
stirred. Even the night fishermen had vanished. Brandy switched
on the engine and the lights, eased out of the slip, and pointed her
prow to the southeast. Navigating for the dark shore would be
tricky, but she was beginning to think she could find her way
blindfolded.

On the return trip the wind was at her back and had lessened.
The boat purred solidly along under a waning moon. No one else
was on the lake. Brandy began to relax. Surely the nightmare had
ended. As she closed on the opposite bank, she turned further east,
and cruised along near the trees, searching in the dim light for the
Able mansion. No motorboat, she noticed, was moored at
Blackthorne's dock. When she spotted the bulk of the boat house,
she raised her flashlight in a high arc, amazed that in Tavares,
almost three miles away, the signal would be visible as a tiny light.

She did not see John's own flashlight beam, but she realized he
might be saving his batteries. She did not like to call out. She was
not sure who might lurk on the other side of the fence. Cutting her
speed almost to idle, she turned off the running lights, and nudged

her way carefully into the slip, surprised that John had not come forward to help her. She could now see him, standing back near the doorway, silent. He's angry, she thought. I've been gone too long. Switching off the engine, she picked up the flashlight again and reached overhead with the other hand, prepared to steady herself by holding to the cross beam.

"Don't," John said, his voice low and strained. "Don't move. Don't touch anything."

Above her she heard a sickening, slithering sound.

She froze, then shone the flashlight upward. Glistening in the shaft of light, she saw the long, fat body, the upraised head, and the gaping white jaws of a cottonmouth moccasin.

TEN

Facing her, the snake's head swayed slightly, its eyes like steel drills. Brandy stifled a cry. John's flashlight flicked on and froze on the heavy coils and the lifted, triangular head. The mouth yawned a fleshy white. "The warning posture," he whispered. "Don't make a sudden move. Going to try to knock it into the water."

She put one foot behind her and stepped slowly backward, grasping for the console, while John advanced, crouching, in one hand a long, narrow board. The black snake head turned. When he had almost reached the boat, he slammed the board up and sideways. But the cottonmouth was quicker. Like a bullet, its body uncoiled and shot forward. Brandy's eyes widened. She screamed, "No!"

At the same instant, the moccasin's fangs sank into John's hand. She gave a sob, sprang out of the boat, and rushed toward John as the moccasin drew back and slid over the edge of the pier into the water. John had dropped to his knees, supporting his wounded arm with the other hand.

She tried to remember the snake bite first aid she once learned in a health class. "Lie down," she said, "be absolutely still." She turned back, lifted a boat cushion off the front seat, and kneeling beside him, helped him stretch out with his head raised on the cushion.

"The kit," he muttered. "Under the first seat." In the dull light he was deathly pale. Perspiration beaded his face. "Hurts like hell."

She climbed back into the boat, pulled the first seat forward, and found a small plastic first aid kit. Kneeling once more beside him, she laid a hand on his clammy forehead. He squirmed. "Thirsty," he said.

Already the small round holes in the back of his hand were turning dusky. Brandy dampened a piece of gauze with disinfectant and gently wiped around the wound, then dried it as best she could with clean gauze. "A deputy should be here right away. He'll call an emergency response team on his car radio. They'll get you to a hospital in no time."

She felt the inside of his wrist and counted. His pulse rate was fast but weak. She had to protect him from shock. Standing up quickly, she pulled off her jacket and tucked it around him, then yanked up her shirt, stripped it off, and tore a wide strip out of the back, willing herself to stay calm.

"Got to make a tourniquet," she said. "Tie it above the wound and below the pulse." She twisted the cotton strip into a band and knotted it loosely between the darkening holes and his wrist. Please, God, she thought, send the deputy now.

John turned his head from side to side, his chest heaving, his teeth clinched. "Going to be sick."

"You mustn't go into shock." She found a bottle of aspirin in the kit, scrambled back onto the boat, and opened the Styrofoam cooler behind the captain's chair. In a few seconds she knelt again beside him, holding a can in one hand and a fistful of ice in the other. Lifting his head slightly, she managed to get two tablets down his throat. His voice was faint. "Pop tastes good," he mumbled. "So thirsty."

Wrapping the ice in another strip of cloth from her tattered shirt, she passed it across his cheeks and forehead and held it there. He's got to have anti–venom, she thought, and soon. He stared up at her, silent, the muscles in his face tense with pain.

She murmured, "Just look what I've done to you."

"Wasn't you. Moccasins are night hunters. Shouldn't have come without a gun." His own eyes glazed. She could barely hear his voice. "Sylvania warned us."

Brandy remembered. Sylvania had said water moccasins were the biggest danger in the lake. Because of them, she didn't go to the boat house.

Brandy turned off the flashlight. The moon had gone behind clouds building in the west. She sat in darkness. A bullfrog——or maybe a 'gator——bellowed. Around them crickets and night insects whirred and trilled.

Supporting John's head against her lap, her gaze strayed to the fourth floor dormer windows. She had glimpsed a shape there when she pulled away from the boat house. Now it was too dark to see. Behind her under the floor in the dark and the dampness the skull lay waiting. Was there a connection, a danger?

Finally in the distance she heard the brief squeal of a siren and a few seconds later, the crunch of tires in the parking lot. Next door the Dobermans set up a storm of barking. She could hear them now, rushing along the fence. She eased John's head back onto the cushion, and seizing the flashlight, signaled wildly. At that moment a figure emerged around the left wing of the house.

"Over here!" she called. "We need help!"

But before she could swing the beam to the left, she heard a voice from the opposite direction. "Sheriff's Office," it said. "Deputy Martin. What's up?"

Confused, she focused the light to the right and picked up a uni-formed deputy striding toward the boat house, ignoring the dogs that lunged along beside the barrier of chain link, and following the beam of his own flashlight.

"Cottonmouth bite!" Brandy shouted. "Emergency!"

The deputy half–slid down the slippery bank, grasped a pier railing, and stepped onto the platform. Squatting on his heels beside John, he tilted back his hat and shone his light on John's hand. The wounds were now puffy and almost black.

He gave a low whistle. "Son–of–a–gun. Got you bad. Looks like you took good care of him, little lady." He stood up, a tall well–made man of perhaps thirty with the sunburned complexion blond people often have in Florida. To Brandy he looked like a saint.

"I'll get on the horn pronto," the deputy said. "EMS will carry him to Leesburg Regional." He jumped down into the weeds along the shore. "I'll be sure they bring anti–venom."

As he started toward his car, Brandy called after him, "Isn't there another deputy with you?" The figure she had seen on the lawn to the left had not arrived.

He looked back over his shoulder. "No partner tonight," he said. "Just me, Miss."

Brandy swung her light across the lawn under the dormer win-dows, highlighting the pale, straight trunks of the cypress, the stretch of ragged grass, the boarded up alcoves of the first floor. In the warm night she shivered. Nothing else was there. Perhaps the first figure had been her imagination.

When the flashlight beam began to fade, she switched it off and knelt beside John. "Hang in there," she whispered. "The troops are on the way."

In silence they waited until the matter–of–fact form of Deputy Martin re–emerged along the right fence. He swung back up on the pier. "I'll need to see about that skeleton the sergeant reported."

Brandy nodded toward the open boat house door behind them. "In there, deputy," she said. "I think the moccasin went into the lake, but be careful where you walk. In places the floor's almost gone." A few minutes later she heard the creaking of boards as he moved around, then his low whistle. He must have seen it.

He eased his way back outside. "I'll secure the place as soon as the response team gets here," he said. "Odd place for a burial, all right." He tugged a small spiral note pad and pencil out of his pocket. "We got a little time. I guess I ought to get your statement, Miss."

With the tail of her shirt Brandy wiped John's forehead again. Professional of the deputy to pretend he didn't notice the whole back of her shirt was missing. "I'm with the Tavares *Beacon*," she began and described as completely as she could how they had found the bones. "The Sheriff will probably want to know if anyone's missing around here," she added. "The answer is, yes." She glanced up toward the dormer windows. "A girl——her name was Eva Stone——vanished here in 1945."

The EMS van's siren keened in the distance. By the time they could hear it bucketing down the lane and see the reflection of its blue light against the metal fence, John's chest was heaving again. Deputy Martin leaped once more to the grassy slope and strode toward the parking lot.

To Brandy the medical team's efficiency seemed awesome. Attendants in white uniforms swarmed up onto the platform. As John was eased onto a stretcher at last, her eyes again filled with tears. Sick and weak, she leaned for support against the boat house wall.

"This your boyfriend?" a technician asked.

"Not exactly." Her voice came in a whisper. "A good friend."

He stooped to pick up one end of the litter. "Now don't worry. He'll get treatment on the way to the hospital." In seconds they were bearing John back across the lawn.

She trailed behind to watch the van door slide shut and the white emergency vehicle spurt back down the lane out of sight, siren wailing. Brandy suddenly remembered the girl on John's dresser. She ought to be told, as well as his brother and his parents. On the way back to the pier she realized she was bone weary, but her task was far from over. The deputy had taken a roll of yellow and black tape from his car and was carefully stringing it around the boat house.

"Marking off this whole area," he explained. "The medical examiner will be here in the morning. He'll tell us the sex and age of the skeleton." He drove a stake into the soft ground and attached the last section of tape. "Detectives will want to inspect everything. They'll need to reach the home owner, if they haven't found her already."

Brandy ducked under the tape and started for the boat slip. "Mrs. Langdon's husband is at the Comfort Inn," she said. "They're separated, but he may know where she stays in town." She dragged herself through the boat's aluminum gate. "I've got to take this boat back to a trailer park on the Dora Canal. Then I'll be going on to the hospital to see how Mr. Able's doing."

Deputy Martin grinned. "I think you'll be safe on the way back. The sergeant says you were followed when you came across the lake to report the bones. If anyone was trying to scare you off, they'll know it's too late. By now everyone in the area's been waked up. A motorcycle race couldn't make more noise than the dogs and EMS. Signal if you have any more trouble. I'll alert the sergeant to have someone watch for you."

After Brandy had lifted the lines from the posts, she edged the boat out of the slip without looking back. She no longer trusted her senses. The moon is down, she thought. Time for night's black agents. After half a century, was someone still trying to hide a bloody secret?

Yet the danger to John, not a ghost or a murderer, drove her across the black waters. As the boat plunged on toward the dim shoreline, she gripped the wheel and focused on steering toward the tall, lighted cylinder of the old Tavares courthouse.

In twenty minutes she had signaled to a deputy on shore and received an answering wave of his beam. Cruising on for a quarter of a mile, she nosed into John's boat slip, tied up, and clambered onto the pier. Before his trailer steps she paused. In the loose dirt around them were a man's footprints. A fine detective I'd make, she said to herself. I can't even tell if they're John's or someone else's.

With the last of the three keys on John's ring, she unlocked the door and was swept by last night's emotion, by the feel of being whirled in his arms down the hall. Again she saw the high plane of his cheek, the warmth of his glance ——but this would not do. She tried to think instead of Mack, but she knew what Mack would say about tonight. On the lake at night with another guy? Breaking into a boat house? A cottonmouth? He'd warned her.

For a few minutes Brandy slumped on the couch, bone tired. Then bracing herself, she picked up John's kitchen phone and called home. Before her mother could unleash her full outrage at the hour, she explained that John was in the hospital and that she planned to stop there before she came home. Next came the Sheriff's Office, where she asked a deputy to be sure John's brother Steve knew about the injury and alerted their parents.

In the bedroom Brandy studied the photograph. In one corner "Love, Sharon," was inscribed in tiny, precise letters. No flare for imaginative language, she thought, but she felt a thickness in her chest. Last night's indignation had melted with her first look at John's wound. In the living room she noticed the yearbook and annual she had thrust under the coffee table the night before. Surely John wouldn't care if she took a look at them now. He had said to take them. They might reveal insights into the people she had to interview. But tonight, she had to know he would be all right.

Books under one arm, she locked the door behind her and climbed wearily into her car. But within thirty minutes she had plowed into the emergency room parking lot, adrenaline again pumping. At the desk a duty nurse told her John was being moved to a private room, that he was in serious but stable condition, and that, after rushing so hard, she would simply have to take a seat in the waiting room. She was not family. She dragged herself into a chair. She owed the family an explanation. In the meantime, she would examine Brookfield Able's 1938 high school yearbook. She was much too wired to sleep.

The slim, fifty–two year old annual had a magazine format consisting of class pictures, black and white photographs of the Spanish stucco high school building, and short articles by classmates about one another. She turned to the senior class page. Brookfield Able stared back, a somber looking youth whose interests were listed as football and hunting. He had been senior class president and an officer in the Honor Society.

His photograph was not as commanding as the likeness in the fireplace portrait, but its forerunner was clearly visible——the high forehead, the black hair brushed neatly back, a thick jaw, a firm if heavy mouth, and a challenging gaze into the camera lens. He bore some family resemblance in bone structure to John, but the angles of John's face were more refined. She turned the next page and recognized the photograph she had seen in the *Leesburg*

Commercial, Eva Stone as high school senior. Her classic features, framed by long, dark hair, dominated the page. Eva's activity and interest list was much shorter than Brookfield's: home–economics; child care. Well, Brandy thought, in 1938 that was to be expected.

Brookfield's sister was younger. Brandy looked in a back section and found Sylvania's much smaller picture among the sophomores. Brandy could easily identify the big head, the prominent features, the cropped hair. Next she turned to the yellowing index: Blackthorne, Axel C.,p. 3. On page three in the junior class she found the developer, youthful but strangely unaltered. His hair was thicker and darker, but the round face and the gap between his front teeth were unchanged. Brandy recognized him immediately. They all must've known each other. It wasn't surprising. Tavares was a small town.

Before setting down the yearbook, she turned on a hunch to Notables. Here she was surprised by a small photograph of a couple standing together, the boy's arm around the girl's slender back, her head against his shoulder. "Most Popular Couple:" read the caption, "Brookfield Able and Eva Stone." She sat back, stunned. Sylvania certainly hadn't mentioned her brother's connection with the dead girl. The fact that Brookfield was Eva Stone's boyfriend in 1938 didn't make her a ghost in 1945——or a skeleton. But it was something to go on.

Grace Able would not be part of the high school group. The news clipping had given the Southerland address as Leesburg, but she would probably appear among the family photographs. Brandy lifted the black leather album into her lap and began turning pages until she came to a group photograph on the back lawn of the Able summer home.

The family members stood before a great, blooming bougainvillea: white–bearded Great–grandfather Able in a black suit, his diminutive wife at his side, next to them John's grandfather and grandmother. Behind them towered a young Sylvania. Next to her, Ace's grinning face was barely visible above the elderly man in front. Brookfield and Grace stood apart from the children seated on the ground before his younger brother. Brookfield, as always, was ramrod straight and unsmiling. Brandy peered at the tiny photograph of Grace——slight, short hair tightly curled, face a sallow oval, hands clasped before her. She had a rather melancholy expression, Brandy thought.

Brandy had set aside the books and begun jotting in her note pad every detail of the night's experience she could remember when a disheveled Steve Able hurried into the room. He was shorter and sturdier than his younger brother, his features more blunt, but Brandy recognized him immediately. As soon as he had checked at the desk, she tucked her note pad away and introduced herself as the *Beacon* reporter involved in his brother's accident.

He frowned and nodded toward two chairs near the desk. "The doctor will come out soon," he said. "Until then, you might as well tell me what happened."

He rocked back in the seat, one ankle resting on the other knee, and listened, interrupting only to ask for more details about the skeleton and the snake. When she had finished, he shook his head. "A bad business. You both took too many risks. Still, the bones will call for a full investigation."

Brandy sat back, limp. This was the second night she had gone with almost no sleep. "You realize John was trying to protect me. That's why he was struck."

Steve stretched out his legs. "Because of John, I doubt Sylvania will make a stink about the break–in."

"Would you try to keep me informed, about the case, I mean? I'll pass on to the Sheriff's Office any information I get. Some people I plan to interview may talk more freely to me than to a detective."

Steve leaned back and locked his hands behind his head. "If it's okay with the detective in charge. I don't know how John will feel about you when he comes through this——but Dad will be mad as hell."

ELEVEN

Brandy checked her watch. Four. A few minutes later a slender young physician with a tired slouch came into the room to give John's brother Steve his report. "A pretty severe necrosis," he said. "We're giving Mr. Able anti–venom intravenously and keeping a careful watch. If the poison has gotten into the muscle, we may have to excise the area and remove the dead tissue. The swelling is going to shock you, so be prepared." The doctor glanced at his clipboard. "He's getting morphine now for pain, so you'll not get much of a visit, but family can go in for a few minutes."

Brandy looked so stricken that Steve took her arm and led her with him. John lay on his back, face white and drawn, tubes running into him from suspended bottles, the swollen hand loosely bandaged. Restless even under sedation, his body twitched. Brandy bent over him. "It wasn't such a good idea I had, after all." There was no response.

Steve touched his shoulder. "Mom and Dad are on the way. Had a little trouble reaching them. I got to report in early this morning, but I'll be back after my shift, okay? Next time, duck." Brandy thought John tried to smile.

As they walked back into the hall, Brandy said, "I'll wait. I owe your folks an apology. But do give me a call if you hear anything."

Steve ran a hand through his hair. "I'll stay in touch."

Brandy remained, still unable to rest. On her note pad she had begun doodling snakes with pin prick eyes and pointy fangs when John's parents arrived.

The retired Captain charged into the almost empty room like a steam engine, head pushed forward, a heavy set man with a growing paunch. He bore out John's description of "Old Spit and Polish." Even at that pre–dawn hour his graying hair was slicked back and his slacks sharply creased, like his son's.

A few paces behind trotted a thin woman with nervous hands. Clearly, she expected her husband to lead. He halted in mid–charge and turned to his wife, who recognizing some subtle signal, produced a pair of eyeglasses from her purse. After he placed them over his sizable nose, he advanced again, better prepared to conduct an inspection.

"So you're the little lady broke into Sylvania's boat house tonight with John. Just what did you expect to find?" He had a commanding voice, barely controlled.

Brandy met him midway across the room and extended her hand. "Brandy O'Bannon, *Tavares Beacon*. I'm sure Steve explained that we did find something important, but I'm truly sorry about your son."

Temporarily derailed, the captain gripped her hand and then dropped it almost immediately. "It's not like John, a fool stunt like that. Not like him at all. He thinks things out."

From the rear John's mother spoke up. "He's always been a careful sort of boy." Her frail figure moved closer. "Let's ask for the doctor, please."

The captain grunted and spun toward the admittance window. Brandy heard herself saying, "Have you notified John's girl friend?" She tried to sound off–hand.

A smile flitted across the older woman's face. "Sharon will get here from Ocala sometime this morning. She's on summer vacation from college. A nice steady sort of girl. You know her?" Brandy shook her head, the weight again in her chest. Apparently, the relationship was close.

The captain turned and motioned his wife to follow. Then his gaze dropped to the album and the yearbook on a side table and he scowled. "What are these doing here?"

"Research. I didn't think John would mind." Brandy reached for them, adding not quite honestly. "He showed them to me. For my story about the Able mansion." She extended the books toward him. "Here, I've finished."

His heavy face flushed. "We'll pick them up at the desk, thank you, Miss O'Bannon." Before a startled receptionist, he shoved them onto the counter. Mrs. Able scurried after him through the swinging door.

Brandy peered again at her watch. Time to catch a few ZZ's at the house, freshen up, and call Mr. Tyler. She didn't want to hang around and meet the exemplary girl friend. Clearly, Sharon was not a woman who had to be pulled from the lake one night, and on the next, urge a normally cautious son to break into a deserted boat house.

As for Brandy, she hadn't aroused a warm response from John since he plucked her out of the lake. Sighing, she shouldered her canvas bag and stepped out to her car.

       *   *   *

For three hours at home Brandy slept fitfully, tossed some more, then finally gave up and showered. Still wired, by nine o'clock she had punched the flashing button on her office answering machine and listened to Mack's irritated message: "What's the matter, kid? I called the house last night and your mom couldn't tell me squat. Your looney tunes job is messing up our plans. I got something to show you."

She hesitated, then phoned the Buick agency and was relieved when the secretary said he was out on the lot. Good old reliable, well–heeled Mack. What was the matter with her? A bird in the hand, she thought ruefully. She would have to call back.

Gathering up her notes, she knocked on Mr. Tyler's half open door, then sailed into his office. Even if she hadn't cornered a ghost, she could report her discovery of the skeleton. Maybe the Sheriff's Office would let the paper report the medical examiner's finding. She expected the editor to be pleased.

Instead, he listened to her story about the buried bones with a languid stare, snuffed out the usual cigarette, and sank back in his chair. "The dailies will be full of your skeleton in the morning," he said. With exaggerated care, he peered at his desk calendar. "We go to the printer on Tuesday. It takes a day to print and distribute, remember? Those bones will be old news by Wednesday. By then you'll need something fresh." He began hunting through the papers on his desk. "But I guess the good news is that you broke into the boat house with the owner's relative, so maybe the paper won't be sued."

No need to point out that, technically, Blackthorne had already bought the boat house land. "Monday I'll have the story I promised," she said, subdued. "And with a human interest focus." She paused, then went on in a rush. "My research was delayed. When John Able was helping me last night, he was bitten by a cottonmouth. He saved me from being struck. Now he's in the hospital."

The editor wagged his head, apparently at the foibles of the young. "You better hang on to the guy. By my count, this is the second time he's pulled your chestnuts out of the fire."

Brandy looked down at her notes. "I'm going to line up several interviews, but I doubt Mr. Able will be helping me any more."

As she rose to leave, the editor pulled a memo from under a sheaf of papers. "I did get a message you'd be interested in. The Sheriff's Office will hold a briefing on the case tonight. Just for the hell of it, you might like to be there." Brandy detected a familiar glint in the shrewd blue eyes. Old fire–horse, she thought. He didn't give me any other assignment, either.

"Eight o'clock. I'll be there."

When Brandy called Curt Greene's office a few minutes later to ask for news of the mansion's sale, the architect wasn't in. His secretary was sure Mr. Greene hadn't located a buyer. Bad news for John.

Brandy had dressed that morning in a cool denim dress and her freshly cleaned pumps, ready once more to make a professional impression. She didn't dare call Sylvania, who would be furious about the second trespass on her property. She wondered what Sylvania's estranged husband would say about the discovery under the boat house. The morning dailies wouldn't have the story until tomorrow. She looked up the phone number of Ace Langdon's motel.

On the telephone his voice sounded slightly slurred. She told him she was talking to people who had been at Brookfield and Grace Able's engagement party. Then she asked to see him. He was silent for several seconds.

"No problem," he said at last. "But there's not much to tell. Be glad to talk to you, though, little lady. The room's Number 270. Come on and we'll drink a wee toast to age and beauty." She could almost see the lift of his eyebrows, the flirtatious smile.

"I'll meet you in the coffee shop," she said firmly. "At eleven."

His voice raised an octave. "Coffee?"

"Coffee." He chuckled, but he agreed.

Brandy finished the work on her desk, and promptly at eleven pulled into the Comfort Inn lot. The old gentleman was already ensconced in a booth, nursing a mug of coffee, a paper cup on the side.

He raised his mug when he saw her and flashed his dimples. "Irish coffee. A little whiskey improves the taste."

Brandy slid into the opposite seat. She had decided to wait until the end of the interview to spring her news bulletin. She signaled the waitress.

"You'll remember I'm writing a feature about the Able homestead," she said, "because it may be torn down. I'm doing the historical research, but I also need an account of Eva Stone's disappearance, including the rumors about it."

Brandy let Ace reflect while she ordered decaf and a dish of frozen yogurt. While she pulled out her note pad, he poured a dollop of clear liquid into his mug, then rubbed one ear. "I remember your assignment well enough, but I can't tell you anything that's not already on record."

Brandy gave him a dead level look. "Let me be the judge of that. I plan to find the maid who saw Eva Stone walk into the water——Lily Mae Brown. If she's still alive. I want to talk to all the witnesses at the party. I hear Eva still has family here."

He sighed and looked down into his cup. "Oh, yes. I was there all right. Gorgeous girl. Terrible pity, her death."

"Can you shed any light on why she'd kill herself?"

"I thought what everybody else did——she was nuts about Brookfield. Went over the edge when he announced his engagement to Grace." He gave a short laugh. "Not that she couldn't have had any other man there. Me included."

"Had you known her before that party, then?"

"I came here with Brookfield on leave the year before. That's when I met the Moose." He grinned. "Pardon me. I mean Sylvania." He took a slow sip of coffee. "Brookfield and I both saw Eva a few times, alone and together. But, well..." His mouth twisted down suddenly. "She didn't succumb to my considerable charms. She and Brookfield had an old romance going way back."

Brandy remembered their yearbook picture and nodded. "What about Grace?"

"Oh, these Southern folks are real big on Daddy fixing up the marriages. Or they used to be. Kind of medieval. Didn't exactly force anyone, of course. But Daddy could really push the advantages of the right match. And Grace Southerland was already smitten with Brookfield. He was seeing Eva as well as Grace then. But the Southerland Fruit Company combined with Able Citrus made a tempting package. Eva couldn't compete. Financially, I mean. Old Man Able tempted me, too, I admit. Later Brookfield's daddy gave us both employment. Me, of course——" his voice dropped,"——on a much lower level. In order to qualify for the job, I had to accept a certain——"he glanced away—— "a certain handicap."

Poor Sylvania, Brandy thought, her marriage doomed from the start. She might even have been in love with the brash young pilot, her beloved brother's best friend. But it was Brookfield's relationship with Eva Stone that Brandy wanted to probe. "Then Brookfield didn't propose to Grace when he was in town the year before?"

He elevated one eyebrow. "You're a very nosy young lady. Why should I tell you that?"

"Because, Mr. Langdon, we're trying to figure out what happened to Eva Stone. You say you cared about her."

Ace sighed and fingered his cup. "He probably wrote her a letter when we got back to England. With a little long distance prodding from Daddy, of course."

"Why was Eva Stone invited to the engagement party, then? It seems cruel."

Ace gave a short, barking laugh. "She wasn't. I'm sure the Moose wouldn't tell you that. Eva had been out of town. She heard that Brookfield's parents were giving him a welcome home party and turned up to see him. I don't think she knew about the engagement. She thought his folks just hadn't included her. Able family——all snobs, you know. Would've made Eva mad."

"Did you talk to Eva much that weekend?"

Ace looked toward the door. "Eva never gave me a tumble, so I cut a deal with Old Man Able." Brandy pictured the pitiful contrast between the two young women. "But the Moose is right about one thing. Don't rake it all up now."

Brandy ignored his advice. "I've heard a lot of stories about the house. About unusual sightings. You lived there for years. Would you comment on those stories?"

Ace was still for a minute, looking down at the counter, twisting his now almost empty paper cup. "The Moose doesn't like to talk about those stories," he said at last. "But I'll tell you this. There's something strange in that house. The Moose sleeps downstairs on the second floor. When I was invited to move up to the third, I took the room farthest from the stairs, and I didn't go up to the fourth. Now that's all I'm saying. I'm speaking just for myself. I ought to get a medal for going up those stairs at all." He pushed his cup away. "I've enjoyed being grilled by a beautiful reporter, but I think I've said enough."

Brandy savored a spoonful of her yogurt. "Something new has come up. The old case is re–opened." He raised a quizzical gray eyebrow again. "A skeleton was found last night on the property."

No need, she thought, to tell where. "It's been there long enough to be Eva Stone's. It's bound to be identified soon. The story will be in all the papers tomorrow. If it's Eva Stone's, you know what that means."

His mouth turned down in a glum line. His curiosity aroused, he seemed to forget he was ending the interview. "Yeah. People don't usually bury themselves."

Ace raised his hand to the waitress for a second coffee. "In light of this discovery, Mr. Langdon——Ace——what else can you tell me about Eva Stone's last hours?"

He emptied a packet of sugar into the new cup, stirred it, and rubbed his chin. "No reason to hide anything I know about that day." His hand was tanned and solid for a man his age, his opal ring at least as expensive as Blackthorne's sapphire. Able Citrus bought that, Brandy thought, and felt a pang of sympathy for tall, awkward Sylvania Able.

"It was a weekend celebration, you know," he said. "I didn't go hunting with the rest of the fellows the morning after the big party. Kind of hung over, for one thing. I was also hoping for other fish to fry." He winked. "When I woke up, the Moose was busy helping her Mama tidy up downstairs, and getting lunch ready for the other girls." Ace took a pack of cigarettes out of his shirt pocket and searched his trousers for a lighter. "Keep trying to quit, but no dice." He didn't strike Brandy as a man who could give up any addiction——cigarettes, alcohol, or women.

"And did you see Eva?" To jog her memory later, Brandy scribbled a few words. Ace didn't appear to notice. Once he'd started, he seemed to relish telling his tale. "I went looking for her late that afternoon. I won't deny it. Sweet little thing, but feisty." He cocked his head, appraising her. "You remind me of her a lot. Same shape face and hair length." His glance traveled down her blouse. "Same figure."

She found the table a comforting barrier between them. "Let's get back to Eva Stone. Did you find her?"

"Briefly." He sighed. "Before the war her father ran a two–bit café down town. He closed it to move up near Camp Blanding during the war. Opened a place there. Afterward the family moved back to Tavares and he re–opened his place here. She worked in the business. That's why she was back in town.

"The party was my chance to get her alone without Brookfield horning in." He grinned at the possibility for a pun, but Brandy's stern expression pushed him on. "You look like her, but you're more prim, I think.   What I did that afternoon is no secret. I told the cops then. Anyhow, I caught up with her in the living room. She was setting her suitcase down by the front door, but she didn't act like she wanted to leave yet. The other girls had gone home, all but one with car trouble. I figured Eva was hanging around, waiting for Brookfield, but so was Grace. Eva didn't have any time with him at the party, which was fine with me."

"Where was Grace?"

"Out by her car by then. It was a friend of hers had the flat tire. The yard man was up under the car, trying to get the jack to work. Eva thought I ought to go out and help him."

Brandy couldn't imagine even a youthful Ace Langdon lying in the sand to change a tire. "And did you?"

"I went out there, but the old fellow was about through with the job. He'd got the tire off. He found a spare that would fit and some tools in the trunk of Grace's car. About all I could do was throw the tools on the floor of Grace's Buick. The Moose and her mother had piled the trunk full of towels and sheets to go back to the Southerlands. I guess Grace left then. I went back in the house to try to find Eva. I didn't. Instead I shot some pool by myself in the game room. You know the rest."

And no one to witness that solitary game, Brandy thought. "Were you one of those who swam out looking for Eva?"

Langdon had gotten the cigarette going with a hotel match, and for a few seconds he watched the smoke rise between them. "I'm not a good swimmer. The Moose was the first one in. She was a strong swimmer, still is. I waded out some, but it was hopeless. No one could tell where Eva had gone down. The water there's like brown soup."

"If the skeleton belongs to Eva Stone, now we know she didn't drown."

"A puzzle isn't it?" He shook his head of lush gray hair.

"When did Brookfield and the others get back?"

Straggled back in pick–ups and on foot about the time the deputies arrived. Old man Able tried to use the dogs to pick up Eva's scent from her suitcase and clothes. The dogs just churned around in the yard. They were no help at all."

"Could Brookfield have been on the grounds when Eva went into the water?"

Langdon stood and mashed his cigarette into an ashtray on the table. "That I couldn't say. I've told you all I know. I can't remember everything that happened forty–five years ago."

Brandy pressed further. "What about Brookfield's fiancée? What about Grace? Where was she at the time?"

"I believe one fellow said Grace's car passed him while he was walking back." Ace faced the coffee shop doors, then turned and added. "If you're planning to see Grace, last I heard she went into some kind of depression after Brookfield's death. Kept a tight rein on his wife, Old Brookfield did. You wouldn't have approved. After he died two years ago, she kind of fell apart."

Ace tapped his gold watch with well–manicured fingernails. "Look, I've got a date. I don't usually lose out to the other guy. Eva Stone was an exception."

Brandy remembered her flower show appointment with Grace Able at four. She hoped the widow would be as talkative. First she might have time to search for Lily Mae Brown.

"I mean to find out what happened to Eva Stone," Brandy called after Ace. She noticed he wasn't still smiling as he sauntered toward his vintage Porsche. Before she looked for a phone, she watched him spurt out of the parking lot. Time to check with her office, then see if she could locate the witness to Eva Stone's fatal walk into Lake Dora.

TWELVE

I'm tired of mixed signals about Brookfield Able, Brandy thought, as she approached a phone booth in the motel lobby. According to his sister, Brookfield was a saint. According to his old war buddy Ace, he was clearly something less. For one thing, he'd been courting two women at the same time.

Now Ace said his friend was a controlling husband. At Sylvania's he'd also said Brookfield was a better buddy than boss. But Ace was clearly jealous of Brookfield. He had also paid a price for the job his friend arranged at A & S Citrus ——marrying Brookfield's unappealing sister. More than most, Ace Langdon was a man who valued a pretty girl.

Time to check with the office. She punched in the code for her answering machine. Steve Able's gruff voice came on, keeping his promise. "Thought you'd like to know we finally reached Sylvania. She was staying in a guest room at the retirement center. There's something else. You might as well know now what the medical examiner says. You'll get details later. It's off the record until the briefing, but the back of the skull was smashed in."

Brandy leaned against the wall, suddenly weak. Eva Stone had been dead so long, others didn't seem to consider her important. But Brandy had seen her photograph, seen that skull. In 1945

Eva's life was just beginning. That life was as important now as it had ever been. At that moment finding who killed Eva Stone became more vital to Brandy than her feature story. Even if John would never believe that fact.

In her hatchback once more, Brandy dragged her county map out of the glove compartment and opened her loose leaf notebook on the seat beside her. The 1945 clipping about Eva's disappearance gave an address for Lily Mae Brown. She had to make a start somewhere. For once Brandy was grateful that Tavares was small.

Within an hour she had located the one–story shot–gun house in a neighborhood of dirt streets and barren yards. The last forty–six years had not been kind to the house, yet it still stood, crumpling slightly to one side on its squat concrete pillars, like a man gone lame in one leg. She pushed a doorbell, and then, hearing no sound, knocked loudly.

Around the corner of the house a black boy of about five appeared, pulling a wagon loaded with tomatoes. In his pinched little face, suspicion waged a losing battle with curiosity.

"Ma's out back," he announced at last.

She followed him through the loose sand into the back yard where a short, plump woman was holding an apron cupped in one hand and throwing grain with the other to some hens in a chicken–wire pen.

"I'm looking for a Lily Mae Brown," Brandy began. "She used to live here back in the late forties."

"Lordy," the woman said. "How I know who lived here all that time ago? Nobody by the name of Brown live around here anymore." She emptied out the last of the grain and, facing Brandy, put her hand on her hip. Brandy waited. "Why you don't go down the street to old lady Wilson's house? She been here forever." She pointed toward the road to her left. "She's setting on the porch."

Brandy eased her car along the ruts and parked in front of the Wilson house. Mrs. Wilson sat in a swing, moving slowly back and forth, shelling peas and dropping them into a big iron kettle. Her eyes appraised Brandy from a face as golden brown and dry as a tobacco leaf.

Brandy repeated her question.

"I think I recollect the Brown family," the old lady said in a high, thin voice. "That family didn't have but two girls. Why you want to know?" She peered up at Brandy, cautious.

"I'm writing a story for the *Beacon* about that big house the Ables own up on Lake Dora. Lily Mae Brown used to work there."

"Guess that's all right, then," the old woman said. "I recollect the Brown family moved a long time ago to Mount Dora. Old man Brown got a job near there for a fruit packing company." Her busy fingers paused. "That girl, Lily Mae——if my memory be right——she married a fellow there, a fellow named Hall. Don't recollect the first name. Last I heard they still lived in Mount Dora. Maybe that'll help you, young lady."

When Brandy reached into her purse, the old woman waved her away. "Might not help you," she said. "It's all I know."

Thirty minutes later Brandy stopped at a fast food restaurant on the edge of Mount Dora, wolfed down a hamburger and coke, and borrowed the telephone book. The number of Halls was daunting, but she did find a Martin Luther King Center listed on the east side of town. It was worth a try.

By three she was standing at the front desk in a one story, white concrete block building, staring hopefully at an elderly black woman in a paisley dress. In a larger adjoining room two teenagers in baggy jeans cracked ping pong balls across a table tennis net.

The woman raised her eyebrows and looked up. "Lily Mae Hall?" she asked, her eyes behind her glasses as thoughtful and reserved as the old lady's on the swing. "Let's see now. Seems like I recollect…" She pulled a notebook from a shelf behind her and flipped through several pages of handwritten names.

Was she stalling? "I would like to interview Mrs. Hall for a story I'm writing for the *Beacon* newspaper. I don't think she'd mind. I want to ask a few details about an old house where she worked years ago."

The woman paused and placed one finger on a name. "If she's the lady I'm thinking of, she's a supporter but we don't see her here much. Don't think she's been right well." She turned the book toward Brandy. "You might want to take down the number, see if she's the lady you want."

Quickly Brandy jotted down name, address, and phone number. Trotting back down the sidewalk toward her car, she checked her watch. There was barely time for the drive back to Tavares for Grace Able's flower show. She would have to telephone Lily Mae tonight.

When Brandy entered the spacious home of the garden club member, she asked for Grace Able, then waited by French doors in a foyer that opened onto the north shore of Lake Dora. The judging had concluded. Grace came mincing in from an adjoining room in high heels, her face flushed. "Miss O'Bannon, I believe." In the living room, she drew Brandy aside.

"Color Under the Sun" read a large placard on an end table. Plumes of red bottlebrush thrust up from a vase on the other end piece, a sprightly pot of golden marigolds brightened a coffee table, a mass of deep pink bougainvillea cascaded from a bowl on the mantel, and a cluster of bromeliads lifted scarlet blooms like inverted bells from a wide pot on the piano.

Grace directed Brandy's attention to the last arrangement. "The judges criticized the size of my container," she said in a low voice. "Too large in proportion to its location." She waved a dainty hand at the bright blooms and the tracery of green Swiss cheese and snake plants that filled in the pot.

Inwardly Brandy smiled. Grace's huge diamond and wide platinum wedding band could also be called out of proportion to her slender finger. The well–bred voice quivered. "I grow bromeliads in my little patio. You can see my design is easily the most pleasing and certainly it has the most exceptional plants."

Brandy glanced from the oval face with its cream complexion and pained blue eyes to the bromeliads on the piano top and their red ribbon. A blue one dangled from the mantel.

Grace sniffed. "Bougainvillea takes no effort in Florida. Excellent balance and proportion, indeed!"

She was almost too thin in a pale silvery green dress with a wide swinging skirt, but well–proportioned, if her arrangement was not. Against the soft folds at the neckline lay a strand of pearls.

"Of course, this is just a local placement show. I should take a first place at the county show next fall in Eustis. The regular shows end in May, but the girls thought a little June summer flower show would be fun." Her voice dropped conspiratorially. "I'm not really surprised at the ribbon, though. They've got new judges this year. Just trained. And they don't like me to compete. I'm too old. They think I ought to step aside for newer members."

She touched the careful waves in her blonde–white hair. "Of course, there's the Able and Southerland Company thing. People in a small town hold money against you, you know." She gave a mirthless little laugh. "As if any amount of money could compensate for the loss of my husband."

Brandy seized on the reference to Brookfield Able's death. "I heard you say you didn't care about the Able homestead, but it was your husband's. For my story, you must have some pleasant memories of it."

The older woman laid a graceful hand on Brandy's arm and led her toward an isolated love seat. "Brookfield didn't like it any better than I. Too far out of town. Too gloomy."

"Your sister–in–law feels the same. It's a pity. It's such a part of county history."

"Poor Sylvania." Grace looked down, a tiny lift to the corners of her mouth. "She never cared much for me, either. Such different interests! Doesn't cherish beautiful things. You've seen her garden, or the lack of it."

"Did you dislike the house when you lived there?"

Grace's eyelids drooped. "I don't know how Sylvania and that dreadful man she married stayed out there so long."

"After Eva Stone disappeared into the lake, you must have heard rumors about unusual sightings there."

The almond–shaped blue eyes opened wide and inspected Brandy for a moment. "I've heard," she said at last quietly.

"I understand you were the guest of honor that weekend. What can you tell me about Eva Stone and her drowning?"

Grace paused, her eyes still averted. "I didn't know her at all well. The drowning happened after I'd already left. A dreadful tragedy. Spoiled our engagement party. Afterwards, it was all people could talk about. If the girl were going to drown herself, I wished she'd picked another time and place." She smoothed the silky skirt across her lap. "I can tell you this. I would not stay in that house again."

Brandy wondered if she had a quotable witness at last. "What exactly did you see that makes you say that?"

Grace's delicate fingers fluttered. "It's only a feeling, really. Like a presence, especially upstairs. A coldness in the air." She shuddered.

"Ever see anything on the lawn? Or near the boat house?"

Grace rose, stepped to the piano, and picked up the red ribbon. "No," she said after a pause. "The family doesn't like to talk about it. Brings gawkers around, you know. Maybe if Sylvania has the house pulled down, that will put a stop to the talk."

"May I quote you?"

"Oh, no, please. Sylvania doesn't like me now. She'd really be angry if I commented to a reporter about——you know ——those stories."

She tucked the ribbon in a tote bag and lifted her pot carefully with both hands. "Just say I haven't lived in the house for over forty years and have no sentimental attachment to it."

Brandy sighed and reached for the pot. "Let me help you to the car. I ought to tell you the case is being re–opened. There's been a new development."

Just as Brandy's fingers tightened around the pot, Grace released her hold and one hand flew to her mouth. "Oh, dear. Must they bring all that up again?"

"I'm afraid so." Brandy said. "Last night a skeleton was found buried near the house. There's a chance it's Eva Stone's." No need to tell Grace about the damaged skull. She might refuse then to talk at all. "I'd like to ask you some questions about the weekend she disappeared."

"We certainly can't speak privately here, Miss O'Bannon." Grace cocked her head and looked at Brandy. "O'Bannon. I believe I met your mother once or twice. Barbara O'Bannon?" Brandy nodded. "Last time was at a Garden Club round robin where we had dessert at different houses. She didn't stay active in the club. Had no free time, people said. I thought teachers got their summers off, and school's over by three or four in the afternoon."

For once Brandy wanted to defend her hard–working mother. "Teachers work after they get home. Especially English teachers. She's a summer school teacher, too."

"So nice to know we have a few good ones," Grace said. Obviously Grace thought her remark a compliment.

Brandy followed her to the Mercedes at the curb and set the bromeliads on the spacious floor behind the driver's seat. She handed Grace a card. "The discovery of human bones will be in the morning papers. May I call on you later if I have more questions?"

Grace put the card in her purse and slid behind the wheel. "I'm sure I can add very little to what you already know," she said, but her hand trembled as she lifted her car keys from a small purse and cut on the engine. Still, at her age, Brandy thought, many people are shaky. "Mabel Boxley and I leave for Canada next week." Grace lowered the window a few inches. "We go to Banff every summer. The Florida heat, you know. Mabel's there now, getting the cottage ready. Until then I'll be at my condo. The Lakeview Arms near Leesburg. You'll need to give my name at the gate."

As the car pulled away, Brandy realized Grace Able had yet to reveal anything useful.

Before going home, surely she should inquire about John. In Leesburg she stopped at a record shop, pawed though its classical offerings, and bought Chopin's Etude in E Major. John didn't need anything heavy, but certainly he needed the soothing effect of great music. At five–thirty Brandy turned again into the hospital parking lot and took her small tape recorder out of the glove compartment.

She had reached the corridor near John's room when she saw Steve Able's solid figure in a dark green uniform closing the door behind him. His greeting was morose. He shook his head. "John's awake again, but there's not much change. This is going to take time."

"I feel responsible," Brandy said.

He ran his fingers over the crown of his deputy's hat. "Don't be so hard on yourself. Moccasins are attack snakes. We all know that." He twisted the hat in his hand and looked away. "Doctor says they'll observe him closely for a while. He hasn't recommended surgery. Anyway, not yet." His tanned forehead crinkled in a frown. "Sylvania's fit to be tied. Reporters from Leesburg and Orlando picked up the patrol car's calls last night. They're swarming all over her place today. Now the Sheriff's Office has asked her to come in for questioning. She says she doesn't know anything about a skeleton and doesn't want to hear about it. She's afraid of what the publicity will do to her sale."

"I got your message this afternoon," Brandy said. "Thanks. When I interview people, knowing the skull was bashed in helps, but I haven't told anyone yet. I'm going to the Sheriff's Office briefing at eight." She moved a step closer. "I suggest the Sheriff's Office find out if Eva Stone's dental records are still around."

Brandy felt a surge of optimism. She was developing her own sources of information. "Did you tell John about the injury to the skull?"

"Not yet. He didn't ask."

"Is he alone? I'd like to look in, say 'hi.'" Steve nodded, then strode on down the hall.

As she opened the door she realized that Sylvania's prediction had been right. Delving into the disappearance of Eva Stone had already caused pain, to John most of all. She slipped into the room and crossed to the bed where he was stirring, his face turned toward her.

"You're looking good," she said. She wished she could talk everything over with him, but he appeared too weak, the planes of his face too white and sharp against the pillow. He could barely raise his head.

She bent over the bed and tried not to look at the black, swollen hand and the puffiness that ran up his arm.

"If it weren't for you, I'd be the one lying there," she said.

His voice was thick, as if his mouth was still numbed by morphine. "Don't blame the snake," he whispered. "It was his territory."

"I know. Territory you're trying to preserve."

His brow furrowed, remembering. "Call Curt Greene, about the house. Tomorrow's Friday."

"I did. No one's made an offer yet." She scooted a chair up to the bed. "By the way——" she fluffed her short hair with one hand, "Ace Langdon thinks I look like Eva Stone. I checked her picture in the old yearbook. It's a compliment."

She saw the flicker of a smile. His voice grew stronger. "Well, Ace Langdon's the world's greatest authority on women."

She lifted the tape and player from her canvas bag. "I hope this will help pass the time. I couldn't bring you a suitable math book, but maybe this is as good. Music is math with emotion, I think you said." She set the two on his bedside stand.

His eyes brightened. "That's really nice. I'll listen after you leave. No one's moved into the other bed yet. If they do, I'll probably have twenty–four hours of T.V. trash." The screen looming near the ceiling was now blank.

"I don't know if you're interested anymore," she said, "but Steve told me the back of the skeleton's skull had been smashed.

He drew a deep breath and then said softly, "Not an accident then."

"If this turns out to be Eva Stone, the alligators are off the hook. And it wasn't a drowning either."

His brown eyes clouded. "An awful thing happened there. Don't keep pushing. Leave it to law enforcement." His voice sank, more feeble now. "Someone may want to stop you."

"I'll be careful."

He sighed, started to speak again, then gave up and closed his eyes.

She wanted to touch him, to thank him for caring. But it was in character for him to caution her. He was a cautious man. She thought of the ghost story that, for very different reasons, had brought them both to the boat house. She had never told him that she saw a movement in the fourth floor dormer window the night before, and later a figure below on the darkened lawn. Had he seen anything himself while he waited for her to return? There hadn't been a chance to ask.

She bit her lip. If she tried to describe what she had seen to him, he would say, "Imagination. You see what you expect to see." Without another witness, better to say nothing.

She looked at her watch. Time to grab a bite in the hospital cafeteria before the briefing. "Tomorrow we'll talk all this over," she said. "This afternoon, you need rest." Slowly the taut lines of John's face relaxed. She thought of pressing his hand before she left, but decided against it.

His voice had sunk to a whisper. "Before you leave, would you switch on the tape?"

She listened with him for a few minutes, then moved quietly out of the room as the étude began to rise toward its lyrical climax.

Passing the nurse's station in the hallway, Brandy noticed a young woman draped over the counter. Something looked familiar about the artful tangle of pale hair, the saucy nose. The photograph in John's trailer——Sharon, of course——Sharon with a filmy mauve scarf at her neck, a white silky dress, a mauve and white tapestry bag, heels.

"I'm a teeny bit late," she was saying in a breathless, little girl voice. "I'm here to see John Able. He's expecting me." When a nurse pointed to John's door, Sharon smiled brightly. "I won't stay long, I've got shopping to do in Mount Dora this evening."

Brandy halted, drew a deep breath, and pretended to search her canvas bag while Sharon swished, heels rapping, down the hall. In her baggy cotton shirtwaist Brandy felt like a hippie frump from the sixties. The little girl voice floated though John's open doorway. "Did we get bitten by a nasty old snake?" Brandy waited several seconds. The étude abruptly ended. Then she heard the excited yelps of a television game show.

Men, she thought starkly. They always go for the pretty air heads.

THIRTEEN

When Brandy reported for the Sheriff's Office briefing a few minutes before eight, reporters had already crowded into the front room, along with two television crews. Mr. Tyler was right, Brandy thought. This news story would hardly be her exclusive.

A hulking lieutenant with thin–rimmed glasses entered from a side door. "Gentlemen——and ladies," he said, "I'm Lieutenant Albert Brady, Criminal Division. You're all here about the skeleton found last night. You probably already know it was buried at the old Able home site on Lake Dora, but we've had a couple of new developments."

Brandy looked for the familiar faces of the sergeant or the sandy–haired deputy. Neither was there. The case had gone higher up the command ladder.

"The medical examiner found a blow to the head that would've caused death," the lieutenant began, laying a spiral notebook on the podium. "He says the pelvis indicates a young woman. From the long bones, not very tall. It's been there at least thirty years but not as long as fifty. The time estimate has to do with the lack of soft tissue and the pockets of calcium phosphate he'd expect to

find in fresher bones. But he says there's none of the mineraliza-
tion our soil should produce after fifty years."

A cog has shifted into place, Brandy thought.

"This afternoon the remains have been identified," he continued. His eyes shifted behind his glasses toward Brandy. "We had a
useful tip. For forty–five years we've held this missing person's
file. It includes dental records. The dead girl was Eva Stone."

A murmur rose from the reporters and television crews, cam-
eras whirred. The lieutenant ran a beefy hand through his hair.
"The file was marked 'Uncleared Pending Disposition' and saved.
We're mandated to keep records of missing persons for 99 years."
He turned directly toward Brandy. "We're grateful to Miss
O'Bannon of the *Tavares Beacon* and John Able, whose relative
owns the property. They found the skeleton." Brandy stopped tak-
ing notes. All eyes swiveled to her.

When the lieutenant took up his account again, their attention
swung back to their notebooks. "The dead girl had been judged a
probable suicide. Disappeared into Lake Dora on a Sunday afternoon in November, 1945. But apparently, the girl didn't drown
herself after all. We're hopeful your stories will turn up some useful information. Maybe some of the people who were there at the
time will come forward." The lieutenant tucked the note pad into
his pocket, a look of satisfaction on his square face. "We're getting ready to excavate the whole area. Any questions?"

The *Leesburg Commercial* reporter's hand shot up, higher than
the others. "Does she have any surviving family?"

"Yes, Eva Stone's mother is still living, as well as a much
younger brother. Mrs. Stone's a very old lady, about ninety–three.
Not very well. We broke the news to her today. We didn't want
her to see it in the papers first. Her son wants to protect her from
you people as much as he can. This has been a terrible shock to
her. I suggest you contact the son, Weston Stone. He's the local

restaurant owner. Mrs. Stone's very frail. She's in an assisted living home in Tavares." The son's name rang a bell. Brandy remembered him as the environmentalist at the Chamber of Commerce meeting.

"Any sign of the weapon that killed her?" It was the *Orlando Sentinel's* Lake County reporter.

"We're still looking for the proverbial blunt instrument."

Another hand near the front. "Isn't that the house that's supposed to be haunted?" Snickers greeted this question.

"I couldn't comment on that," the lieutenant said.

"What about the woman who lives on the property now, Mrs. Langdon?" It was a voice from the rear. "What does she say?"

Brandy heard a commotion around a door to the hallway and a tall figure burst through. "Mrs. Langdon says nothing!" The tone of the familiar voice was fierce. Sylvania swept past them, large head erect, angular body wrapped in her usual long, shapeless dress. Her gray eyes settled for a moment on Brandy, and she paused in mid–stride. Again her voice rang out. "The house will be sold and torn down. Unfortunately, the sale is temporarily postponed." Clearly she directed the next remark to Brandy. "When this search is over, the house goes! That's certain."

"I'm sure you want to know the truth," Brandy said. "I mean to find out what happened there."

Sylvania's lips tightened and she hurried on past. She was not alone. Behind her loomed the burly form of Axel Blackthorne. Catching up with Sylvania, he pushed aside the reporters, took her arm, and as he began shepherding her back through the doorway, Brandy followed.

She thrust her way through to his side and called out, "I've got some questions for you, Mr. Blackthorne." Furious eyes met hers, then he ducked his head and plowed on toward his Cadillac at the curb. With a shrug, Brandy turned back to the briefing and squirmed her way to a spot near the lieutenant. Blackthorne would be tomorrow's interview——if she could get into his office.

Sylvania must've already been questioned at the sheriff's office. Clearly she was as irritated as Steve said. The lieutenant continued as though Sylvania had not appeared. "I understand Mrs. Langdon's home will be torn down as soon as our investigation is completed," he said.

A voice from the rear. "Any suspects or clues?"

The lieutenant flashed a brief, patronizing smile. "A case this old is difficult. The physical scene has obviously deteriorated. Witnesses are hard to find. Any leads have been cold for years. Many of the people we'd like to question are deceased."

Brandy had the sinking sensation that Eva Stone's fate was no longer a high priority at the Sheriff's Office.

"We'll just have to 'trace their shadows,'" she muttered, forgetting she stood at the lieutenant's elbow.

He glanced down at her. "What's that, Miss O'Bannon?"

"We'll have to trace their shadows with the magic hand of chance," she answered, coloring. "The poet John Keats."

He paused, puzzled, removed his glasses and rubbed his eyes. "That's all, ladies and gentlemen," he said at last. With a brisk wave he strode back through the door and closed it behind him.

Brandy was jostled as the others massed at the outer door. "You're the gal who found the bones, aren't you?" It was the tall *Commercial* reporter. "The *Beacon's* a small weekly, right?" He squeezed her arm and grinned down at her. "I'd like to talk to you. Maybe we could collaborate."

Brandy lifted her head and shook her arm free. "Some other time, thank you. I've got my own story to write."

Outside she unlocked her car and started home. At least the Sheriff's Office had confirmed that Eva Stone was murdered, but she had collected little other useful information. Her probing had alienated half of Tavares——Sylvania, both of John's parents, John himself, her mother, even Mack, whose morning call she must return. Even Mr. Tyler was still poised to drop the guillotine.

But she did still have work to do. She wanted to talk to Blackthorne, she hadn't heard Grace's version of the disastrous weekend, hadn't talked to the most important witness, Lily Mae Brown, maybe now Lily Mae Hall. She also wanted to interview the new lead, Eva Stone's aged mother.

For the moment Brandy's own mother would be holding her supper, if not her temper. She turned off the main road and drove down her darkened lane under a heavy canopy of Spanish moss. Fleetingly she remembered John's warning. But who of these elderly people could possibly try to stop her?

As she passed the sole neighbor's corner house, she was glad Mack's pickup was not out front. She did not want to admit to him yet that she'd searched the Able boat house with John. He'd either be jealous or insist again that the Able family was all crazy. Or both.

Instead Meg's lively bark greeted her as she parked behind Mrs. O'Bannon's seven year old Buick in the driveway. In the summer her mother threw open the doors to the old single–car garage to make a potting shed, and in the winter closed them to protect her delicate plants. The cars stayed outside. When Brandy caught a whiff of the confederate jasmine on the fence, she thought of Grace Able and the flower show. Maybe Barbara O'Bannon would've been winning ribbons herself, if her husband had been a citrus magnate instead of a teacher.

When Brandy opened the kitchen door, she found Mrs. O'Bannon sitting at the dining room table, correcting summer school paragraphs. She laid down her red pen and gave Brandy her long, authoritative stare. "An English teacher's taking maternity leave when the regular term starts in August. Senior level," she said and sat back. "You could probably qualify for a tempo-rary certificate. You'd make far more than you're making now. It's not too late to change your mind."

Brandy rolled her eyes at the ceiling. "I'm not stuck at this salary forever. I'm still working on the story I told you about. If I do a good job, I'll get a promotion."

Sighing, her mother rose and opened the refrigerator. "I grocery shopped, but I haven't stopped to eat yet. I can set the hibachi on the table outside and grill some fresh fish, toss a quick salad."

"Sounds good. I'm starved." Brandy opened her bedroom door and watched Meg disappear inside. She would brief her mother at supper, prepare her for the morning paper, and before she went to bed, transcribe her disjointed notes into her looseleaf notebook. It was too late to try to reach the number for Mrs. Hall, but she did have to make one call. Reluctantly she picked up the kitchen phone and dialed Mack. Better to tell him about her discovery now than have him read about it in the morning.

*   *   *

At eight the next morning Brandy was pulling on a pair of crin-kle cotton slacks when she heard the blast of Mack's horn. She had agreed the night before to see him before work. It wouldn't take long, he'd said, for him to show her his surprise. She cast an apologetic look around the room. Clothes still lay in piles. How did people find time to clean their rooms? Or iron their clothes? Apparently John did. But she mustn't start thinking about him.

She pulled on the matching blouse, chosen like the slacks because it didn't need ironing, while she waited for Meg to scoot out from under the bed. Then she let the retriever into the yard and strolled over to the powerful Sierra pick–up throbbing in the driveway. As she took the high step into the cab, she wished just once he would ask his dad for a sports car.

"What's so mysterious?" she said. "I've got a busy schedule."

He leaned toward her, wrapped one barrel–shaped arm around her shoulder, looked through the rear window, gunned the engine, and rocketed backward into the lane. "We've had an understanding for a zillion years," he said, uncoiling his arm and wrenching the wheel around. "It's about time we made some definite plans." He patted her knee. "Time's a–wasting. I found just the place for us." They shot past down town, curved north, and slowed before a pair of concrete block walls connected by an arch labeled "Forest Heights." Beyond lay row upon row of new concrete block houses, a few sodded yards, a few scraggly slash pines. There were no other trees and no rise to the ground.

Mack eased the Sierra under the arch. The houses all gave the same impression——heavy, pitched roof porticos above massive front doors, pride of place given to big garages, a walled–in look, a diminished house size in the rear——mini–fortresses. The builder had been at pains to provide small differences, mainly in planters and window treatments. Mack drew up before one much like its neighbor. "Got the down payment for this baby in the bank right now."

Brandy floundered for words. She remembered the photograph in John's living room of the quintessential cracker house, its wide porches, breezeway, openness. Yet these tract homes were expensive, far better than any she had ever lived in. Mack, for all his bluster, was a good man, an attractive man. He could date any girl in three cities. John had his own girl friend. What was wrong with her?

"Mack, it's a lovely house. You're too generous." She kissed one sunburned cheek. "But I told you, I don't know if I'm ready yet for the suburban routine."

His blunt features gathered in a scowl. "God almighty, I guess it's that frigging job you got. If you want to work a few years, do like your mom says. Teach here in town. You'd have better hours."

Brandy didn't bother to tell him what her mother's at–home hours were. It was true they were more regular, if as long, as a reporter's. "I have to think about it, Mack, okay?" She reached up and ran her fingers though his close cropped blond hair. "I have to turn this story in Monday. After that, I promise I'll give you an answer."

An hour later Brandy sat at her laptop in the *Beacon* office and typed the first draft of a lead for the story she had promised Mr. Tyler:

> "The skeleton of a long–dead girl, rumors of a ghost, and the sale of a historic Lake Dora home all con- verged at a dramatic Sheriff's Office briefing in Tavares Thursday afternoon."

She bit her lip, leaned back, and inspected it. Maybe she should start with the main point, what her journalism professor had called the "nut graph." She typed another opening:

> The report that a reputed spirit slipped into a locked boat house at night led to the skeleton of Eva Stone, a girl who disappeared forty–five years ago on the prop- erty of Tavares pioneer Brookfield Able, Sr. A Beacon reporter, accompanied by the grand–nephew of Brookfield Able, Jr., investigated the sighting and spot- ted the long–buried bones that have re–opened the missing person's case, according to Lieutenant Albert Grady of the Lake County Sheriff's Office.

What would John think when he read her story? She would have to name him. When Brandy persuaded him to look into the abandoned boat house for family mementos, he had suspected her of a hidden agenda. Now it would be there, stark and clear. For the third time he would feel manipulated. She would have to try to make him understand.

Quickly she jotted down the topics that would follow and conjure up a personal, human interest spin. Typing rapidly, she elaborated on how the skeleton had come to light, how she was chased across the lake by another boat, how John was bitten by a cottonmouth.

When she had rapped out the completed draft, she poked her head into Mr. Tyler's office. "See what you think of the first paragraphs of the Able mansion story."

Wordlessly he pulled it up on his computer screen, scanned it, and sent her a summons. "Did you get the names of the two fishermen that followed you across Lake Dora?"

"I hadn't time to ask their names. I was trying to save my skin and report what we'd found."

"You need a confirming source, Miss O'Bannon. You can't prove that another boat tried to run you down. As it happens, the unfortunate Mr. Able can vouch for the way you found the skeleton. Except for those details, every paper in the area printed the same facts in the morning paper."

Squelched again, Brandy murmured, "They don't have the ghost." But without a quotable witness, neither did she. Brandy didn't tell him that she herself had seen a wispy shape in the window and later on the lawn, not without photographs or another witness.

"By Monday I'll have interviewed almost everyone who was there the day Eva Stone died," she said. "So will the Sheriff's detectives, but I have personal contacts, people who will talk to me. I can add some facts that'll give the story pizzazz. And I do have some leads about the murdered girl."

Leaving his cigarette burning in his ashtray, Mr. Tyler pressed the tips of his fingers together and peered over his glasses. "Don't get too big for your britches. Leave the criminal stuff to detectives." She nodded, but as she turned to close the door behind her, she noticed he still had not picked up the cigarette.

At her desk she opened her note pad to the phone number she had been given at the Martin Luther King Center and placed the call. After six rings, she was ready to hang up when a breathless woman's voice answered.

"I'm a reporter on the *Beacon* staff in Tavares," Brandy began. "I'm researching the old Able homestead on Lake Dora. If you're the Mrs. Hall who worked there once, I'd like to talk to you about it."

For a few seconds the voice on the other end was silent. "I reckon that'd be okay, young lady," the woman said finally. "Let's see now. I be gone this afternoon, but I be home tomorrow afternoon. Got to baby sit my grand baby."

Brandy felt a charge of excitement. Here was the last person to see Eva Stone alive. "Could I see you about two?"

"I reckon so." Mrs. Hall repeated her address.

Out of a sense of duty to John, Brandy also called Curt Greene's office again. Greene still had not persuaded anyone to make a bid on the house. Too much work to do on it, too little time to arrange financing, too little utility for a place so far from town. In spite of the zero with Greene and her editor, she could try her next source, Brookfield's widow. Then she had a chance to hit one out of the park with Lily Mae Hall.

FOURTEEN

Grace Able had an unlisted number, but by exaggerating her press credentials on the phone to the condominium manager, Brandy eventually reached the widow's apartment. She remembered that the indispensable Mabel Boxley was in Canada but eventually Grace picked up the phone.

"I see very few people," the widow said, "but we've met and I know your mother. I suppose I've got to talk to some newspaper person. I saw the story about the skeleton in the Leesburg paper this morning. Shocking. Then I had a call about it from someone in the family." Her tone sank. "The news brought back terrible memories. If Mabel had been here, she would have handled everything."

Brandy remembered Grace Able's bland, oval face in the old photograph album, the disappointed look in her blue eyes when she took a second place for her bromeliads. Brandy had not seen her talking to others at the flower show. Ace Langdon said Brookfield kept a "tight rein" on her. In the family picture Grace had looked subdued beside her husband, perhaps dominated. Yet she seemed devoted to Brookfield's memory. She might've developed a similar dependency on Mabel Boxley.

Brandy found Grace's building about a quarter of a mile from busy Route 27. She identified herself to a security guard at a station, drove through a retractable gate, and parked before the lake. In the thickly carpeted lobby she stopped at a reception desk and announced herself.

Grace's apartment, down a north corridor wing and past the entrance to the pool and sauna, had a door labeled with the logo of A & S Citrus Company. After Brandy punched a bell in the shape of a camellia, a stout woman in a maid's apron opened the door. She was not the indispensable Mabel.

From the other side of the room, Brandy heard Grace's genteel Southern accent. "Do come in, Miss O'Bannon. Join me by the window. Alice is just fixing tea."

Brandy entered a generous-sized living room, its square lines softened by mint green carpets and drapes. Before a bay window two needlepoint chairs were drawn up beside the small Duncan Phyfe table facing the lake. From one of the chairs Grace set aside a knitting bag and gestured for her guest to sit down.

Although Brandy noticed the ruffled ivory blouse, the tiny pearl earrings, she was most struck by Grace's unlined face. Brandy had forgotten how much younger Grace looked than she had expected.

"Such a serene place," the older woman said when Brandy complimented her on the apartment. "I'm so fortunate to have it. And so fortunate to usually have my dear Mabel to help me, and Alice to clean."

The pink blossom of a double hibiscus floated in a crystal bowl on the table. Through a sliding side door lay the flagstones of a patio, bright with salvia and marigolds. Grace Able had apparently found harmony after her husband's death.

Outside Brandy saw residents strolling along a sidewalk beside a row of crepe myrtle or sitting on benches beside the sunlit water.

Grace folded her slender fingers. "The news about the skeleton is a shock, of course. My place here has been a haven from the cares of the world."

Alice put her head out of the small kitchen. "I'll serve you ladies tea, and then I need to scoot down the hall. Mabel asked me to return some things to the desk in the lobby."

"So tactful, you see," Grace said, leaning forward. "I expect Alice knows we need to talk privately." The smooth brow furrowed. I simply wasn't prepared for such dreadful news. I couldn't believe it."

The widow's glance drifted to a bookshelf along the opposite wall and a portrait of Brookfield in his Air Force uniform, a rakish tilt to his billed cap. Beside the finely tooled leather frame hung a plaque that displayed a first lieutenant's bars and a pair of silver wings. "I keep thinking there must be a mistake about the skeleton."

Brandy needed to bring up more unpleasant facts. "I'm afraid the remains were identified positively as Eva Stone's," she said. "The worst part is that she may have been killed." The word "murdered" was not easily said to Grace Able.

Grace fingered her pearls. "I was afraid of that. Such a lovely girl. I hardly knew her, but like everyone else, I liked her."

Even if she spoiled your engagement party? Brandy thought but did not ask. The delicate brows rose. "I understand you have an interest in this tragedy?" It was a polite question, but the words had an edge.

The maid carried in a tray with a silver tea pot, fragile China cups, and a plate of tiny cinnamon pastries.

"Partly, I suppose, because John Able and I found it."

"Sylvania must be quite upset." As Grace poured the tea, the hint of a smile showed on her lips and vanished.

In their first interview Grace had admitted that the two women did not like one another, even though Grace had married the one person in the world Sylvania cherished. Maybe the marriage had caused the animosity. "I'm troubling you with all this, Mrs. Able, because I'm trying to find out just what went on that afternoon forty–five years ago when Eva Stone disappeared. I'm trying to interview everyone I can who was there."

The older woman allowed herself a glacial smile. "In other words, you want to know if we all have alibis." She rested her head against the back cushion of the chair and closed her eyes. "Well, let's see what I can remember. We all had to talk to the deputies then." In a few seconds she sat forward and spoke in a regretful tone.

"The last thing I did at the house that afternoon was to help Brookfield's mother gather up the linens. I was to take them to the laundry in town the next day. She'd borrowed some of our towels and sheets, too." Grace crossed her arms in her lap. "Let's see, we'd had a late lunch. Most of the girls had already gone home. I do recall that Eva Stone's car was still there."

"I believe one other girl left late because of a flat tire."

"Yes, that's so. I remember now. Poor thing hadn't come with a spare or a jack. I got the yard man, and he managed to get the tire changed. He found what he needed in my car."

"Do you remember Mr. Langdon there then?"

She gave a lady–like little snort. "Oh, him! He was no good for anything then, and he hasn't been good for anything since. He came out after the poor old yard man had finished the job. Didn't get up in time to go hunting with the other men." Her lips turned down at the corners. "I suspected he stayed around to flirt with Eva Stone. He couldn't take his eyes off her all weekend."

"Sylvania must have felt hurt. Mr. Langdon was her date."

"I expect she was. She didn't talk to me about it. Of course, I was so excited about my own engagement, I didn't notice much else."

"I understand Brookfield and the other men came back shortly after you left."

"I guess that's so." Daintily she nibbled a pastry. "I remember driving off after we put the linens in the car and I'd gotten my tools back. I passed one or two of the fellows on foot. I didn't see Brookfield until that night when he came in town to tell me what had happened. I went out to the house the next day and stayed all night to try to comfort Brookfield's mother and help with the Stones." Her account tallied with Ace Langdon's.

"Mrs. Able, this is difficult to mention, but I'm trying to get all the relevant facts. Were you aware then that Eva Stone had once been in love with your fiancé?"

The older woman looked down. "He knew her before we began dating, of course. Before I met Brookfield in college. Brookfield and I hadn't put her on the guest list. She just came, I suppose to see Brookfield. When she showed up, I felt sorry for her. She worked in her father's little café, you see. She was never a part of our crowd. I thought maybe Sylvania or her parents had invited her at the last minute."

The door creaked ajar and Alice poked her head into the room. "I need to finish in the bedroom, Mrs. Langdon."

"Of course, Alice. Come on in. We're about done."

Grace had not really said whether she knew about Brookfield and Eva's romance. Brandy decided that she probably had.

"The fellow who's buying Sylvania's house was there too," Grace said, briskly, as though eager to finish. "The developer Axel Blackthorne. I'm sure Sylvania asked Axel. Brookfield said they'd been friends a long time. She must have realized she couldn't count on that dreadful Ace Langdon as a partner, not for dancing and all."

Something else to follow up, Brandy thought. "And you weren't worried about Eva Stone as a rival?"

For a moment a look Brandy could not identify flickered in Grace's eyes. Fear? Sorrow? Pain?

"Brookfield and I were always a solid team. We didn't need anyone else," she said at last. "I never doubted him, and he never gave me reason to." Her eyelids fluttered down again. "Thinking about all of this has been hard, Miss O'Bannon. It was terrible when Eva's parents came out to the house that night. Brookfield was just frantic. The tragedy clouded our whole first year. Everyone seemed to think she killed herself because we were getting married. I couldn't stand the place after that.

"Brookfield loved hunting and boating, and his dad expected us to live there. His parents were getting too old to use it much, but in the end we decided not to. I didn't go back after we moved out."

Brandy rushed in her next topic. "You must have heard rumors that the house was haunted. When did they start?"

Grace dropped her voice. "I really don't know exactly. After we married, I would never go back up to the fourth floor. We'd all slept there the night of the banquet. That was the last place I'd seen poor Eva alive. The atmosphere in that house..." She gave a tiny shiver. "There was something dark there, something evil. I'm telling you that in confidence. Sylvania would kill me." Her voice trailed into silence.

"Did you ever see anything unusual there?"

Her eyes widened. "Just shadows, really. Brookfield said they were my imagination. But I was glad to leave."

Alice re-appeared in the bedroom door, flourishing her dust cloth. "I need to get into the living room, M'am."

Grace stood, the ivory skin around her eyes suddenly drawn. Brandy recognized the signal. The interview was almost over. "Did Brookfield ever tell you anything that might help the Sheriff's Office uncover the truth?" she asked.

Grace shook her head slowly, her mouth still tense. "I can tell you this. Brookfield would never have let anything or anyone come between us." As she moved toward the door, Brandy studied her. How did she manage to create an impression of fragility? Grace was not frail, only lean, and as tall as Brandy. Some Southern women cultivated the gift—— if it was one.

Grace opened the door. "Please excuse me. I really must get to work on my column for the condominium newsletter."

Alice picked up a stack of books on the bookcase and swished her duster under them. "You want me to turn in these library books, Mrs. Able?"

Grace shrugged. "No, I'm not quite through with my research."

What research, Brandy wondered, would interest the reclusive Grace Able? She seemed to read Brandy's mind. "My gardening column, you see," she said. "It does take work."

Brandy stepped into the hall. "The Sheriff's Office will probably call you, but they may not spend a lot of time on this case. It was all so long ago. I plan to keep digging until I find out what happened."

Brandy walked thoughtfully back down the hall. Did Grace realize what she had said a few minutes earlier? She had identified her husband as a possible threat to the murdered girl, said he would let nothing come between them. Had Eva tried to do just that? The two sources she had questioned, however, all agreed on the order of events. Brandy had never discussed that 1945 afternoon with Axel Blackthorne.

At the lobby desk she borrowed a Tavares telephone book to look up the developer's office number. His secretary said her boss

would be in his office until about three. Then he had an appointment at the site for manufactured homes on Lake Dora. Brandy
did not give her name. She knew he would be hostile.

She filled the time gap by stopping for a sandwich to eat in the
car, then parked behind the brick building that housed the Lake
County Historical Museum. Her story needed more background.
From a volume about Tavares pioneers, she read that Sylvania's
grandfather had come to Lake County from Georgia in the 1870's.
He had ferried materials for his first house down the Oklawaha
River and hauled them overland by ox teams. For the house in
question, he used the recently built railroad and cut local cypress,
now logged out except for a pristine patch along the Dora Canal.
That fact, she thought as she closed the heavy book, probably
accounted for John's love of his trailer location.

When Brandy pulled up a little after two in front of the yellow
brick building of the Blackthorne Construction Company, she
reminded herself that the difference between a poor reporter and a
good one was often the difference between timidity and assertive-
ness.

Mr. Blackthorne's secretary turned out to be a plump, motherly
soul with iron gray hair. Brandy announced flatly, "Tell your
employer that I'm the person who found the skeleton on his Lake
Dora boat house property, and that I need some answers."

FIFTEEN

Ignoring Brandy's abrupt comment about the skeleton on the developer's property, Blackthorne's secretary gave her a cordial smile. "Your name, please? I'll let Mr. Blackthorne know you're here." After the woman stepped into his office, Brandy could hear his muffled bark. The secretary returned with a regretful shake of her head. "Sorry, Miss O'Bannon, is it? Mr. Blackthorne's too busy to see you." Brandy braced her shoulders.

"I called earlier," she said pleasantly. "I'll take only a few minutes of his time. It's important for me to speak to him about a story I'm working on for the *Tavares Beacon*. He'll be mentioned." She brushed past the secretary and into his office through the open door.

The wall beside Blackthorne's desk was covered with an architectural drawing of the new Lake Dora development——row upon row of identical little gray houses, packed together in a metallic rabbit warren. Blackthorne did not rise from behind his desk to greet her.

"I might've known it'd be you," he growled. "I asked my girl to tell you I was busy." She'd forgotten how wide the gap was between his front teeth. Under the heavy brows his eyes smoldered.

"She did tell me," Brandy said. "But I think you owe me some explanations, Mr. Blackthorne." She took a seat in a straight chair across from his desk and looked at him directly. "Wednesday night when John Able and I found the skeleton, I was chased across the lake by a motorboat from your pier. No mistake about that. There wasn't another motorboat on the lake, and I saw it leave the shore." She thrust her head forward. "And I have witnesses." No need to tell him that she didn't have the fishermen's names and had no idea how to reach them. "I want to know why your boat tried to run me down."

Blackthorne leaned back in the swivel chair, his fleshy hands toying with a pen on his desk. "I wanted you to leave Sylvania Langdon alone," he said at last. "No secret about that. She'd come to a decision and you were making it hard for her. You had no business on her property either night. I don't mind saying I left orders with my night watchman to stop your prowling, especially while she was gone."

Brandy's eyebrows lifted. "Stop me? Drown me is more like it!"

"My man may have been overly enthusiastic."

"Just like the night he turned the dogs on me."

Blackthorne did get up then, walked over to the window, and stood looking out, hands clasped behind him, a bulky silhouette against the early afternoon sunlight. She waited.

"I'm going to retire when this Lake Dora job is done," he said, more subdued. "I'm turning the business over to a nephew. I'd like to buy Sylvania's lot before I leave. It will help us both."

Brandy took her note pad out of her bag. "Surely the best thing for her would be for the publicity to end. And that will happen when we know the truth about Eva Stone's last afternoon." She caught his eye and he looked away. "I've talked to almost everyone who was at the weekend party when she disappeared. The bones have been identified as hers, so we know she didn't drown.

Or if she did, who buried her? I'm trying to find out as honestly as I can what went on that afternoon."

Blackthorne walked back to his desk, a wry smile pulling at the corners of his mouth. "I wonder who constituted you to represent the law?"

"I'm not representing the law, Mr. Blackthorne. I've no doubt the Sheriff's Office will ask the same questions. But I'm writing a story about the house, and I've come to care very much about what happened to Eva Stone. If people who were there will talk, maybe Sylvania can finally put the tragedy behind her."

He ran his hand through the thin hairs above his forehead, either trying to remember or trying to decide how much to tell. Finally he made his decision. "Sylvania called me the day before the party, very much upset. She asked me if I'd be there because she needed at least one friend she could depend on. I was surprised. I thought she was being courted by the young man Brookfield had brought home on a visit the year before."

He looked out the window again.

"But you did go for the weekend," Brandy prompted.

"Oh, yes. I went. Eva Stone came along at the last minute, too, but I didn't see much of her. I guess you know by now that all the fellows were after Eva, especially Ace Langdon. I think Syl found out that Ace had seen Eva on the sly, maybe even asked her to come. That's probably why Syl wanted me there. Someone she knew would show her some attention."

He slumped back in his chair and picked up the pen again. When Eva Stone disappeared, Ace turned back to Syl and made up with her." A sigh escaped through the space between his front teeth.

"I'm trying to find out where people were that afternoon," Brandy said gently. "I understand you went hunting with the other men."

"Sure, I wanted to be one of the guys, not like Ace Langdon. He hung around to prey on the girls. I didn't bag anything, as I remember." His face twisted in a smile. "I don't know if Ace did. I went in a pick–up truck with Brookfield. I wasn't as close a friend of his as I was of Syl's, but he did ask me to ride with him. He started home early, said he had an appointment and he had to get back to the house, so I got out and walked through a field west of the Ables' place, trying to scare up some quail. I wanted something to show for the afternoon's hunt. He drove on alone."

"So he got back to the house before you did?"

"Well, I guess he did. When I got there, everyone was looking for Eva Stone."

"Did you see Grace Southerland's car when she left?"

"She passed me on the road as I was walking in. I didn't say anything to her. I didn't know at the time there was any problem, and I guess she didn't either."

"And did you go into the water to hunt for Eva yourself?"

"Oh, yeah. Almost all of us did. Syl had been the first one in. Just like her. She was the best swimmer of us all. Brookfield was ahead of me. None of us could find a trace of the girl."

A possibility suddenly occurred to Brandy. "Later on, did Brookfield or Sylvania have an interest in your construction business?"

He looked at her sharply. "That's a matter of record," he said after a short pause. "Brookfield invested in my company when I got it started about a year later. I'd been working off and on since high school for a construction company in Leesburg. I knew the business, and my work in the Seabees during the war helped. The investment certainly rewarded Brookfield well. The years right after the war were prosperous for builders. Did Syl have an interest in it? No. It was strictly Brookfield's money, and he sold his interest long before his death."

Brandy rose. "If you think of anything else that might help us learn the truth about Eva Stone's death, I hope you'll call me or the Sheriff's Office. John and I never meant to hurt Sylvania."

He looked up at her, bristly brows drawn into a scowl. "You could fool me," he said. "What you've done so far has made her life almost unbearable. She's certainly never been hauled into the Sheriff's Office before."

He shifted papers from the out–basket to his desk and tapped them. "This is the contract for Sylvania's house. Just as soon as the Sheriff's through digging, Syl will sign it. Then she'll finally be rid of the house and all that goes with it. And another thing," he added, his words measured, "if your news story even suggests that I knew anything about that skeleton or Eva Stone's death, I'll sue you and your paper for slander."

Brandy had meant to shake his hand, but that no longer seemed appropriate. "I don't intend to slander anyone," she said. "But I do intend to go on talking to people. Tomorrow I'll see the woman who watched Eva Stone walk out into the lake. And maybe I'll be able to interview Mrs. Stone, too. She's still alive. I do intend to find out what happened to Eva Stone."

As Brandy stepped into the reception room, Blackthorne's secretary moved behind her and closed the developer's open door. "Before you leave, Miss O'Bannon," she said quietly, "you need some background information I'll tell you that Axel won't."

Brandy paused, intrigued.

"Don't judge Axel from those threats until you know the whole story. He's my cousin. After my husband died, he helped by giving me this job. I've known him all my life, he and Sylvania."

Her expression softened. "Down through the years Axel watched that woman suffer. In school kids made fun of him because he was too fat and Sylvania for being too tall. It was the two of them against the world. Their misery made them close friends and they stayed close. Then along came Ace Langdon. He had glamour. He'd been a bomber pilot during the war, and the girls always went for pilots. Axel had sweated out the war in construction on islands in the Pacific. And Ace was good–looking. All the other girls thought he was a real catch. When he proposed to Sylvania, that must've been sweet revenge."

The secretary eased back around her desk and sat down, but she wasn't finished. "Sylvania's folks were all for the marriage. Mr. Able probably thought he had an old maid on his hands. And Ace was supposed to come from a fine family up North. Blackthorne's father operated a shoe repair shop on Main Street. That should tell you something. After a few years, Axel married, too, but it didn't last. His heart wasn't in it. Neither had any children. It was hushed up, but several years after her disastrous marriage, a cleaning woman went in early one day and found Sylvania with her head in the oven. Axel vowed then never to let her reach that level of despair again. If she wants to sell her house, he'll see that she can, and for a hefty price."

She gave Brandy a warm smile. "Don't leave thinking Axel Blackthorne wants that property just to make money. He may not even get his investment back. Sylvania's always been too proud to accept help, but now Axel can see that she lives comfortably the rest of her life. That's the reason he has tried so hard to get her to sell to him. He'd do almost anything for Sylvania. When you write your story, these facts should make you see Axel in a different light. I believe they call it 'deep background.'"

She's given me the dignity of an experienced journalist, Brandy thought. Clever. As she thanked the secretary and vowed to be discreet, she felt more sympathy for Blackthorne than she ever thought she could, in spite of his ugly houses and his threats. At least he was capable of a devotion she had not suspected.

Thoughtfully, she drove through a rising wind to a fast food window and bought a hamburger and a coke. She had seen Sylvania in her role as Woman of Steel, she had never seen her as suicidal. Her one-sided love for a hotshot philanderer may have given her reason. Was a guilty conscience another? On that long-ago weekend, could she have rid herself of a troublesome rival? And if Blackthorne would do anything for Sylvania, could it include eliminating that rival?

There was only one place Brandy really wanted to go, and under gathering clouds her car raced there almost on its own. Just don't let me run into the exemplary Sharon, she thought as she finished her lunch in the hospital parking lot.

Sixteen

Brandy found the door to John's room open, the dresser crowded with a cactus garden and a huge spray of irises and peace lilies, and no sign of Sharon. The game young doctor stood at John's bedside, trying to listen to his heart, while John pled to go home. The doctor insisted that he had to keep a watch on John's puffy, discolored hand——"proud flesh" he called it—— and his swollen arm as well. Brandy cornered him in the corridor as he left the room.

The doctor halted, plainly still under the impression that she was family. "Today will tell whether we have to remove the dead muscle tissue. We'd rather not operate, but the main thing is to prevent gangrene. Mr. Able's still getting anti–venom. It's some better, and I'm encouraged. Maybe we can avoid surgery."

Brandy stepped back into the room and crossed to John's bed. He seemed less feverish. "Hi," she said. "Waiting's the hardest part, not knowing what will happen."

"Hi, your own self." He rubbed his forehead with his good hand. She was pleased to see the Chopin tape had been played.

"Nice surprise. Didn't expect a visit from Brenda Starr, girl reporter. Thought you'd be too busy."

She accepted the remark as an invitation, perched on a chair beside the bed, and pulled her spiral note pad from her bag. "I came to take your mind off your hand. I had an informative talk with both Grace and Blackthorne. Interested?" She thought she detected a glimmer in his eyes and opened the note pad. "I also learned something new at the briefing. Eva Stone had a much younger brother. Name's Weston Stone. He owns the Pub on the Lake and some other waterfront places, too."

John nodded toward the foot of the bed. "The early edition of the *Commercial* is out. It has a story about the briefing."

Brandy picked up the paper. "I've hardly got a scoop, have I?" The front page featured a photograph of Eva Stone that she hadn't seen before, one with shorter hair and a more mature face, although Brandy instantly recognized the arching forehead, the luminous eyes, the full lips.

Under it was the account given by the lieutenant and a follow–up interview with Weston Stone. "He's quoted as saying he was adopted after Eva Stone's death," she said, skimming the story. "He never knew her."

Maybe John did care about Eva Stone's fate, Brandy thought. "I need to talk to Weston Stone," she said. "We'll probably like him. He spoke up for preserving the lake view at the Chamber of Commerce meeting. He could give me access to his mother."

John raised his head. "Surely you don't want to bother the poor old lady now."

"We'll see if it's necessary," Brandy soothed. "Help me draw up a list. We need suspects, motives, and opportunity. It's always done in murder mysteries."

He stared at her with wonder. "I think you're actually enjoying this. You're not paying the least attention to my advice. Leave crime to the professionals."

Brandy dredged a pencil up from the depths of her bag. "They'll never solve it in time for my deadline. I'm not doing anything dangerous. And I've already got Sylvania mad at me. I don't suppose she's been to see you?"

He frowned. "Not likely."

"All right. Number 1 suspect would be Brookfield himself. Motive: fear Eva might upset his plans to marry Grace, a marriage that meant a great increase in wealth. His whereabouts at the time of the disappearance are unknown, but the developer says Brookfield had an appointment at the house, apparently before Eva disappeared. Brookfield drove on home alone, earlier than the other men. Later he was seen in the water searching for the body. He went on searching for days."

She stopped writing and bit her lip. "But the motive's a trifle weak. Why would Eva present such a serious threat?" She scribbled furiously again for a few seconds.

"Number 2 is Sylvania." She held up her hand. "Now don't get upset. Everyone has to be a suspect. Eva represented a threat to Sylvania, too. Even though Sylvania had accepted Ace Langdon's proposal, he made it plain he would ditch Sylvania for Eva. If he'd done that, pardon me——but according to Blackthorne's cousin Sylvania would've been more of a laughing stock than she was already.

"As for opportunity, she was there helping her mother. Then she was the first in the water during the search. She was the best swimmer. That could've given her more opportunity to hide the body. We have to consider that poor Eva may have been dragged under, half–drowned, taken ashore, and bashed for good measure. Of course, anyone searching for Eva might've pulled that off."

For the moment John entered into the spirit of the chase. "How could that happen with everyone else out looking for her?"

"I've considered that carefully. There's the spit of land in front of the house with a huge bougainvillea growing on it. It's in the old photograph. Someone could conceal a body there for a short time."

"Very risky," he said.

"Number 3 is Grace," she went on. "Her motive: She expected to marry Brookfield and could've seen Eva as a dangerous rival. Maybe Brookfield said he was still in love with Eva. Maybe he was going to break their engagement after it had just been announced. That would be devastating to a woman everyone says is so sensitive. Her whereabouts? That's the catch, of course. She was seen leaving before the search got well underway, so she seems to have an alibi."

"Grace seems awfully mild to go about bashing skulls."

Brandy nodded. "Then we have Ace Langdon as Number 4. Motive: Maybe he wasn't so unsuccessful with Eva. We only have his word for that. Maybe he'd been fooling around with her and she came there to blackmail him. We know he's always been an incorrigible woman chaser. Maybe he'd had an affair with her and she threatened to tell. After all, he was planning to marry into a wealthy family and have a cushy job for life. That could be a powerful motive.

"His whereabouts at the time of Eva's disappearance? Unknown. He says he was alone in the billiard room. Earlier we know he had been with Eva." She paused to take more notes.

"And last, we have the ever–popular Axel Blackthorne. This afternoon he was surprisingly forthcoming, considering how he hates us both. He was devoted to Sylvania, but I don't see why that gave him a reason to do away with Eva Stone. There's one plausible motive. A commonplace in crime forever. Maybe he was paid to do the killing.

"Blackthorne himself says he was with Brookfield that afternoon. If Brookfield wanted Eva dead, he might've persuaded Blackthorne to do the job."

"And how would he be paid without anyone knowing?"

"By providing financing for Blackthorne's new construction company. Brookfield backed the developer's business the following year. How else would a poor boy just out of the service be able to start up a construction company?

"Blackthorne had the opportunity to find Eva in the water. Maybe he was only supposed to discourage Eva, the way Blackthorne's man tried to discourage me. He could've followed her into the water, got carried away while everyone was milling around, and killed her in a panic. Physically he's a brute of a man. Blackthorne as a hired killer makes sense."

Brandy looked up and closed her notebook. "We have motives and opportunities here, but there's still something that we don't know. There's a piece of the puzzle missing. I feel it."

John turned partly on one side to face her. "Steve says the Sheriff's Office has taken down the boat house plank by plank today. Tomorrow they start excavating the area, looking for——dare I say the word——clues. You don't have to do their job."

Brandy tried to reassure him by patting his arm and smiling. Mentally she tallied up her activities for the next day: a call to Weston Stone to set up an appointment with Eva's mother, a visit to the boat house site, the two o'clock session with Mrs. Hall.

He looked down at his swollen hand. "I don't suppose you've found any time to check up on my interests. Have you talked to Curt Greene?"

She nodded. "Still hasn't found a buyer. Tomorrow's contract signing was postponed, but Sylvania says she's going ahead with it as soon as the Sheriff's Office is through digging on her property."

She closed her bag. John looked tired, his coloring grayer, his body under the cover thinner than two days ago. Maybe she had worried him further. "I was hoping to cheer you up."

"By telling me half my family may be killers?" But he gave her his rare smile.

She grinned back and started for the door.

"Brandy." John's voice startled her. When she turned she noticed the name tag on the large arrangement of flowers on the dresser. She recognized the tidy, precise handwriting and the two word message, "Love, Sharon." In a way John's girlfriend had been with them after all.

He raised his head while she paused before the flowers. "There's something I need to explain..."

Brandy interrupted quickly. "No need. I understand about your girl friend. Don't worry. There's Mack, you know." Of course she understood. What happened between them was a thing of the moment, a release of nervous tension after a crisis. No need for him to feel guilty. No need for her plans with Mack to change. But again she felt the lump of lead in her chest.

As she pulled the door partially closed behind her, she could see him lie back, a troubled look in his dark eyes.

Outside the wind had died down and the sky grown overcast. A fine mist hung in the low spots of the parking lot. The Florida dusk would be short and night fall like a trap. As Brandy drove down the darkening streets, she tried to push from her mind all thoughts of Sharon and Mack, and even of John. She could do nothing about Sharon, and she still had a few days to decide about Mack.

If she ever had a chance with John, she had certainly ruined it. She had gotten him dunked into the lake at night, bitten by a poisonous snake, and in trouble with all his relatives, especially the great–aunt whose support and trust he most wanted. Brandy clinched her fingers around the steering wheel. Suddenly she needed very much to be home, to be alone with her loose leaf notebook on the case, thinking only about the mystery of Eva Stone.

Fog had settled over the tall pines in the vacant lot next to the driveway, around her mother's Ford, and along the chain link fence in the back yard. When she heard Meg's happy, welcome–home bark, she knelt for a moment and stroked the coppery head before letting herself into the kitchen. Her mother sat at her usual place at the dining room table, wielding a red pen over a stack of papers. She looked up, lips pressed together.

"Well, have you beaten the detectives at their own game and solved the murder? I read the evening paper." She stood and crossed to the telephone stand. "A weekly paper doesn't pay much. It shouldn't require you to put your life on the line."

Brandy mumbled something about still working on the same story, and stayed in the kitchen to set a cup of instant coffee into the microwave.

"You had two messages," Mrs. O'Bannon said. She tore a note from the memo pad on the dining room table and handed it to Brandy. "A man called about five."

"Mr. Hyer from Hyer's Retirement Home," Brandy read. "Mrs. Stone wants to talk to the reporter from the *Tavares Beacon*. She won't talk to any others. Call at the home tomorrow at four." Her mother had scribbled down a Tavares address.

The older woman crossed into the kitchen. "He said Mrs. Stone had a doctor's appointment in the morning and then had her lunch and took a long nap. Said she'll see you after that. I guess it's good news for you." She pulled an iron kettle out of a cupboard. "Mr. Hyer said Mrs. Stone wants to thank you for finding her daughter's remains." She lifted her chin and cut her eyes sideways at her daughter. "A doubtful pleasure, I'm sure. After all these years, it must have reminded her of her painful loss. Why not let sleeping dogs lie?"

Brandy couldn't resist a pun. "Because someone's been lying about Eva Stone for years." She took a sip of the hot coffee. The times would work out tomorrow if she hurried, Mrs. Hall at two, Mrs. Stone at four. "And the other message?"

Her mother handed her an envelope with no stamp and no return address. "This was in the mailbox when I got home." Brandy slit the envelope with a paring knife and unfolded a single sheet of cheap bond paper with a few lines of type and no signature. "*I have important information for your investigation,*" she read silently, "*but I can't reveal my identity. I'll leave a package of documents in your garage tonight by midnight. If I see anyone watching, I won't stop and I'll destroy the evidence.*"

Hello, Brandy thought. Things are looking up. What kind of documents might relate to Eva Stone? Surely something that tied her to her killer——letters, legal papers? The note came in a plain white envelope, the kind carried in every drug and grocery store. Its style sounded formal, but Brandy had met no illiterates in her investigation. She tucked the note into her canvas bag and decided not to discuss it with her mother. She could imagine her reaction, surely something sarcastic about Sherlock Holmes.

Brandy glanced out the window. The fog had not lifted. The garage was a blurry, peaked shape at the rear of the lot. After a supper of Mrs. O'Bannon's homemade vegetable–beef soup and muffins, Brandy nipped outside, through the gate, and past their cars in the driveway. When she switched on a small bulb above the open garage doors, a faint glow spread over the counters of potted plants and bags of potting soil—— a clever, out of the way place for her correspondent to stash the treasure. Brandy had been pleased with Steve Able as a source, but the note had brought her another, even more valuable.

She considered leaving Meg outside, where her barking would signal the visitor's arrival, but she decided to let the grateful dog slink through the kitchen and into her bedroom. Meg might frighten Brandy's benefactor away.

In her room Brandy changed into a shirt and jeans, ready to dart back out to the garage around midnight. By nine–thirty she was at her desk, transcribing notes into a loose leaf binder while the interviews with Ace, Blackthorne, and Grace were still sharp in her mind. Meg scrambled under the bed, her chew rag in her jaws, her feathery tail thumping, and they settled down to wait. About ten Brandy heard her mother's door close. Summer school started early.

By eleven Brandy began straining to hear a car. Almost none ever turned down their street. But the only sound was the monotonous hum of the room air conditioner. Her eyes grew heavy. She laid down her pen and nodded at her desk. About eleven–fifteen Meg growled deep in her throat and poked her creamy muzzle out below the bedspread fringe. Brandy turned off the desk lamp and peered through the venetian blinds.

She could see no headlights, no figure, only the bulk of their own cars, blocking her view of the garage. Beyond the driveway nothing moved except the fog around the pines and wax myrtle in the vacant lot. Meg squirmed out from under the bed, paced back and forth, whining, and laid her chin in Brandy's lap.

"You know something's amiss," Brandy whispered, "but we don't dare go outside and scare the person away." Surely, she thought, she would be able to figure out from the documents themselves who had left them. Brandy waited until eleven–forty–five. Then she quietly peeked into the hall. From the crack under the other bedroom door, she could see her mother's room was dark. Meg's damp nose pushed forward, but Brandy petted her, then gently shoved her back into the bedroom. "Can't have you barking," she said, and closed the door.

Outside the sky was blanketed with clouds, the mist thicker than ever. She had depended on the garage door light and not thought to bring a flash. Now she hesitated, turned on the back porch light, and decided she could see well enough with the two.

She felt her way around the cars and stood for a moment under the pale bulb, peering into the dimness of the garage. One of the double doors had been shut. She didn't remember seeing the change earlier in the evening, but she hadn't looked. Maybe her mother wanted to protect some fragile plants from the wind.

When Brandy stepped onto the littered garage floor, she first examined the shelves and counter top near the entrance. No parcel. Her benefactor had been more secretive. She was conscious of a familiar odor——charcoal briquettes burning. Maybe her mother hadn't completely doused the coals in the hibachi last night, then set it inside in case the rains came. Brandy would have to check before she left the garage. It was not like Mrs. O'Bannon to be careless.

After stumbling over a large bag of pine bark, Brandy felt her way along the counter past two metal cans of weed killer, almost tripped over a rake, and banged her shin on the lawn mower. At last through the shadows she saw a tall cardboard box she had never seen before, standing beside paint cans on a low rear shelf.

She had reached the box, had put her hands on the sides, then groped inside, when something creaked behind her, and she was plunged into sudden darkness. It took a minute for her to realize that the other garage door had swung shut. She hadn't been aware of a rising wind. While she stood, startled, staring into blackness, the outside locking bar rattled into place.

She stood, shaking, in an inky pit. Wind could not shift the bar. How could the door have closed? The odor now was much stronger. She felt muddled, headachy. In the corner she had seen a clump of fiddle leaf plants and a large, potted bougainvillea, all recuperating from last winter's freeze. The smell came from behind them. She could see no flame, but in the absolute night of the garage a ruddy glow shone through the leaves, not enough to give light——the hibachi.

She dragged herself back in the direction she thought led to the door, halted, tried to remember where the lawn mower and the bags of pine bark were. Now she had trouble getting her breath, felt nauseated. She needed to rest a minute and gather her thoughts. No one could hear her bang on the door now.

Maybe she would have to wait until morning when her mother left for work. Then she could check the box. As she lowered herself to the concrete floor, closed her eyes, and dropped her head between her knees, she heard one sound from a great distance—— a faint barking.

SEVENTEEN

Brandy was first conscious of a strong light and her big red dog vibrating with excitement beside her, then of the round face of a woman in a white uniform above her. She lay in the night air on a hard, damp surface. She must be on her back in the driveway. Her head throbbed.

"A near thing," the woman said, and placed an oxygen mask over Brandy's nose. "Move one of those cars so we can get the van in here. We need to get out before the rain starts."

"Will she be all right?" Her mother's voice anxious, then a more reluctant, "If it hadn't been for that dog... Her barking woke me up. I looked and my daughter wasn't in her room. The dog led me to the garage." More insistent. "Is she all right?"

The woman nodded and straightened up. "You got her into the air in time. A dog's nose comes in handy. Ask the cops." She motioned to someone behind her. "We'll give your daughter a hundred per cent oxygen for a while, let the doctor check her out." The medics lifted Brandy on a stretcher and carried her as they had carried John. Brandy dropped one hand and felt the retriever's silky back. She was surprised when her mother knelt beside the ambulance and put her arms around Meg, fleas and all.

Before the door slammed shut Brandy saw a deputy jump out of his car at the curb and come toward them. "I need to get some facts here," he said.

One of the medics turned. "Talk to the mother. Carbon monoxide poisoning."

Then another loud, familiar voice. "What the hell is going on here?" Oh, lord. Rumpled and unshaven, Mack stalked out of the darkness.

Her mother close to her ear. "I called him, dear."

She had a brief view of Mack's tall form, his face perplexed and angry. "I want to know how this happened."

The box of documents, Brandy thought, she had never checked the box.

The door closed. A woman sat beside her while she breathed oxygen.

*   *   *

Brandy tried to orient herself, to decide what was real. She had been asleep, had dreamed she was trapped in a box struggling to breathe. She was sure something like that had happened. Yet this was a hospital. In the dream the lid had closed on her, shutting out the air. But she knew there was something important about a box. She breathed deeply, and found she was now receiving her oxygen in a nose tube.

At the foot of her bed the plastic curtain slid aside, and a stocky, middle–aged man in street clothes came toward her. He flashed a Sheriff's Office badge. "Detective Morris," he said. "We need to talk. You okay?"

Brandy shook off the momentary terror and looked around. "I'm okay," she said. "I was groggy, but my head's clear now. Where's my watch? I've got appointments this afternoon." She noticed that someone, probably her mother, had laid fresh clothes over the foot of the bed.

The balding detective leaned so close that Brandy could see the hairs in his heavy brown mustache and eyebrows. It was not an unpleasant face, but purposeful. "It's only nine, Miss. You're in the hospital emergency wing. Doc says they're letting you go soon." He sat on a padded stool beside the bed. "Look, I talked to your mom before she left. She told me someone put a note in your mailbox yesterday, while you were both at work. She found it in your bag."

Brandy pulled the pillow up behind her and sat up. "The big cardboard box on the rear shelf..."

"Blank paper on top, this week's newspapers underneath."

Brandy slapped her hand down on the blanket. "Of course! I was so muddle–headed I didn't know what was happening."

"Common with carbon monoxide. That's why it's so dangerous."

Her voice rose. "Any prints on the note or the box?"

He grinned. "Everyone expects fingerprints. We dusted, but I don't think so. Whoever did this knew about fingerprints. Also your only neighbor was away last night. She did hear the dog barking yesterday afternoon, but she didn't go outside to check. Looks like that's when the perpetrator moved the hibachi from the picnic table to the garage. Your mom would've been at work then. The perp knew what he was doing. Even used WD–40 on the garage door hinges."

Brandy remembered the sudden blackness. "I couldn't find the door. I got so disoriented."

"Burning briquettes can fill a small, closed space with carbon monoxide fast."

She clinched her fingers around the covers. "Any luck tracing the note?"

"Since you saw it, I guess I can tell you it's a computer print–out. Hard to identify."

"Any footprints in the vacant lot next door?"

"On pine needles?"

Brandy realized the intruder probably parked down the block and came across the lot. Any tire prints would be washed away by rain early that morning.

He poised a pencil over his spiral note pad. "I want you to fill in the details."

Brandy folded her hands before her and explained all she knew. Her poking around had clearly made enemies, maybe at least four——Axel Blackthorne, Sylvania Langdon, Ace Langdon, and Grace Able. The detective stared back at her, his eyes grave. "My recommendation, Miss, is to forget this case."

"Somebody wants me to chill out, all right. Maybe I'll let them think I have. But I won't give up my interviews this afternoon." She smiled. "Anyway, you'll have the case solved before my little feature story comes out."

He sighed and stood up. "Stay available. And stay with people." He glanced toward the wide doorway. "Somebody else out here wants to see you mighty bad."

Her heart lifted. John was in the hospital. Maybe he had heard, maybe Steve or someone else in the Sheriff's Office had told him. He might be allowed to come downstairs. But as the detective left through the open door, Brandy heard a nurse speaking rapidly, then that familiar voice again, loud. "I got to see her. She's my fiancée. I want to know what the hell's going on."

Mack, of course. He'd followed her to the hospital. She lay back against the pillow and tried to look wan. If he thought she was going to stay here, he wouldn't shadow her. She had heard Detective Morris's warning. She would be more careful, but she would not give up on Eva Stone. Obviously she was close to some fact of enormous danger to someone. Mack would never understand, but she had to know what the sheriff's men were finding near the boat house.

She greeted him with an exhausted smile. "I'm weak as a kitten," she whispered. "I think I'll be here quite a while." He gave a nod of satisfaction. John had said she was manipulative. Maybe she'd proved him right.

A few minutes later he blundered out, not much enlightened. When the doctor looked in on her again, she persuaded him to let her go. No real damage had been done to her red blood cells, he said———thanks to her mother and a certain golden retriever.

She stepped into the rest room, changed into shirt and slacks, and stuffed the jeans from last night into a plastic hospital bag. In the waiting room she found an in–house phone and called John's room. When he answered, he sounded restive. In the background she could hear———not the lyrical strain of the Chopin etude——— but the rhythms of an evangelical preacher's voice. Apparently a roommate had a strangle hold on the television remote. John said the doctor had just made his rounds and told him he could go. He was ready to dial his folks to pick him up. Brandy wondered if Sharon and his parents planned to drag him off to their lair.

"I'm going to your Aunt Sylvania's this morning," she said. "Check out what the Sheriff's Office is finding. Even with the rain, they must be well along with the digging." She would be in no danger with law enforcement officers around———especially if John would go. Outside the window she saw blue sky through patches in the clouds. "Want to go with me? Might as well re–visit the scene of the crime. It could be interesting."

He paused. "I ought to see Sylvania," he said, his voice mournful. "I need to apologize for trespassing."

She looked at her watch. "I plan to go right away. I could drop you off wherever you say afterward."

He might feel used again if she said Detective Morris told her not to be alone. Neither did she mention her own near miss. Time for that later.

In his room John sat beside the bed, dressed in short–sleeved shirt and jeans, his overnight bag packed, his fingers drumming on the arms of the chair. On the television screen above the two beds a disheveled girl was now shrieking and jumping up and down. Although John's skin still looked unnaturally white, his cheeks gaunt, Brandy could see his swollen arm was a lighter purple.

He glanced down at it. "The doctor says I can handle this now with antibiotics." He slipped the Chopin tape into his bag and handed her the player. "A life–saver when I could use it. Let's get out of here."

In the lobby she stopped to call her mother's school and leave word that she had been discharged.

On the long ride past pastures, a newly planted grove, pines and palmettos, to the south side of Lake Dora, Brandy did not raise the questions about Sylvania, but John's great aunt must know something. Why had she tried so hard to keep Brandy away? Why was she so eager to see the house destroyed when there was surely enough Able money to fix it up? Why, indeed, had her brother Brookfield built that boat house in such a hurry and then left it so promptly? Maybe because of the buried body. John might get Sylvania to talk. Brandy did decide to tell him about last night. Better he heard the account from her. She did not explain that she might have died, only that someone had——as he predicted——tried to stop her.

At the Able homestead two deputies' cars were pulled up in the parking area. Brandy recognized the reporter from the Leesburg *Commercial* lounging against a long leaf pine with a bored expression, watching the two men in uniform.

All seemed quiet on Blackthorne's side of the fence where the uprooted water lilies still lay rotting in the damp air.

The officers had strung yellow and black tape around the plot where the boat house once stood. Here the earth had been divided with cord into grids of about five feet each. The deputies knelt within them, digging methodically with trowels and throwing the dirt into screens, where it settled in moist piles and slowly sifted through into a tray below. On the lawn beside them lay a tarp, and on it the few items that had been culled from the site.

Brandy sauntered ahead of John and recognized Deputy Martin, the officer with the sandy complexion who had responded the night the skeleton was found. Apparently he had been allowed to follow up on the case.

"Uncovered anything of interest?" she asked.

Martin stood up and gave her a friendly smile. "Glad to see you again, Miss," he said. He nodded toward the tarp. "You can see what we've found so far. There's some brass buttons and a brass belt buckle. Some glass beads, too."

Brandy and John squatted beside the canvas to peer down at the pathetically few remnants of Eva Stone's clothing. They had been rinsed and lay drying in the feeble morning sun, a few yards from her burial site. Brandy tried to suppress the grisly memory of the skeleton.

Leaning forward, she inspected the cache. The number of greenish buttons surprised her. She counted ten. "These must have gone all down the front or back of a dress," she said. A piece of corroded metal might once have been a buckle. Beside it, a cluster of beads caught the light and, through the dull film that coated the surface, shone a soft blue. But Brandy looked hardest at the pinkish scrap of material. The witness Charlotte who saw the ghost said it wore something white at the neck, and then something red.

"Funny thing," Martin said, tipping back his hat and scratching his head with one hand. "These things weren't found where we expected to find them." He gestured toward the area where stakes marked the site and dimensions of the bones. "They weren't where the skeleton was. We found them over here, a good distance away and all bunched together."

"What do you think that means?" John asked, rising.

"Well, to put it bluntly, it looks like the dress wasn't on the victim when she was buried."

Brandy wondered about a possible rape, impossible to prove now. She turned to another concern. "There's been a lot of rumors about unusual sightings here," she said. "Anything interesting to report in that line?"

The deputy paused, then looked directly at Brandy, his eyes troubled. "I'll tell you, Miss, after last night, I'll be glad to be finished with this job."

Before she could ask more, the trowel wielded by the other officer clanged against metal. The man bent forward, peered at the soil, then exchanged his small tool for a spade. Under the cypress tree the *Commercial* reporter perked up and ambled over. Carefully the deputy inserted the sharp blade under an encrusted object, lifted it up, and laid it on the tarp.

It took Brandy a minute to recognize what it was, but John's eyes were immediately alert. Rusted through in several places and stained black, lay a long, thin tube–like bar, flared at one end like a shoe–horn and pointed at the other like a chisel.

"Don't see many of them anymore," the deputy with the spade said.

"It's what we were looking for, all right." Martin dropped his trowel and knelt beside it. "Any blood or hair would've disappeared long ago. But this would've done the job."

"Of course," said John. "As the weapon, it makes sense." He turned to Brandy. "You've got another piece of your puzzle."

And then Brandy finally realized what she was seeing. She remembered that the yard man changed a tire before Eva disappeared, that the tools came from Grace Southerland's trunk, that Ace Langdon claimed he returned them to the floor of Grace's back seat. She was looking at the crucial tool—— the tire iron.

At that moment around the corner of the house came the tall figure of Sylvania Langdon in a flapping shirt and a pair of loose–fitting slacks.

Deputy Martin stepped forward. "We need to let you know what we've found here, Mrs. Langdon." She halted in her stride and glanced down sharply at the twisted piece of metal. "Looks like a tire iron," he went on. "We believe it was used to change a tire the afternoon the young lady disappeared."

"I know nothing about that," Sylvania answered quickly. "I only heard about the flat tire later. I know nothing about Eva Stone's actions that day until the maid called for help."

"We think it was after you heard the maid that someone killed Eva Stone," the officer said.

John edged toward his great–aunt. "We were on our way to see you," he said. "We just stopped in the yard first to speak to the deputies."

"They're certainly here all right," she said, waspish. "All over my property. Even had me down to the Sheriff's Office! That was humiliating."

John ignored her remark. "I came to say I'm sorry I didn't get your permission before I investigated the boat house. But you were gone."

Her keen gray eyes glared down at his arm. "Next time I warn you, maybe you'll pay attention."

Tactfully the officer turned away and began helping his companion put away their tools. When the reporter from the *Commercial* produced a notebook and began asking questions, Martin referred him to a spokesman at the Sheriff's Office. John and Brandy walked beside Sylvania toward the house.

Brandy, slogging through the wet grass beside John, spoke up first. "We couldn't possibly have known what we would find that night. We just wanted to see what was in the boat house before it was knocked down. I'm sorry, too, for coming here without your permission." She couldn't resist adding, "But it's a lucky thing we checked it out. We uncovered a brutal crime."

"Can you think of anybody who might have known the skeleton was there?" John asked.

"As far as I know, anybody could've known," Sylvania snapped. "The fact that the boat house was built in that spot was just a coincidence. I imagine the body was buried hastily. Brookfield cleared a lot of shrubbery on the land he chose for his boat house. It could've been buried under those bushes. It was logical to put the boat house on that spit of land where there's a natural harbor."

"Did he ever say anything to you about the boat house specifically?"

She halted. "Of course not. I only know that he always disliked this house after Eva Stone disappeared. He didn't want to live here himself. After the tragedy he didn't enjoy fishing here, and I guess hunting reminded him of it, too. It's easy to see why he would've wanted to move away. On his deathbed he told me I needn't hold on to the house, even though he left it to me. He said to get shut of it. He knew the land would be valuable. And that's an end of it!"

Overhead clouds again blocked the sun, and the smell of rain hung in the air. When Sylvania did not ask them in, John started back toward the car with Brandy hurrying to match his stride. "I tracked down the maid who saw Eva go into the lake. I see her at two."

"I don't imagine she has anything to say that you don't already know."

She glanced up at him, hoping he wouldn't disapprove of her second interview. Maybe he'd think it was ghoulish to interview the mourning Mrs Stone. "I've got another appointment later to talk to Eva Stone's mother. Maybe she knows something we don't."

He did disapprove. "My God," she said. "Can't you reporters respect a mother's grief?"

EIGHTEEN

Before Brandy's car reached the highway, the summer rain had begun again, blurring the vague shapes of cabbage palms and live oaks along the roadside. As they neared the Dora Canal, she suggested they pull into a fast food restaurant for an early lunch before she dropped him off at his trailer. Over a grilled fish sandwich, she summoned the courage to ask John a question, one she'd wanted to ask ever since Deputy Martin admitted he didn't like guarding the boat house site.

"While you were waiting for me Wednesday night, did you see or hear anything out of the ordinary, anything that would explain the ghost story?"

Outside the wind had risen and the rain blew in gusts against the windows. She expected a raised eyebrow and a derisive laugh. Instead John rubbed his forehead with his good hand in that familiar gesture of uncertainty. At the hospital he had lost weight. Now his face looked leaner, his cheeks sunken, and his eyes unusually bright as he studied her face, as though unsure how to answer.

"At first when you left me that night," he said slowly, "I just listened to the sound of your engine, and then I heard Blackthorne's boat start up. I could hear two boats about the same place, and I saw two moving lights in the distance, but I couldn't tell what was going on out there. So at first I didn't pay any attention to the house itself. Later, everything got very still and dark. I couldn't see into the upstairs window from where I was standing, but I guess the power of suggestion got to me."

He gazed out at the thin, bending trunks of slash pines beside the restaurant, then set his hamburger down and stared into his coffee cup. "I thought I saw something move down on the lawn. I knew Sylvania wasn't there, and everything was quiet next door. I never heard a car come or go. I remembered the story, of course, and I thought I saw somebody come around the corner of the house. A human shape. Then I lost it. I know the imagination plays tricks. Maybe I saw the shadow of a tree."

His fingers massaged his forehead again. "Then quite a while before you got back, the cottonmouth came out of the water. When it slithered up on the deck and onto that beam, it got my full attention." He moved his still swollen hand. "Remember, by then the moon was down and I was standing there alone with that skeleton behind me. Even if I believed I saw something, I'm hardly a credible witness."

Brandy caught her breath. "But I thought I saw the same figure. Only I didn't dare tell anyone."

"Doesn't prove anything. Just that two of us fell under the spell of suggestion."

Outside the fronds of a palm tossed against the window. Brandy had the overwhelming sense of another world out there, waiting.

"I told you I did some reading about this kind of thing," she said. "When I knew I wanted to report on the ghost story, I spent several hours making notes in the library. I haven't studied enough physics to understand most of what I read. That's more your field. But apparently physicists don't know why time seems only to move forward. According to the laws of physics, at least as they're understood now, time should move backward as well as forward." Her eyes widened. "What if occasionally something that happened in the past re–plays itself? What if time sometimes does go backward?"

"That's absurd," John said.

"If you don't like that one, there's another theory: there's a lot dimensions besides the ones we know. Usually we don't have a way to experience them, but sometimes there's a shred in the fabric of our own dimension. It lets us sense what's going on in another. Actually, the theories kind of mesh. One book says that many worlds could cohabit something called superspace at the same time, and that past, present, and future coexist simultaneously."

His lips turned up in a wry smile. "What happened to your theory about a traumatic event impressed on the atmosphere?"

"That's still another explanation. According to that theory, there wouldn't be any consciousness in the thing we're seeing. The image would be like a photograph repeated over and over again."

He shook his head. "Like a shadow, hanging around to point to the killer? Come on. I don't like to think vengeance is that strong."

She frowned. "It's all so confusing. But even I know the physical world is made up of nothing but different forms of energy."

John shifted in his seat, more serious now. "I've been honest about that experience, but I don't like to talk about it. I don't believe all that hocus–pocus about other dimensions. I'd rather live in the world I know."

Brandy thought of the world she had known too briefly Tuesday night. "Amen to that," she said. But then, Sharon was in that world, too. And Mack.

After they had ducked through the rain to the car, she settled again under the wheel and waited for him to fasten his seat belt. "You're probably right that I can't put the supernatural element in my story. Maybe it's just as well. It seems flippant to call what we saw a 'ghost.' Grace Able called it an evil presence, but it seemed more poignant to me."

As Brandy pulled into the trailer parking lot, she glanced down at her watch. It would take at least a half an hour to reach Mrs. Hall's Mount Dora address. "I'll call you tonight," she said. Maybe I'll have something new to report from Mrs. Hall." She didn't mention Eva Stone's mother again.

No sign of Sharon at the trailer, she thought, but there was always the phone.

John pulled his overnight bag out of the back seat. "I need to let the folks know I'm home. And I expect your boy friend would like to hear you're still okay, and out of the Able family's——"he paused——"sinister hands." He was smiling, but perhaps she had hurt his family pride. Or maybe he wanted to remind her of her boy friend. "Thanks for the tour," he added. "The doctor says I can drive again soon." He ducked through the rain, then glanced back from his narrow porch. "Be careful."

"I'll be with people. Not to worry." She left him unlocking his door.

But on the way to Mount Dora the wiper slashing across the windshield seemed to echo his warning. She drove past foggy outlines of trees and buildings, listening to the murmur of the rain and feeling vulnerable. Only a few people knew she was unharmed in the garage, but when she thought of the figure in the mansion's dormer window and the shadowy form on the lawn, her fingers tightened around the wheel. Beyond the wet streets yawned that unknown world.

Brandy shook her head, as if it still needed clearing. She needed to be rational, like John. That note had been typed with mortal hands. How many of her suspects had access to a computer? Blackthorne, certainly. She saw one in his office. He had admitted he was responsible for the chase across Lake Dora. Maybe he was up to his old tricks.

Sylvania probably did her genealogy research on a library computer, and Ace Langdon dropped into the office of A & S Citrus now and then. It would have computers. Even Grace Able helped produce a newsletter. Logic seemed to get her exactly nowhere—yet.

By the time Brandy reached the outskirts of Mount Dora, the rain had been replaced by a sullen, overcast sky. She tucked a rain hood in her bag, and within a half hour was walking between beds of pink impatiens up the porch steps and knocking on the door of a trim, concrete block cottage on the east side of town.

"Brandy O'Bannon, Tavares *Beacon*," Brandy said when the door opened. "Mrs. Hall is expecting me."

The woman before her was of average height, stylishly dressed in a tailored cotton suit and hose, a shoulder strap bag slung over one arm, and plainly too young to have been an adult in 1945. Her voice was formal and guarded, as the old woman's and the small boy's had been yesterday.

"I'm Mrs. Hall's daughter," the woman said. "We just finished lunch, and Mama's lying down. I'll ask if she's ready to see you." She retreated into an adjoining bedroom and in a few minutes reappeared, guiding an older woman by one stout arm.

Mrs. Hall moved to a rocking chair near the kitchen. "I been kinda poorly lately, but you come right on in. I recollect you called. I reckon visitors is always welcome."

Her daughter opened the screen and stepped aside for Brandy. The linoleum on the living room floor was immaculate, the oil heater in one corner and the small end tables dusted, and another rocker invitingly set to face Mrs. Hall's. On an uncluttered shelf lay a Bible.

"I was just fixing to leave," the daughter said. "I need to grocery shop for Mama on my day off."

Her mother looked up. "Go along, child. I'll be fine. I don't mind talking to this young lady." Toward Brandy she turned a pair of gentle, intelligent eyes. She was heavy set, her hair slate gray. With crooked fingers——probably bent by arthritis and hard work, Brandy thought——she reached for a needlepoint hoop on a side table.

"My childrens, I declare, they sees to everything for me these days, now I retired." The old lady looked again at her daughter, her voice even more insistent. "Go along now, girl. You got your Saturday chores to do." Her attention shifted once more to Brandy. "My daughter's got a big position at a Leesburg bank. Proud to say all my childrens got an education."

Embarrassed, her daughter glanced down and then locked eyes with Brandy. When Brandy gave her an understanding smile, her daughter opened the door. "If you need anything, Mama, call, you hear?"

"Bobby'll be here directly with my grand baby," Mrs. Hall said. "I might as well get my lazy self up now," She laughed, throwing back her head. "I reckon I won't be laying down when little Sammy get here."

As the door closed, Brandy settled into the chair opposite Mrs. Hall without setting up a tape recorder or pulling out her tattered note pad. She did not want to inhibit her witness. She would have to trust her memory.

Brandy began forthrightly, but not with the discovery of Eva Stone's skeleton. Perhaps Mrs. Hall had not read about it yet. "I'm researching the history of the Able homestead," Brandy said.

"I understand you worked there years ago. Maybe you could help me reconstruct the period of the nineteen forties."

Mrs. Hall studied her needlework, shrewd eyes lowered. "I expect you wants to hear about Miss Stone," she said simply. "I was the onliest witness, worse luck. I had a lot of talking to do in those days with newspaper folks."

Brandy kept her voice quiet. "Perhaps you'd tell me as much as you can about the weekend she disappeared."

With sure movements, Ms. Hall's needle began to puncture the fabric, working a blue thread into an intricate floral design. "In the first place, old Mr. and Mrs. Able didn't live out there all the time——only in the summers to get away from the heat in town, or in the fall for the hunting. Times like that. But Lordy, what a weekend that was!

"The party was just fine until poor Miss Stone done such a terrible thing. Mrs. Able had me and another girl tricked out in aprons and caps like we was really something." She giggled, remembering. "I was as young as the guests that weekend, but I was supposed to take care of the upper floor where the girls all stayed, and then help serve the dinner that night.

"I had to be up and around the next morning early to help with their breakfast and then clean up after they'd all gone. I was busy, I can tell you. They had a woman to cook that big dinner and another girl to help me serve it. And old Henry Washington—— God rest his soul——to take care of things outdoors and to help the menfolks."

She set her needlepoint in her ample lap, eyes alight at the memory. Brandy settled back. At last she would hear an impartial account.

NINETEEN

Mrs. Hall rocked back, smoothing the colorful fabric over one knee. "We had us seven couples of young folks that weekend, and then old Mr. and Mrs. Able and the Southerlands, though they didn't stay the night. They just come for the dinner, and the announcement about their daughter's engagement to Mr. Brookfield. Somehow there was an extra girl when Miss Sylvania decided to stay. She'd been threatening to leave all week. She hated parties, and small wonder. Land, she was one girl didn't have none of what Mrs. Able called the social graces."

"Did you notice Eva Stone much that first day and evening?"

"I was the one that had to meet the girls at the door when they got there and show them up to that big attic room—— like a big dormitory it was——with double-decker beds and some cots. Henry met the gentlemens and took them to the third floor. Most of the girls, they come together two or three to a car. But Mr. Brookfield's fiancée, she come first by herself. They had lots of planning to do. She brought the towels and sheets from her mother's for the guest rooms. Miss Grace was nervous, anyway, and anxious, I reckon, for everything to be nice. That evening all the girls——or most all of them——bunched around her and helped her dress and took on like no one ever got engaged before.

"Eva Stone, poor little thing, 'bout as big as a minute ——she come last, by herself. She didn't look happy the whole time. But she was the prettiest girl there, for a fact. I couldn't make out exactly who she was supposed to be paired with. Maybe her date couldn't come. Some of the young folks had gone to high school together and some of them, like Miss Grace, had got to know Mr. Brookfield later, before he went into the war." She looked toward the spotless kitchen. "Lord–a–mercy, I didn't even offer you a cold drink. Be glad to get you some soda pop or iced tea."

Brandy smiled. "I'm fine, thank you."

Mrs. Hall nodded, satisfied. "Mr. Brookfield had a buddy, too, come down from up North. A Lieutenant Langdon. 'Ace,' they called him. He'd visited once before when Mr. Brookfield was home on leave. Didn't have much family left. They said his daddy had a big name but not a lot of money. Him and Mr. Brookfield had been together in the air forces, and they'd just gotten out after the war. I think the Langdon fellow was supposed to be Miss Sylvania's date." She laughed again and shook her head. "Now wasn't she a caution at a big party like that! All the girls with their pretty long dresses, and poor Miss Sylvania with no more figure than a hat rack."

"Still, she did marry."

"Oh, yes, m'am. Later she marry that same fellow Mr. Brookfield carried home from the war. I heard that Lieutenant Langdon had tried to court Miss Stone hisself, but I reckon old Mr. Able could offer a young fellow some pretty good prospects in his citrus business. I expect where Mr. Langdon come from, he didn't have the chances old Mr. Able gave him here. I reckon that could change a fellow's mind. Miss Sylvania, well, I don't think she ever had what you'd call a real beau around here. Thing was, that big, strong build her brother had looked good on a man, but, lordy, it was a sight on a woman. Miss Sylvania's skinnier now, last I seen her, than she used to be.

"Onliest person she really seemed to care for was Mr. Brookfield hisself. I reckon he was a mighty good brother to her. She was as glad to see him again as anybody. He'd only gotten home on leave a couple of times since he went in the Air Forces. And after his last visit he'd been overseas for about a year."

Mrs. Hall looked away, eyes still shining. "What a dinner that was! Hams and candied yams and roasts and I don't know what all, candles on the tables, everybody so gussied up, and the smell of gardenias coming in through the windows. Old Mrs. Able had the place so pretty then. In the late fall that purple bougainvillea just covered the south side of the place. You couldn't even see the scrub lands and the woods for that bougainvillea."

Gently Brandy pulled her back to the crucial night. "So neither Eva Stone nor Sylvania seemed happy that weekend?"

Shaking her head, Mrs. Hall studied the blue and pink pattern in her hands. "From what I could see, I don't reckon so. I figured Miss Eva was sweet on Mr. Brookfield herself, the way she looked at him. But Miss Grace, she just cozied up to him the whole time, until the mens went bird hunting the next morning. Miss Eva could of had a bad shock that night. I understand she'd been out of town. The announcement about the engagement was suppose to be a surprise, but I think Miss Grace had told some of her friends. I don't think Miss Eva was one of those girls."

"What happened the second day, after the dinner dance?"

"Well, the mens got up real early. You know what a to–do it take to get mens off hunting. I was sleeping in a little room off the kitchen. I could hear them traipsing around in the kitchen in their boots, and the dogs yelping in the dog–run out back. They got breakfast and loaded theirselves and the shotguns and the dogs in some pick–up trucks and were gone before sun–up. They was just going into the woods over there towards Lake Beauclair, hoping to get some quail or doves and maybe some wild turkeys. Old Mr. Able and Mr. Brookfield, they was awful crazy about hunting.

"Day before, in the afternoon, some of the young folks went out on the lake in an old rowboat they kept tied up there in front of the house and tried some fishing. But I don't recollect that Miss Eva went."

"What did the women do that morning?"

"Oh, they was sleepyheads, you can bet. It'd been a late night. They come straggling down all those stairs——have to be half mountain goat to keep house in that place, I can tell you——and just picked around at their breakfast the cook got ready. Some of them went out and sat around in the lawn chairs for a while, but I reckon the pleasure was gone out of the weekend for them when the mens went off. After a while they straggled back upstairs and began giggling and packing up their things. Throwing clothes around, I declare, I never saw girls leave such a mess.

"The cook fixed some sandwiches and soda pop for lunch, and then they commenced leaving like they'd come, mostly in two's or three's.

"I recollect one car was late getting away. When the girl got ready to drive off, they found it had a flat tire. Poor old Henry, rest his soul, had to get down in that sandy road and change it. The girl who owned the car was a regular little ninny. She drove plumb out there in the country and didn't have no spare tire or a jack or any tools in her car. And the mens and their trucks gone! Henry got what he needed from Miss Grace's big old Buick, and they finally got off. One of the mens was still around, and he helped some, but I don't recollect who it was."

Ace Langdon, Brandy thought, remembering his own account of the flat tire. He'd said Eva asked him to help.

Mrs. Hall began working with her needle again, more slowly. "I seen Miss Eva go downstairs with her bag after that. We found it later by the back door. About that time Miss Grace was getting ready to leave, too. She'd waited around a little while, helping me gather up a big basket of her sheets and towels. I think she was hoping Mr. Brookfield would get back, but when he didn't, I reckon she left. That would've been before we started searching for Miss Eva. Miss Eva's was the onliest car still parked in the road then."

"Tell me what you saw from that upstairs window."

The older woman sighed, all merriment now gone. "I declare, I'll never forget that long as I live," she said softly. "We'd already toted the bed clothes down to Miss Grace's car. I went back up and was putting clean sheets and pillow slips on the beds upstairs. Then I heard the sound of that bell that was down there by the boat. It made an awful racket. The Ables used it to call folks in off the lake for meals. When they was fishing, you know, but no one was out in a boat then. Nobody ever admitted ringing that bell. We figured later that maybe poor Miss Eva had knocked against it when she went into the lake. Or maybe she'd stumbled over the rope you was supposed to pull to make the bell ring." Mrs. Hall paused, then went on, wonder in her voice. "If it hadn't been for that bell, no one would've known she drowned."

New information to process, Brandy thought. An odd note. Was the bell ringing important or just an accident, as the authorities then supposed.

Mrs. Hall's fingers paused. "Anyway, I looked up and I saw——clear as I see you now——Miss Eva walking straight out into that water. She was wearing a red dress with a big, floppy white collar."

Brandy felt a chill in the pit of her stomach. The teen witness, Charlotte, had said the figure she saw wore something red, with white around its neck. That very morning Brandy has seen a pinkish scrap of material, buried all those years in the yard.

Lost in her telling, Mrs. Hall did not notice Brandy's eyes widen. "I saw Miss Eva dressed that way at lunch and later when she went out the back door, so I knew right away who it was. She was right stylish, even if she didn't have the money those other girls had.

"She was just moving forward into the lake. She never looked back. She kind of raised her arms up a little when the water reached her shoulders. She wasn't calling for help or nothing."

Brandy shivered. She had taken her own terrifying walk into the lake, had herself stepped into nothingness.

"Well, I can tell you, I was struck dumb," Mrs. Hall said. "And then I shouted out to her, but she didn't turn around. The windows was open, you know. No air conditioning in those days.

"And then I run down all them stairs, fast as I could, yelling for someone to stop her. I knew there was a drop off when you went out far enough. Henry heard me about the same time as old Mrs. Able did. He run down to the water's edge and jumped in that little boat and rowed out and kept sticking the oars over the side, prodding and calling out. By then Miss Eva had gone under. He was most crying hisself. He couldn't swim a lick and neither could I. I got down the stairs and I don't even remember running across the grass. I just remember wading out as far as I could. I was already bawling.

"Miss Sylvania was the strongest swimmer there, I reckon. She swam out, but she said the weeds was something terrible and she couldn't see a thing. You knows how brown the water is around cypress trees. Old Mrs. Able called the Sheriff's Office in Tavares and Mount Dora both. But, lands, by the time they got there, there was no way Miss Eva could still be alive."

"When did the rest of the men get back?"

"Oh, I reckon 'round about the same time as the deputies got there. The Sheriff's cars come tearing up the road, maybe thirty minutes after Mrs. Able phoned. And then the pick–up trucks come next, one at a time, not all together. All the mens, I think, went out looking for Miss Eva. Some swimming, some in the boat. Some of them beat through the bushes all along the water's edge. Later, when we looked, all we found was Miss Eva's overnight bag at the back door and her purse in her car."

She shook her head mournfully. "Mr. Brookfield and the Ables, they went into town early that evening to tell her folks what happened. Lordy, I was glad I didn't have that job! The Stones, they come out the next day and just sat and waited.

"The Southerlands felt terrible, too. Miss Grace come back out herself the next day, while the search was going on, and she stayed all night to help Mrs. Able. I was afraid the old lady would have a heart attack, she was so upset. And I guess Miss Grace tried to cheer up Mr. Brookfield, too, but lordy, she was so high strung herself, she didn't help much.

"Mr. Brookfield, he went out day and night along the lake and in the boat, trying to find the body. After a few days, the sheriff's men kinda give up. They left it to Mr. Brookfield. They said to call if anything washed ashore like clothing, but it never did."

She dropped her voice. "Well, I reckon you know why they figured no one found the body. They needed to find it the first day or two. After that, I don't think anyone would have reported what they found, anyway. It was kinder that way. You lives around these lakes. You knows what 'gators can do." They sat for a short time in silence.

The blue thread began once more to outline a needlepoint flower. "Miss Grace, she never liked the house after that, even after they got married, and I can't blame her." She sighed again. "Miss Sylvania, she's let the place run down something terrible.

My son Bobby took me fishing out there in his little ole' Jon boat last fall, and I saw all her mama's pretty plants is gone. Miss Grace didn't take no interest either when she lived there a spell. And Mr. Brookfield, all he did was to buy hisself a big boat and tear down that pretty bougainvillea to build a boat house. Now its falling down itself."

"The boat house is gone now," Brandy said. "And the whole house will probably be gone soon. Making room for a new development." She leaned forward, hands clasped. "And why do you think Eva Stone drowned herself?"

"I reckon some gals, they just can't stand to lose a man to another gal. That's the onliest thing I could figure. Not that folks thought Mr. Brookfield was fixing to marry anyone but Miss Grace."

Brandy looked squarely into the older woman's eyes. "I ought to prepare you for news you may see in the papers. An awful discovery was made two nights ago. A woman's skeleton was found on the Able property. The medical examiner says it's been there between forty and fifty years."

One plump hand flew to Mrs. Hall's mouth, she gasped, and her dark eyes went moist. "My Lord. Got to be that poor child. But how could she be buried?"

"We'll have to leave that to the Sheriff's Office," Brandy said. "They're working on it. I have one more thing to ask you about." She looked down, phrasing her next question carefully. "You've probably heard tales about that house, Mrs. Hall. About what some people claim they've seen there."

The older woman laid her needlepoint in her lap and sat still for a moment. At last she said, "I don't mind telling you, I wouldn't go out there to stay again——even if I didn't know about them bones. That's a fact. Now I'm a good Christian woman. I never seen nothing peculiar there myself. But I've known good folks say they have, and I won't say they didn't, just because I never did. There's more things in this world and the next than folks know about."

A reasonable, if unsettling, point of view, Brandy thought—— one Hamlet hadn't phrased much better.

Lily Mae's bent hands were now busy with her pattern. "Mess of white kids from town claimed they seen a ghost there by the lake last year. But folks just made fun of them."

Brandy nodded. Charlotte and Seymour and company.

Mrs. Hall laughed. "Lordy, I notice, though, that nobody else has gone out there since. After dark, anyway. Except family, of course."

Not even the family, Brandy knew. "Is there anything else you can tell me about Eva Stone, Mrs. Hall?"

The old lady's dark forehead creased in a sudden frown. "They's one more thing I might say, young lady. Mr. Brookfield never seemed to satisfy hisself that Miss Eva's body could disappear so fast, even with 'gators around. He kept looking, day and night."

Outside a car slowed in front of the house. Mrs. Hall set the needlepoint on the side table and pushed herself up out of her rocker. "I reckon I wasn't satisfied neither. Now looks like we was both right."

She trudged to the door and opened it. A Ford station wagon was pulling into the driveway, a toddler behind the driver in a car seat. He crowed and waved his arms at the sight of his grand-mother in the doorway.

"Thank you for your time. I'm truly glad I had a chance to know you," Brandy said and meant it.

"Why, you're more than welcome, young lady." With a wide smile, Mrs. Hall turned toward the car. "There's my grandbaby."

The last Brandy saw of her, she was lifting him out and holding his round, happy face close to hers.

Brandy drove a few blocks, parked in front of a strip shopping center, and scribbled the most important details of Mrs. Hall's story in her note pad. Tonight she would record them more fully in her loose leaf notebook. She had learned more specifics, but Mrs. Hall's account matched the others——except for one detail. Neither Grace nor Ace Langdon had mentioned the bell. Certainly Sylvania hadn't.

She glanced at her watch. She had thirty minutes to make her appointment with Mrs. Stone.

TWENTY

A light shimmered behind the clouds as Brandy skirted Lake Dora and pulled up to the Hyer Retirement Home in Tavares, a gracious white building with colonial columns and a wide veranda. As she walked up the steps, the *Lake County Sentinel* reporter was sitting morosely on a porch swing, and his companion from the *Commercial* was standing with his back to the front window, gazing out at the street. When Brandy rang the bell, the door was opened by a thin, lean–faced man with glasses and a nervous smile.

"Miss O'Bannon?" he asked.

When she nodded, he swung the door wider for her, smiled and lifted his shoulders in a helpless shrug at the two reporters on the porch, then closed the door behind her. "It's hard on the others," he said, "but Mr. Stone's orders are quite explicit. She's not to be bothered by reporters. She's not in any condition to answer their questions. But she feels an obligation to you."

Brandy followed him across a living room. Through French doors she could see into a Florida room where several elderly people were playing cards.

"Mrs. Stone's room is on this floor. She doesn't do the stairs anymore." He lowered his voice. "Short of breath. Emphysema.

It's not rare at her age. She's ninety–three, you know. Such a lovely woman! We hope we can go on keeping her here. She doesn't require any special care yet, and she likes our family setting. Of course, Mr. Stone would be glad to put his mother in any facility she wanted."

They walked down a carpeted hall and stopped at an oak door. "We have suites here," he said. Our guests usually have their meals together in the dining room." He rapped gently, and hearing a signal from inside, opened the door. "Mr. Stone is with his mother now," he said.

So I'm to meet the restaurateur again, as well as his mother, Brandy thought, remembering him from the Chamber of Commerce meeting. For Mrs. Stone the news of her daughter's skeleton must be traumatic. She probably needed her son's comfort. They stepped into a small, old–fashioned room with high ceilings and an oriental rug.

From the doorway Brandy could see into a bedroom where a patchwork quilt covered a woman in a four poster bed. On this dull afternoon a wrought iron lamp cast a circle of light around her. Mrs. Stone lay beside a bay window facing the lawn and propped up on several pillows. A huge magnolia tree rose before the window, its waxy blossoms a ghostly white through the mist.

At the foot of the bed stood a tall man, perhaps in his late forties, in a well–tailored navy blue suit, his dark hair graying at the temples. His brown eyes and the set of his head and shoulders looked like someone she'd seen before, not just at the Chamber meeting. Maybe also at The Pub on the Lake or another of his waterfront restaurants. Now he came forward, the lines in his forehead showing strain, and held out his hand.

"Miss O'Bannon," he said. "I'm Weston Stone. Obviously, my mother must speak to someone from the press. We realize you're not with a daily paper, but I expect they'll get the news they need without badgering Mother."

Brandy turned toward the fragile figure on the bed. She was the oldest person Brandy had ever seen. Across the sharp edges of her cheeks and forehead, her skin was almost transparent, but her eyes shone a clear, lively blue. They searched Brandy's face.

When the old woman spoke, her voice trembled and her fingers plucked at the quilt. "You found Eva." She reached out an unsteady hand. Stepping forward, Brandy took it and with the other hand pulled up a chair. Weston Stone turned toward the window and looked out at the dying daylight, the muscles in his jaw working in a way that Brandy couldn't yet understand.

"I'm sorry if I've caused you pain," Brandy said.

The old lady's eyes blinked rapidly. She shifted her head and Brandy followed her gaze. On the dresser sat the familiar yearbook photograph of Eva Stone, and next to it, the other portrait, the one that had been in the newspaper the night before. It revealed an older Eva Stone with the same delicately modeled features, the same large eyes.

"She was a beauty," her mother said simply. "But she had inner beauty, too."

Brandy leaned forward. "Was there something you wanted to tell me?" she asked.

The old woman looked up, not at Brandy, but at her son. "I finally had to talk to someone," she said. "I should have long ago. I had my reasons. But now..." Her lips quivered. "Now after you found——what you did, I can see that Eva didn't take her own life. Everything is so different than I thought. In a way, it's more painful, in another way it's not."

Weston took a tentative step forward. "Mother..." He hesitated. "You don't need to say anything."

"No," she said, "I should have told the truth long ago. I should have told everything I knew, but I simply couldn't at the time. Now I've told Weston and the detective. I intend to tell Miss O'Bannon, too."

Brandy's bewildered glance veered from one to the other. Weston turned back to the window as Mrs. Stone pressed Brandy's hand. "You seem like such a nice young lady," she said. "You remind me of my Eva."

Brandy shook her head slightly. It was the second time she'd been told that.

"You're about the same size and about the same age. You look very much like her. She was a spirited girl, you know, like I think you are." She sat up straighter, gently withdrew her hand and laid it beside the other on the coverlet. "The truth is, I know why Eva went to the Able house that day. I know what she went there to do. She was in love with Brookfield Able."

"Yes," Brandy said quietly. "We know that."

"Oh, but that's not all. Not nearly all. They had an understanding. At least, Eva thought they did. When he was home on leave the year before the war was over, they were..." She paused, almost painfully, then forced herself on. "They were together a lot. They'd been so close in high school. She'd never cared for anyone else, even when he went away to college. Eva was always sure Brookfield would come back to her, even after he was sent overseas."

She lifted her chin. "Today things would be very different. But when Eva found she was going to have a baby, it was a terrible crisis. She wouldn't write Brookfield. Her father and I were the only ones she told. In those days girls were likely to feel guilty. Eva took the blame on herself."

Her lips compressed in a bitter line. "Brookfield was in England flying bombing missions every day. She didn't want to add to his worries. She thought that when he came home, everything would be all right, that he would be delighted they had a child. She hoped it would be a boy."

The old woman groped under the pillow for a handkerchief. "Nobody seemed to guess why Eva's father and I left our business here and moved up near Camp Blanding. We had family in Jacksonville, and we started up another café. We took care of her there. The baby was born in Jacksonville just two months before Eva died." Mrs. Stone's voice quivered. "The son she wanted."

She stopped for a moment to wipe her eyes. "Eva had been concerned because she hadn't heard from Brookfield in several months, but the mail was often late. After her father and I came back to re–start our business in Tavares, we read in the paper that Brookfield was coming home, and she joined us here.

"She left the baby with relatives, until she could sort things out. Right after she got here, she heard in the café about a welcome home party for Brookfield. She thought he didn't know she was back in town, that her mail had probably been sent to her other address. She meant to surprise him with her news. She would go to the party and tell him he had a son. She had no doubt they'd soon be married, and everything would be lovely." Mrs. Stone held the handkerchief again to her eyes.

"Can you imagine," she went on at last, "how we felt when we had the call that our daughter had drowned herself?"

"Mother," Weston Stone said again. "You don't have to do this."

"Yes, I do. It's always wrong not to be truthful. I don't want to die with this on my conscience. Not even Weston knowing."

Brandy looked quickly at Weston Stone. He had his head down, his hands in his pockets.

"Apparently Brookfield had never written Eva that he was marrying someone else. That weekend she believed she was going to his welcome–home party. Instead she found herself at his and Grace Southerland's engagement party. We felt sure she'd been in such despair that she walked into the lake and drowned herself. We held Brookfield responsible."

Her voice broke. "I didn't want to tell anyone about the baby. He was all we had left of Eva. Our relatives kept him for a couple of months, and then we let on that we had adopted an orphan from our family there. Everyone thought that was understandable. Eva had been our only child. It was true we needed to fill that terrible void. From birth we loved that baby like he was our own. We re–named him after my father and brought him back to live with us."

Brandy breathed, "Eva's child and Brookfield's."

"And if I'd told Brookfield that we were rearing his child, do you think we could have legally kept him? In the circumstances we were in? Running that little café? Especially later on, when Brookfield and his wife didn't have any children of their own?"

"But if Eva told Brookfield about the baby," Brandy asked, "what do you suppose he thought happened to his son after she disappeared?"

"I suppose he thought the baby was put up for adoption. He certainly never asked us about any child. I imagine he wanted to forget what Eva told him. If he'd tried to find out about his son, his new wife might've kicked up a row and there'd have been a scandal. She was very high–society. And very wealthy." The thin lips tightened. "I imagine that fact meant more to Brookfield Able than the fact he had a child. You can scarcely imagine how my husband and I hated him for what he caused Eva to do."

"Maybe when she saw he was marrying someone else, she didn't tell him about the baby."

Mrs. Stone's wet blue eyes met Brandy's. "We felt sure she would tell him. Even if she didn't, he caused her death."

Brandy took another long look at the profile of Weston Stone, and now she saw a blending: the fine features of the mother with the sturdy neck and shoulders and the black eyes of Brookfield Able——another reason he had looked familiar.

"So you see," the old lady went on in her faint voice, "I told Weston the truth about his parents today. Weston is not really Weston Stone. He's Weston Able."

She looked up at Brandy, her restless fingers again moving on the quilt. "When you found Eva at last, I realized she must've been murdered. Her father and I... we never could understand, no matter how upset she was, how she could leave her baby. I don't know who knew about the baby then. Or who knows about him now."

Like a signal, a pale ray of late sunlight broke through the clouds and glistened on the window pane. A large piece of the puzzle had slipped into place. As Weston Stone stepped forward and switched off the lamp, Mrs. Stone looked up at him.

"No matter how depressed Eva was, I should've known she wouldn't leave Weston," she repeated. "She was so proud of him. So concerned about him."

"Mrs. Stone," Brandy said after a pause. "Can you remember who told Eva about the party at the Ables?"

The thin white skin puckered into a frown. "I'm almost sure who it was. My husband and I agreed about it afterward. Ace Langdon came into the café and talked to her the day before the party. He was a newcomer in town, so we noticed. We weren't exactly surprised. He'd tried to court Eva the year before, but she wouldn't have much to do with him. I guess he wanted her to come to the celebration for Brookfield. He didn't know the reason she agreed to go."

"I think... Mother..." Stone hesitated over the word. It would be difficult, Brandy thought, for him to call the mother he had known all of his life "grandmother." "I think there's been enough conversation about this. It's distressing for you."

Mrs. Stone reached up and took his hand. "I just feel so bad that I never told Weston the truth until now. There was all that Able money. I deprived him of that."

"That's probably the best thing you and Dad ever did for me," Stone said. "If I'd had Able citrus money, do you suppose I'd have worked as hard as I did?"

Mrs. Stone's eyes brightened. "He's been such a success! He worked in that little café while he was growing up. When we turned it over to him, he expanded until he had restaurants all through the area——in Leesburg and in Orlando and, of course, the Irish pub on Lake Dora here. Such lovely restaurants! Everyone with a different theme."

Brandy remembered Sylvania's interest in preserving the family line. "Mr. Stone, do you have children?"

He faced her, his tone lighter. "Two sons and a daughter. My oldest boy's in high school."

"Such fine youngsters!" Mrs. Stone intoned. "Little gentlemen and such a beautiful little girl. She has Eva's eyes and skin. Weston always thought he was the orphan son of Jacksonville kinfolks. He thought Eva was his distant relative. If he'd known Eva was his mother, he'd surely have seen the resemblance to his own daughter. Until now, I've had to keep that to myself."

"John Able and I are in contact with Brookfield's sister Sylvania," Brandy said.

"Will you ask John to tell her about Weston?" the old lady asked. "I'd hate for her to hear the truth from a detective or read it in the newspaper. I haven't the courage to talk to her now myself, but the Ables are Weston's people, too. They could've done so much for him!"

Weston leaned down and pressed her hand. "You and Dad gave me the best home any boy could have," he said, his voice thick. "It was filled with more love than I ever would've gotten from my father. And I didn't need his money."

Brandy stood up. "What are you willing for me to put in my newspaper article?" she asked. "I don't want to violate a confidence. My story will be on the stands Wednesday."

"I've already told everything to a nice young man from the Sheriff's Office," Mrs. Stone said. Brandy thought that balding Detective Morris would be flattered. "He doesn't plan to release the information about Weston just yet, but it will all come out eventually. The detective says we may never know exactly how Eva died." She glanced up at Brandy with those moist, incredibly blue eyes. "You can use everything I've told you. Just don't say I cried."

Weston Stone walked with Brandy to the door. "My grandmother wants to have a grave side ceremony as soon as the Sheriff's Office finishes with the remains," he said quietly. "She wants you there, and she's asking the Able family as well. She thinks I should get to know them."

As he opened the door into the hallway, Brandy paused. "I've developed a very real interest in your mother. It goes beyond my newspaper story." She said. "I plan to find out what did happen to her."

He nodded, his mouth grim. Brandy had the peculiar sensation that she was looking into the dark eyes of Brookfield Able. "I don't like to say this in front of her," he said, glancing over his shoulder, "but my father may have murdered my mother. He had a motive, and she was buried on his property. It doesn't make me feel particularly friendly toward the Ables."

Brandy remembered Brookfield's appointment at the house with someone that fatal afternoon. It could have been with Eva. She turned without responding and the door closed behind her.

TWENTY-ONE

When Brandy stepped out onto the retirement home veran-
dah, the misty air had cleared. One reporter had gone, but
the man from the *Commercial* still lingered on the porch swing.
He signaled to her, but she only smiled, waved, and hurried down
the front steps. The Sheriff's Office would brief him soon enough.

Nothing to do but call John who would have to break the news
to Sylvania. When she stopped at the *Beacon* at five– thirty, she
spotted Mr. Tyler's Chevrolet at the curb. Old war horse, she
thought. On a late Saturday afternoon he ought to be relaxing.
When she poked her head into his office, he looked up from some
copy, removed his horn–rimmed glasses, rubbed his eyes, and settled them again over the thin bridge of his nose.

"Must be a mirage," he said. "You haven't been in the office in
so long I'd forgotten what you looked like." He glanced down at
the print–out on his desk and sighed. "Fortunately the regular
reporter for city news is still working."

"I have until the end of the day Monday," she said. "You'll
have a terrific feature."

In the editorial room she sat at her computer, but not to write—
—not yet. She wanted a quiet place to think. A bizarre theory had
begun to form, then a plan, its outlines blurry like shapes in the

fog. After a few minutes it took a firmer shape. She pulled out her pad and scribbled a few notes, found herself doodling a tire iron in the margin, then a dress with a wide belt and buttons down the front.

Her thoughts focused on the sequence of events that led to and followed the murder of Eva Stone: her unexpected appearance at the party, Ace's conversation with her, the flat tire, Ace's presence, Brookfield's arrival, the bell that clanged a death knell, Lily Mae Brown's account, Grace's leaving and Blackthorne's arriving, the long search in the water, the bougainvillea hedge, and the new complication of the baby. She nodded her head decisively.

"Makes sense," she said under her breath.

A discount store would have what she needed. She would make the call to John, another to a friend who was a home economics teacher, and then do some shopping. She reached for the phone.

When she called John's trailer, instantly she recognized the lilting, little girl voice that answered. Brandy took comfort from the fact that she heard others in the background. "Oh, you're *that* reporter," the voice said, the emphasis disdainful. "John's coming home with us now."

Brandy pictured Sharon draped over his kitchen counter in something filmy and expensive, maybe draped around John himself. "Tell him I've got important news," she said between her teeth.

"I'll take it." John's voice now. "Doctor doesn't want me driving yet. I'm going over to my folks for dinner. What's up?"

"You may want to share this with your dad. All the Ables will know soon enough. Mrs. Stone had something startling to say." John listened silently. She imagined he rubbed his forehead when she came to the part about Weston Stone.

"I'll talk to Aunt Sylvania," he said when Brandy had finished. "But I don't want to break the news over the phone. You better be there. I'll arrange for us to meet her after church tomorrow. The Congregational Church. She never misses a Sunday service. Maybe we can use the minister's study." He paused." And I'm sure we'll all show our respect by going to the graveside service."

Maybe Sharon couldn't get too intimate with John while his folks were there, although Mrs. Able seemed to be as much of a marriage promoter as Brandy's own mother. Pushing aside that bleak thought, she dialed Mrs. Brewster, the home ec teacher who often sewed for Brandy's mother and herself. On that first day at Sylvania's, if Brandy hadn't made a favorable impression in Mrs. Brewster's apricot–colored frock, the fault was not in the dress. Brandy arranged to stop by Mrs. Brewster's house before supper. Then she made a final call to her mother who, after all, deserved some consideration. Only this morning she had pulled her daughter out of a garage filled with carbon monoxide.

"I'll be late for supper," Brandy said when Mrs. O'Bannon answered. "Not to worry. Just need to run a few errands and make a stop at Mrs. Brewster's about a dress, okay?"

Mrs. O'Bannon's querulous tone had reasserted itself. "Mack's been trying to reach you again. I didn't know you'd be at the office."

"I won't be now. I'll give him a call when I get home. This craziness is almost over. Did I ever thank you for your heroics this morning?"

Mrs. O'Bannon paused, then seemed to remember a current TV commercial. "That's what mothers do," she said.

Brandy smiled. "Feed Meg for me, please. And Mother? Not something on the hibachi tonight."

At the nearest fabric outlet she bought a dress pattern and some cotton material, then shopped at a discount jewelry counter. Back in her Chevrolet hatchback, she had almost reached the dress-maker's house beyond the city limits when she noticed a faded blue sedan in her rear view mirror. When she slowed, it did. When she turned, it turned. At first she thought it might be a plain clothes escort. Detective Morris had warned her not to go out alone. Maybe he had someone checking on her. But the scruffy paint job didn't look official.

Her pulse raced. The car definitely didn't fit into her scheme. Did its driver write the phony note? Or did she have more than one enemy?

She turned into an alley that ran the length of the block. The sedan swerved in behind her, far enough in the rear that she couldn't tell if the figure behind the wheel was male or female. Accelerating, she skimmed around the corner of the next street, ducked into another alley, and pulled up at Mrs. Brewster's back gate. The other car had sped past the second alley, but she could hear it turning around at the end of the block. The driver must know where she had gone.

Brandy grabbed her packages, leapt out of her car, bolted through the back yard, and pounded at the kitchen door. In the alley behind her a car door slammed. And then she heard the shuffle of slippered feet on the kitchen tile and the door opened.

"Gracious," said Mrs. Brewster as Brandy pushed her way in. "What on earth's the matter?"

"Can't explain now," Brandy gasped, banging the door closed behind her and forcing the metal lock forward. She flopped into a chair by the kitchen table and steadied her hands by holding more tightly to her package. "It has to do with a story I'm working on."

"For the Tavares *Beacon*?" the older woman asked, raising her eyebrows.

Brandy nodded. In a minute she rose and peered out the back window. No one was there, at least no one that she could see. Calmer now, she took the pattern and fabric out of the paper bag and handed them to the startled Mrs. Brewster, a matronly figure with gray hair and round cheeks, still staring at Brandy.

"I'll come in the bedroom in a minute," Brandy said, "so you can look at the pattern on me. First, I'd like to borrow the phone."

After Mrs. Brewster had disappeared into the adjoining room, Brandy dialed the Sheriff's Office. Detective Morris was not in, but she left him a message and then asked the dispatcher for Steve Able. In a low voice she gave Mrs. Brewster's address. "I need an escort home. Deputy Able knows about an attack on me last night." She was glad to hear Steve was on duty. The desk sergeant promised a squad car in half an hour.

Relieved, Brandy joined Mrs. Brewster in the bedroom and stood immobile on a small stool while the seamstress adjusted the pattern to Brandy's measurements. "It's awfully short notice," the older woman complained, taking a straight pin out of her mouth.

"If you can cut the dress out tomorrow, I'll pop by late tomorrow for a quick fitting. It doesn't have to be your usual perfect job. I'll pay extra if you finish it by Monday, say late morning."

In the living room Brandy watched though the venetian blinds as Steve's patrol car pulled up. When she slid into the passenger seat beside Steve a few minutes later, he glanced at her, wary.

"Thanks, Steve," she said. "My car's in the alley behind the house. Detective Morris warned me to be careful. Someone followed me here, and I need your expertise."

"Hold on." He stepped out of the car, and Brandy waited while he circled the house, then slipped again under the wheel. "Whoever it was is gone now."

Brandy dropped her voice. "I want to prove a theory about the murder of Eva Stone." He frowned. "I want the Sheriff's Office to know what I'm doing," she added quickly.

Steve grunted, non–committal.

Carefully, she explained her scheme.

"I'm a sworn officer," he said. "I got to be careful. But if you need support, better me than John. He's a bit overworked in the rescue business. Maybe you ought to find a less dangerous career."

He was beginning to sound like Mack. "My plan could work."

The creases deepened on his forehead. "If I don't cooperate, I suppose you'll go to an electronic store for the equipment." He shrugged. "I'll get the stuff to you tomorrow and explain how to use it. It doesn't belong to the Sheriff's Office. It's mine."

"Thanks." Right on, she thought——the first steps of her grand plan completed.

Steve drove into the alley, and Brandy opened the cruiser door. He shook his head. "I hope to hell you know what you're doing. You oughtn't to try it alone. I'm off duty Monday afternoon. I'll ride shotgun." On her drive home Steve followed in his cruiser. Brandy saw nothing more of the battered blue car.

When she let herself into the kitchen, she spotted her mother dropping the living room curtain back into place at the front window. "Sheriff's Office has to escort you home now, I see," the older woman said, coming into the kitchen. "I don't know if that's good or bad."

Brandy was surprised to see Meg come frisking in from the dining room, tail high, and thrust her creamy muzzle up to both of them. She supposed Meg had earned dispensation for services rendered.

"The vet sold me a marvelous new flea remedy," her mother said drily.

On the telephone pad was a message from Weston Stone. His mother's graveside rites would be at eleven o'clock Monday morning. The Stones hoped an early time would draw less attention from the curious. There was also another message to call Mack.

He answered the phone with something between a whine and a growl. "What's going on? Last thing I knew you were laid up in the hospital. I call and you're gone. You're never at your office, and no one knows where the hell I can reach you."

"It's been a wacky week. It should all be over by Monday night, the deadline for this story." Maybe the Stone case would go down Monday, she thought, and with it her association with John.

Mack breathed into the phone. "I'm making plans, kid."

Brandy hung up, feeling melancholy. I've got to realize John's a passing infatuation, she thought, a momentary thrill. Mack's a known quantity, rock solid. Someone she'd known most of her life.

Almost as soon as Brandy put down the receiver, Detective Morris called. "Thought I told you to stay with people." More a bark than a comment.

"I was only alone a short time in my car. Did the people I've been talking to have alibis last night, at the time the garage door slammed shut?"

The detective's sigh was audible. "Not much help there. Mrs. Able went to a concert in Mount Dora with friends from her condo and stopped for coffee afterward." That didn't sound like the solitary Grace Brandy knew, but maybe Grace felt lonely while Mabel Boxley was away. "Trouble is she drove home alone," Morris went on. "Says she got lost, wandered around a while. Not used to driving herself. The gatekeeper checked her in about twelve–thirty.

"Blackthorne says he was home alone all evening, ditto Elton Langdon." That didn't sound like Ace, either, although he might spend a lot more time by himself than he liked to admit.

"And Sylvania Langdon?"

"Left the retirement center about nine and drove back to her house that night, also by herself. No one there to verify that, either."

Brandy wandered back into the kitchen, where Meg now flopped beside the stove, her valuable nose between her paws.

"Sorry I'm late again tonight," she said to her mother, who was slicing a loaf of homemade bread at the counter. Brandy sniffed the pot of stew simmering on the stove. "But I can make a contribution in this case." She began ladling meat and potatoes into two bowls. "I think I know who killed Eva Stone. I'm working on a way to prove it."

TWENTY-TWO

Sunday morning's paper ran a small box on the front page: local journalist unhurt in apparent carbon monoxide attack. Few details. The enterprising Leesburg reporter had picked up the record at the Sheriff's Office. Now Brandy couldn't watch for surprise or alarm when she met her suspects.

At nine she phoned John's trailer. She had expected he might stay at his parents, but he answered. Sharon? Brandy couldn't tell if she was there. No tell–tale murmurs in the background. "I better pick you up to meet Sylvania," Brandy said.

"God, I'll be glad when I can drive. We'll wait for her outside the church. I don't feel up to sitting through the service. I had a rough night."

That puffy arm. If he cuddled up to a girl friend, it might be a handicap. Brandy smiled to herself.

When she called Weston's Stone's home number, his wife's pleasant voice answered. Brandy accepted the invitation to Monday's graveside ceremony.

"Mrs. Stone has a request," Weston's wife said. "Grace Able would like to be there, but her companion will be busy and she feels awkward coming alone. Mrs. Stone doesn't want her to feel left out. Thinks it would look like we're discriminating against

Brookfield's wife. I believe you're a friend of John Able? I took the liberty of saying you two would pick her up. Is that all right? The other family members will be there, too."

John probably had no plans to attend with Brandy, but Mrs. Stone needn't know that. Brandy would be glad to bring Grace Able. She wanted her there, and without the indispensable Mabel Boxley. Blackthorne would surely bring Sylvania. She'd need his support, and Ace would come as a family member out of curiosity. They'd all be together then. Brandy would have a chance to tie up loose ends.

"I'll call Mrs. Able," Brandy said, and looked up Grace's number in her directory.

Grace sounded resigned when Brandy made her offer. Plainly she would rather not go. "Mabel got back yesterday," she said, "but she'll be busy tomorrow morning, picking up our airline tickets. I suppose it'll look rude if I don't go, especially if Mrs. Stone wants me there." Brandy arranged to stop for her at ten–thirty the next morning. To save time, Grace said she would wait on a bench near the gate.

When Brandy drew up before John's trailer and rang the bell, she found his mood not much better than the widow's.

He didn't ask her in, but then there wasn't time. She couldn't see a car that looked right for Sharon. Brandy expected no less than a Corvette.

"I'll go to the funeral tomorrow out of respect for Mrs. Stone," John said as he climbed into the hatchback's passenger seat. "My folks expect me to be there, but I hate taking any more time off. I'm on thin ice at the company as it is. I've got no prospect for a permanent job, and I can't save this one if I don't get the use of my arm soon. I'm not much good as a draftsman now, even on the computer." He slammed the car door. "I haven't had another offer for an internship. And no prospect has turned up to buy Sylvania's house."

Brandy looked at him sorrowfully. It was probably her fault that he'd lost the internship in Leesburg. She was the one who most rattled Blackthorne's cage. It was her fault, too, that he injured his arm. "What does the doctor say?"

"He wants to see me this afternoon. He'll tell me when I can use it then."

Brandy explained Weston Stone's request. "They expect us both to take Grace to the cemetery. It's important to Eva Stone's mother that Grace is there. You probably expected to go with your parents, but Grace will think it's funny if you aren't along. You're the relative, after all. I'm just your temporary driver." Would he call the plan more manipulation?

They rode for a few minutes in silence. "Your boy friend coming, too?"

"Doesn't seem appropriate," Brandy said, thinking more of Sharon than of Mack. "It isn't a social occasion."

"Pick me up then in about half an hour before the thing starts. I'll tell my folks I'll meet them there, but we have to make it short."

At least the summer rains had stopped for the day. Brandy parked on a shady side street near the stone church with steeply pitched roof and narrow stained glass windows. At last the final strains of the organ died away, the rear doors opened, and worshippers began filing out. After the most of the congregation had shaken hands with the minister and strolled to their cars, or clustered outside to visit, Brandy spotted the gangly great–aunt they were waiting for——a head above the rest.

"Wait," John said, and strode quickly over to intercept her at the curb. He spoke to Sylvania for a few minutes, then motioned

Brandy to join them. Sylvania turned from one to the other, her long face set in disapproval.

"Come, come. I'm in the middle of packing. I don't have time for foolishness."

John glanced down at his shoes, as if to collect his thoughts. "Eva Stone's mother asked us to tell you something that may be a shock to you. She didn't want you to read it in the newspaper or hear it from detectives."

"Maybe you ought to find a place to sit down," Brandy said. "The minister's study, maybe?"

Sylvania crossed her arms over her spare chest. "Whatever it is, you can tell me right here. I barely took time for church this morning. I sign the contract on the house tomorrow. John might as well know that right now." She lifted her chin. "The Sheriff's people promised to be through tearing up the yard by then. And that'll be an end of it."

Irritated, John looked straight at Sylvania. "All right then. We'll tell you here. Mrs. Stone has explained to the Sheriff's Office——and to Brandy here——that Eva Stone had a child by Brookfield."

Brandy thought Sylvania should have taken their suggestion to sit. She almost tottered in her black oxfords. Brandy watched her face. Unless Sylvania was a very good actress, her eyes showed surprise.

"A child?" she asked faintly.

"A boy," Brandy said. "He was raised as an adopted son by the Stones themselves. Mrs. Stone never revealed who he was until now. You may have met him. He's prominent here."

"The restaurant owner Weston Stone," John added.

They walked a few steps toward Sylvania's shabby Ford. Then Sylvania paused, her hands clasped before her. "Can that be proved?"

"The Sheriff's Office is probably checking on it right now," John said. "There'll be records. The baby was born in Jacksonville."

Brandy weighed in. "Why would Mrs. Stone make up something like that, after all these years? It certainly won't enhance Eva's memory. Mrs. Stone says she wants to set the record straight while she's still alive. She and her husband concealed the truth because they didn't want to give the baby up to Brookfield. They thought their daughter committed suicide because of him. You'll be convinced when you see how much Weston Stone looks like your brother."

Sylvania's forehead knotted. "If this is so, why in the world didn't Eva tell my brother about the baby? He said nothing to me or anyone else."

John shuffled his feet. "We don't know whether she told him or not," he said.

Then the facts seemed to strike her. She tossed her large head. "That girl couldn't have! She couldn't have! Brookfield would never abandon his own child."

She's ignoring the more terrible possibility, Brandy thought—— that he may have wanted to silence Eva forever. The older woman turned abruptly toward the car, her large hands shaking, her shoulders bent.

Brandy spoke up quickly. "Mrs. Langdon, Eva's mother is planning a graveside service tomorrow. She's very much aware that Weston is Brookfield's son. As his sister, she wants you to come, and the other members of the Able family. I'm sure Weston's wife will call you."

Distracted, Sylvania only nodded as she folded her long body into the driver's seat.

Brandy dropped John off at his civil engineering office, where he hoped to complete some computer changes in a design, then

stopped at a drug store to make a purchase in the hair care department. When she drove home, she kept a watchful eye out for the
faded blue sedan. Apparently its driver had been scared off.

After lunch she called Mrs. Brewster, and half an hour later
stood once more in the home economic teacher's bedroom while
the older woman pinned a garment together around her and knelt
to adjust the hem.

"I don't like working so fast," Mrs. Brewster mumbled, her lips
prickly with pins. "I take pride in my work."

"Think of it this way," Brandy said. "You're a part of an
important investigation." Mrs. Brewster promised to have the
dress ready early the following afternoon.

At home again she picked up the telephone, reached information, then called a Gainesville clinical psychologist's home. "I need
an opinion," she said, after introducing herself to an answering
machine. "I'll be home this evening. You lectured to my class at
the University of Florida a year ago. You said we could call if we
had an important question." She left her phone number. The psychologist had once worked at the mental health facility in
Arcadia. Brandy hoped she would verify a part of her theory.

At her desk Brandy went carefully over her notes on Eva Stone's
murder. About six the psychologist called back. She remembered
the class, remembered the topic. Her cool, professional tone was
reassuring. Briefly, she confirmed Brandy's recollection.

Brandy had one other call. Steve Able promised again to bring
his equipment to the cemetery.

       *   *   *

Monday brought a sky of muddy clouds and oppressive heat.
John was waiting for Brandy outside his trailer. Again he seemed
alone. Maybe Sharon had decided she was not expected at the

service. She would, of course, have impeccable judgment. Or perhaps she would come with John's parents.

"I ordered a small basket of flowers," John said, taking the passenger seat. "Lord, how I hate funerals." He looked fresh and appealing in a crisp, light weight suit. He had managed to pull shirt and coat over his arm. Today, Brandy thought, this should all be over——hopefully the case itself, and sadly, her excuse to see John.

On the road to the Lakeview condominium, Brandy kept her eyes on the rear view mirror. Once she thought she glimpsed the blue car, but she couldn't be sure. If she were being followed, the other driver was at quite a distance. And this time Brandy was not alone. At the security gate, she identified herself to the guard, drove into the complex, and drew up next to the lake where a red–tipped hedge bisected the paved area. They spotted Grace on a stone bench under the pink blooms of a tall crepe myrtle, busy with her knitting needles. Brandy honked the horn and waved.

As John climbed out to escort Grace to the car, she rose, dressed more in the style of the forties than the nineties in a small, navy blue hat, a voile navy dress with white trim, and dainty white pumps. She hung her knitting bag over her wrist, pulled on a pair of white gloves, and took John's arm.

"It's good of you to come," Brandy said as Grace ducked into the front seat, holding her hat in place with one hand. "This can't be easy for you." The older woman's eyes darted in Brandy's direction.

"We were at Sylvania's place yesterday," Brandy added as John seated himself in the back. "When the tire iron was found near Sylvania's house, I mean." She pulled away from the curb. "I suppose you read about it in the morning paper."

"A detective came to see me," Grace said, a sour turn to her lips. "Of course, I know nothing about any of that. The last person to handle the tools was Elton Langdon." She gripped the knitting bag, still watching Brandy closely. "Of course, anyone could've taken them out of the car before I left."

"Did your father ask you later about the tire iron?"

"He didn't say anything to me. I was just borrowing his Buick. I didn't pay any attention to the tools my father kept in it."

Brandy dropped her voice. "I suppose the detective told you about Weston Stone." Grace's hands fumbled with the handle of her bag, and her eyes fluttered downward. "Yes, he told me what Mrs. Stone said. I think he felt it would become public knowledge and perhaps I should be told about it first."

Brandy thought Detective Morris would want to know if Brookfield's wife had heard about Eva's baby. "Had Brookfield ever said anything to you about a child?"

"Of course not!" Her voice shook. "I don't like to speak evil of anyone, especially when their life was so tragic. But it's hard for me to believe that story of Mrs. Stone's. She's just repeating what Eva must've told her." Grace's voice became one of sweet reason. "It would be shrewd for her to claim a rich man like Brookfield for the father."

Brandy didn't respond. Eva Stone as gold–digger or black–mailer didn't match her image of the dead girl.

Grace folded her hands. "I'm just saying, I don't take Mrs. Stone's word. Eva Stone was a very popular young lady. She had lots of boy friends." She looked briefly out the window. "Even if it were true, this has nothing to do with me. Brookfield was acquainted with Eva Stone before our courtship began."

Brandy took this in quietly. Brookfield had proposed to Grace by mail from England, after he'd returned from leave. He must've been seeing Eva and Grace simultaneously while he was home. It didn't make Brookfield appear to be a man of moral integrity. But then, Eva was also seeing Ace Langdon.

Under an overcast sky they rode in silence through Tavares, down a tree–lined street on the outskirts, and through the junipers and brick pillars of Memory Gardens. Here Brandy eased along under a stand of live oaks, their branches heavy with Spanish moss. To the right in the old part of the grounds, tombstones leaned toward an occasional cement crypt. The sun had disappeared, and the graveyard lay under a heavy bank of flat clouds. In the moist air nothing stirred.

They parked on a sandy road beside a long leaf pine. To the left among a newer section of flush headstones, a canopy had been erected over several rows of folding chairs. Before them rested the casket itself, blanketed by a spray of calla lilies and roses. In the front row sat the frail figure of Eva Stone's mother in a wheel chair, her feathery white hair a corona around her head. On one side knelt the minister and on the other stood Weston Stone, his hand on the back of her chair.

As the three of them made their way toward the canopy, Brandy recognized Sylvania's ashen face, rising up in the back row. Beside her, like a bulwark against the world, sat Axel Blackthorne. John nodded to Brandy, then found a seat next to his mother and father. Brandy and Grace slipped into the last row. At one side Ace Langdon approached the mourners. The old pilot eyed the crowd, searching Brandy supposed for an attractive young mourner as a seating companion.

Brandy turned back toward the casket and tried to repress her memory of the stained skull. As the young minister, who never could have known Eva Stone, took his place before the casket, Brandy realized how closely she had identified with the dead girl. She could not think of Eva as a gold digger, as Grace obviously did. But could she be sure her own image was the correct one?

With a flash of iridescent black, a covey of grackles settled in the nearby sand pines to watch as the minister opened the *Book of*

Common Prayer. "Man, that is born of woman, hath but a short time to live, and is full of misery," he began. "He cometh up, and is cut down, like a flower; he fleeth as it were a shadow and never continueth in one stay. In the midst of life we are in death."

The prayer might have been written for Eva Stone. Had she continued here as a shadow? Someone in the rear breathed a heartfelt, "Amen, Lord."

Brandy looked behind her. In the corner of the back row she was startled to see the dark, kindly face of Lily Mae Hall, come to pay her respects to the girl she couldn't save. Maybe this sole witness could help Brandy nail down her theory.

TWENTY-THREE

When the service ended, Brandy took her place in the line filing past Mrs. Stone. Weston stood by her wheelchair, and next to him, his wife, a poised, well-groomed woman with a gracious smile. Then came their two sons, one about seventeen, a slimmer version of his father, and a younger boy, his hair slicked back, his small figure neatly turned out in a jacket and bow tie. Last and fidgeting uncomfortably in the heat, was the youngest, a girl of perhaps ten with dark hair and luminous eyes. Almost an Eva Stone in miniature.

When Brandy's turn came, Mrs. Stone accepted her hand and pressed it, her blue eyes glistening. "It's hard," she said, "but I've finally said good-bye to Eva. All these years I've had a feeling of incompleteness. Now she's come home at last."

Brandy could see the tidy markers of the Stone family beside the casket. Eva would be laid to rest next to her father. Mrs. Stone's own name was already engraved on the same long headstone. Fleetingly Brandy wondered if Mrs. Stone had ever heard the ghost stories about the house where her daughter had died. She would never ask.

"I'm glad finding her remains has helped you," Brandy said.

Mrs. Stone lowered her moist gaze. "The deputy said they even found remnants of the dress she wore that day. I'd made it for her. We shopped together for the wide belt buckle and the buttons that went all down the front. She picked out the beads to go with it."

Of course, Brandy thought. This was a mother who would've made her daughter's clothes. Brandy patted the fragile hand. "I'm sure they'll all be returned to you. They'll be mementos you can keep."

Then she moved on and watched while John introduced himself to Weston Stone. Sylvania held out one hand to Weston next, her gray eyes searching his face, and said rather clumsily, "I'm Sylvania Able Langdon. They tell me I'm your aunt."

Startled, he took her hand.

She looked down from her great height at the younger two. "These are your children?"

"My older son's here, too," Weston said, turning to the youth beside him. The younger ones shook hands shyly, uneasy among the unfamiliar faces, the older boy with more dignity.

Sylvania and Blackthorne passed on quickly. Ace not at all. Among the final mourners came Grace, who bent toward the old lady and spoke softly with a faint smile. Then she stood to the side, twisting her white gloves in one hand, watching the others, then with a slight scowl, focusing her gaze on Brandy. Probably was eager to leave, Brandy thought. Grace was not the only watcher. Outside the canopy and in uniform, the sturdy figure of Steven Able rocked on his heels beside a tall cedar. Nearby a discreet Detective Morris surveyed the guests as they broke into groups.

John drew Weston Stone aside as soon as the final relative shook his hand. Brandy sauntered up to Captain Able and his wife, standing near John under a cluster of sand pines, in time to hear Weston's last remark.

"I suppose I should see the house," he was saying. "After all, it's where my mother died. But I have a strange revulsion at the thought of it."

"That's understandable," John said, "but from an architect's point of view it's a marvelous old nineteenth century home. You really ought to see it before it's pulled down. The Sheriff's office has completed its search."

The captain hooked his thumbs in the pants pockets of his tidy suit. "They'll get to the bottom of this," he said, while his wife gave a quick nod. Brandy half expected her to produce her husband's glasses from her purse so he could better examine his newly discovered relative.

John's lips tightened. "Now there's nothing to hold up the sale of the property."

Sylvania was crossing the pine needles toward them, her walk more tentative than Brandy had ever seen it, her large head thrust a little forward and her hands swinging loosely at her sides. Behind her, even more slowly, came the burly developer.

"I hope she's not as peevish as usual," Brandy murmured to John.

"Not much has happened in her life to make her cheerful."

Sylvania halted before Weston Stone. "I've done a lot of genealogical research. I know all about the Able family," she said in a rush, her gaze probing his face——the dark eyes, the tell-tale high cheekbones. "I've got the Ables back to the seventeenth century in Cornwall. You might be interested, now that you know your relationship to the family."

Weston's eyebrows elevated slightly. "I'm trying to adjust to the news. It's been quite a shock." His tone remained correct but cool.

She plunged on. "You ought to see the house on Lake Dora before it's gone——and the portrait there. I think you'll find it surprising." Her eyes met his.

She isn't like Grace, Brandy thought. She doesn't doubt Mrs. Stone's story. Is it just his resemblance to Brookfield, or something she knows?

John spoke up quickly. "With your permission, I'd like to bring Curt Greene to see the house again with Mr. Stone. Mr. Greene can explain its finer points. He's not only an architect. He's also with the Historical Society. We've been trying to interest someone in restoring the house for the National Register."

A surly Blackthorne wedged himself between Sylvania and Weston and stared at John. "Don't get that started again."

"It's all right, Axel," Sylvania said, laying one hand on his arm. To Weston she added, "I've moved to my new apartment, but most of the furnishings are still there. I'd be glad to meet you at the house tomorrow afternoon."

Blackthorne frowned. "Do you think that's wise, Syl?"

As they turned to leave, Brandy heard her say, "It doesn't matter now, Axel. It doesn't matter anymore."

Weston looked toward Mrs. Stone. "I've got to get Mother — —I should say, my grandmother——home. She's exhausted." He shook hands again with John and the Captain, then spoke quietly to Brandy. "I can't feel friendly toward anyone who was with my mother that last weekend. Not until I know who killed her."

Beside the circular drive Brandy could see Steve standing at his cruiser. He motioned to her and ducked his head inside the car, as John took her elbow and pulled her aside. "You're busy," John said, his face quite close to hers. "I'll hang a ride to the office with my dad. You can manage Grace without me now." He hesitated, and for a minute she hoped he would say something else, but he dropped her arm, turned quickly, and followed his father's broad back toward the drive. When would she see him again? Probably Sharon was waiting at his folks' house——or at his trailer.

Through the dispersing crowd, Brandy saw Steve emerge from the cruiser with a plastic bag, and stop to talk to Morris. Then Ace Langdon marched toward her alone. Apparently the gathering had offered him slim pickings.

He paused before Brandy. "You've got a lot to answer for, young lady," he said. A frown darkened his face. "Had a call from a detective yesterday. Wanted to talk to me about the tire iron." He moved in close. "Seems you told them I was the last one to have it. I put the damn thing in Mr. Southerland's car. That's all I know about it."

Brandy took a step backward. "I wasn't the only one who knew you had the tire iron. Or the only one who knew you had a thing for Eva Stone."

His face flushed. "After all these years, you've stirred up enough trouble. What good does it do now?"

"It brought Eva home to her family," Brandy said.

Silenced for the moment, he ran a well–manicured hand through his gray hair, and then said abruptly, "Before you go prying any further, I've got to talk to you."

"We can't very well talk here." She glanced at Weston Stone, wheeling his grandmother toward his car. "In light of this new development, I was going to ask you for another interview, late this afternoon."

"No problem," he said to Brandy in a voice a little less hostile. "You know I've still got an office at A & S Citrus. I'll be waiting for you. Make it the cocktail hour. About five–thirty." Apparently she still rated a drink, if not his familiar wink. But with Ace, anyone rated a drink.

"By the way," Brandy asked, as he turned to leave, "do you by any chance drive a blue car?"

"You saw my Porsche. I also have an old black Cadillac, a relic from when I entertained for the company." He did not stop to ask why she wanted to know. But if he were following her, she thought, would he use his own car? Wouldn't he or the developer hire someone?

Blackthorne himself had already escorted Sylvania to his Cadillac and was now striding back toward Weston Stone and his grandmother.

"Do you own a blue car, Mr. Blackthorne?" Brandy called out. He whirled, his face contorted.

"You're the one who turned that detective on me!" He stalked closer. "Said I almost ran you down in my boat, made all sorts of insinuations to the Sheriff's Office!"

"Someone's following me again," Brandy said sweetly. "I thought it might be you."

He raised one heavy arm. "If you print a charge like that, I'll sue you and your paper for libel."

She stayed calm, but she found herself taking one step backward. "The Sheriff's Office may ask you some more questions about Eva Stone's last afternoon," she said. "We can't talk about it here. I'll come by your office late today. Be sure to wait for me." He might be angry, but he would also be curious. For safety, she hoped his secretary would still be there.

After threading her way among the tombstones, careful not to step on any graves, she reached Steve. "You brought the goods?"

He opened the passenger door of the cruiser. "Get in. I'll show you how they work. Remember, this isn't Sheriff's Office equipment, but I want it back undamaged." He slipped under the wheel, opened the plastic bag, and removed a tiny lapel microphone from a box. "Never say we don't cooperate with the press."

"I may get something that'll help make a case." Carefully, Steve showed her how to attach the microphone to a small recorder and how to conceal them both, clipped to her underwear. He dropped them back into the bag, handed them to her, and gave her a solemn look. "Conversation you tape can't be used as evidence, you know. We'd have to have a court order——which we don't have the evidence to get. You can't quote anyone in your story, either. Legally, people have to know they're being recorded."

"Understood," she said. "It may not be good in court, but we'll know if I'm on the right track. I'll be able to prove what's said. It'll help the investigation." She slipped out of the car, and turned toward him before closing the door. "Afterward, we'll destroy the tape. You're a treasure. Tomorrow afternoon. I'll count on you to be there."

His square forehead hardened in disapproval. "You're just lucky I'm off then. It's the best I can do for the department, short of locking you up. And I've got no warrant for that either."

She tapped the window and he rolled it down. "May I ask you about something else?" He nodded, puzzled. "How serious is it between Sharon and John?"

He scratched his head. "They've been a hot item for about two years. She's finishing college and he's trying to find a regular job. What's the matter? Is he making your boyfriend jealous?" He threw his head back with a quick laugh and switched on the engine. The only help she'd get from Steve would be mechanical, she thought, starting down the road for her car, the leaden lump again in her chest.

From the back she recognized a stout figure in a black dress and a small white hat, Lily Mae Hall, walking slowly along the cemetery lane after the Stones, alone. As Brandy fell in along the sandy tracks beside her, the former maid looked up and her face brightened.

"I reckon I just wanted to say goodbye to Miss Eva, like old Mrs. Stone did," Mrs. Hall said simply. "Seems like I'm the last person to see her alive. I feel like I ought've been more help."

"You did all you could, Mrs. Hall," Brandy said. "Since the officers found the tire iron, I've been wanting to talk to you again. They're pretty sure it was the murder weapon. After Eva Stone disappeared into the lake, do you remember if Henry Washington ever said anything else about that tire iron?"

"He told me several days later that Mr. Southerland asked him about it. Said it wasn't in his car. Henry told him he didn't know what happened to it. He gave it to Mr. Langdon."

"We know Brookfield said he had an appointment at the house before the others got back. Do you remember if he was home before you saw Eva go into the lake?"

"Lands, let me think." They walked along in companionable silence for a few minutes. Finally Lily Mae spoke up. "I recollect me and Miss Sylvania had already toted the dirty sheets downstairs. I was getting the clean sheets out of the linen closet in the upstairs hallway when I heard Mr. Brookfield come in. His mother called out to him, and he said he was going to change clothes." She stopped suddenly and clapped one ample hand over her mouth. "I declare! He said he was looking for Miss Eva. I remember because I was surprised that he said 'Miss Eva.' I thought he'd be looking for Miss Grace."

"How long was that before you saw Eva walk out into the water?"

"Hard to say after all these years. But it must've been a little while because I went back into the rooms and made up the beds, and then I was picking up when I heard that bell. Next time I saw Mr. Brookfield, he was swimming out there with everyone else, looking for Miss Eva."

Brandy patted her on the arm. "Thanks," she said. "I have a theory about something and that fits just fine."

Blue–black clouds were piling up in the west and a slight wind stirred the dead air. Brandy was hurrying past Blackthorne's

Cadillac toward her own hatchback, where she could see Grace waiting, when she heard a soft but unmistakable noise. She paused and glanced into the car. Sylvania was sitting alone in the passenger seat, her head bowed. The sound Brandy heard was sobbing.

            *   *   *

"I'm sure this has been hard for you," Brandy said later, as she walked Grace into the lobby of her lake side condominium. They had ridden back in silence. Now Grace responded with a tense nod, as if she held Brandy responsible for the ordeal. Beside the reception desk, the solid figure of Mabel Boxley was waiting.

"I have the airline tickets," she said to Grace, waving envelopes above her head. At Brandy she frowned.

In a small alcove off the lobby, two silver–haired residents, one working at a desk with a computer and the other operating a Xerox machine, stopped and motioned to Grace.

Grace gave a tiny sigh. "They're editing and running off the weekly newsletter. Probably want to cut my article on bromeliads. I'll just be a minute. It's one aggravation after another." She hurried toward the two women.

The efficient Mrs. Boxley rounded on Brandy, her plump face flushed. "I can't wait to get her away from here. I can see the strain's beginning to tell." She stuffed the tickets into her purse. "I got us a flight day after tomorrow." Her voice rose. "Her faith in her husband was her strength. And now she hears that her husband fathered another woman's child, and then you tell her she's got to go to that woman's funeral!" As Mabel watched Grace leave the alcove, her indignation changed to guilt. "I should have been here for her."

When Grace re–joined them, her unlined, oval face looked paler than ever. "I don't know why I bother with that column. It isn't appreciated."

Mabel's tone had softened. "We need to get you to your apartment where you can lie down." She started across the lobby.

Brandy placed a hand on Grace's arm before she could follow. "I hate to bother you with anything else," she said. "I know you're tired, but I need your help. I can explain how Eva Stone died, but I'll need to see you again today, privately."

Grace hesitated, then looked down at her gloves, then thoughtfully at Brandy. "Mabel plans to grocery shop about three–thirty or four. If it isn't raining, I'll wait for you on the same bench by the lake. I'll use the time to finish my shawl." She gave Brandy a wan smile. "I hope this will be the end of all the unpleasantness."

As Grace trailed after the indispensable Mrs. Boxley, Brandy counted three more verified facts: Brookfield came back to see Eva before she vanished, any one of the suspects could have typed that phony note, and Brandy had pictured Eva's dress correctly.

She glanced out the lobby's broad front windows at the lake. The water had begun to churn in the wind. I called "a spirit from the vasty deep," like I told John I would, she thought, and it will come.

At the desk she paused to borrow the telephone again and called Mrs. Brewster. "Don't worry. It's like I supposed," she said. "The buttons go down the front."

TWENTY–FOUR

Fortunately Mrs. O'Bannon was still at school when Brandy let herself into the house. She would not be there to ask questions before Brandy left again. She let Meg into the kitchen and gave her red–gold head a pat and feathery body a rub. The retriever bounced through the hall to Brandy's bedroom, picked up her chew rag, and wagged her flag of a tail, hoping for a game. Brandy held her palm up to signal "no," murmured, "I'll make it up to you later," and stepped into the bathroom for a shower. After thoroughly working a dark rinse through her hair at the sink, she flicked on the drier and checked her watch. Two–thirty.

In the bedroom again, Brandy looked over the notes she had made after the clinical psychologist's call, added a few lines about the morning's experience, and nodded. Everything fit. After pulling on a pair of jeans and a big shirt, she paused for a second before the mirror, fluffed out her mahogany colored bob, and gave the ends a flip with the curling iron. To her dad's picture she whispered, "Wish me luck."

Outside the sky continued to darken. She had not considered that the weather might be bad. Still, as she let Meg into the yard and drove a few minutes later back down the quiet streets, there was no sign of the blue sedan. Perhaps somebody had called off the dogs. She shuddered at the memory of the Dobermans. Maybe whoever set her up in the garage knew it was too late now, maybe had only wanted to keep her from seeing Mrs. Stone. Or maybe the person had learned the Sheriff's Office was quite thorough, in spite of the almost fifty year time gap, and stopping Brandy would not help.

By three–thirty she stood on Mrs. Brewster's front porch. The seamstress trudged to the door again in her slippers. "You don't give a body much time," she said, letting Brandy into the living room. "Still, I guess the dress is about as ready as it'll ever be." She looked pointedly at Brandy's once auburn hair. "I hardly knew you. Liked it better natural." She peered out the bay window and pursed her lips. "From now on, I guess I'll have to read the *Beacon* more carefully. Must've been missing something. Will you need a police escort this time?"

Brandy smiled. "In a manner of speaking."

In the bedroom she took her place on the stool while the older woman pulled the red dress over her head, removed a pin here and there, fastened the long row of buttons, and smoothed down the wide, white collar. Then she stepped back with a pleased nod. Impressed, Brandy gaped at her image in the full–length mirror. Just maybe her plan was going to work, she thought, rolling her jeans and shirt into a plastic bag to carry to the car.

Before she left the dressmaker's house, Brandy reached Steve again on the kitchen telephone. He was grumpy, but prepared. In the driver's seat, with trembling fingers, she clamped the tiny microphone to her bra strap, ran the wires down the neckline, under the wide belt, and clipped the recorder to her half slip, concealed by the folds of the A–line skirt.

She would drive first to Leesburg. Thunder rumbled in clouds to the west. Please, no rain. Not yet, she thought. Beside the highway trees swayed in the wind. Still no blue car. She rattled over the

Dora Canal, passed Mack's dealership, and recognized his tall form standing with a customer in the lot. She did not dare wave. If Mack knew her plan, he would go ballistic. Not exactly the life he envisioned for her in that squat house in the suburb. When this case was over, she had promised him an answer. According to her plan, that would be tonight. She pushed the thought from her mind, gripped the wheel, and steeled herself for the task before her.

It was then that she glanced in the rear view mirror and saw the long, black car whip around the truck behind her and swerve in close to her bumper, a solitary figure at the wheel. A chill shot through her. Both Langdon and Blackthorne drove black Cadillacs.

She pressed harder on the gas pedal, changed lanes, tried to put other cars between them. The black car swung around them, and surged close again, its driver hunched forward, a dark shape behind the windshield. She bit her lip. She had not anticipated this, not now. Where was Steve's patrol car when she needed him? And then she remembered the security booth at Grace's complex. Surely the guard would not admit the black car. She could give Grace's name. She was expected.

As Brandy swept up to the concrete block gate house, she flipped on the recorder and called out Grace Able's name and address. A stocky, moon-faced man in uniform thumbed through a list of residents on a clipboard. In the mirror she could see the Cadillac charging up, the figure in it now clearer. Ace Langdon was almost slender. This was the bulky outline of Axel Blackthorne. He threw open the driver's door and jumped out with surprising quickness.

"Grace Able. I'm in a hurry!" Brandy cried to the guard. He looked up.

Blackthorne had reached her hatchback. He thrust his pallid face up to her window. She could hear his breath coming in gasps, see the shaggy brows and the wide–spaced front teeth.

"Get out!" he rasped. "I want to talk to you now."

When he seized the outside handle, her heart gave a sudden thud. She had not locked the doors. She saw the heavy fingers, the sapphire ring.

"Hey, just a minute!" the guard shouted, stepping out of the booth. "I don't think the lady wants to talk to you." Scowling, he strode up to Blackthorne. "I'm letting the lady through. You can get out of here." The wrought iron gate rolled to one side.

The developer dropped his hand and flailed a large arm at the guard, while Brandy shifted into drive and gunned the engine. "I got friends here!" The voice was Blackthorne's.

Brandy sped through the gate, hands shaking, and it clanged shut. In the rear view mirror she saw Blackthorne bull his way into the control booth, his voice still loud. She hadn't expected him. He wasn't part of her plans yet. She meant to see him later. "The best laid schemes of mice and men Gang aft agley," she thought. But she could not bear to turn back. This stage of her performance would not take long. Surely Steve would be here soon.

Along the deserted walkway the wind bent the crepe myrtles and lashed whitecaps on the surface of the lake. Grace sat on the same stone bench working stoically on her knitted shawl, a large rain coat folded beside her. She was dressed as she had been for the funeral, her hair held in place by a tidy scarf, her knitting bag in her lap. Brandy parked in an isolated spot near the red–tipped hedge, climbed out of the car, and glided on sandals toward her.

"I'm here again, Grace," she called. For a few minutes she stood before the bench, the dress whipping around her knees, the dark hair blowing about her face, and looked down into the drawn, unhappy eyes of Grace Able. "I have bad news for you. It's about Brookfield."

Grace's hands quivered slightly, but she did not appear surprised as she gathered up her needlepoint, laid it in the knitting bag, and threw the raincoat like a cape over her shoulders.

"I've been expecting you," she said. She looked toward the thick clouds in the west. The sky was the color of charcoal and heavy with the smell of rain. "Perhaps we should sit in my car. I parked near the bench. Mabel will be back soon. She might interrupt us in the apartment." She turned her pale, perfect face toward Brandy. "I'll be leaving town day after tomorrow."

They lowered their heads against the wind and Brandy followed Grace to her white Mercedes, nervously glancing about for Steve——or Blackthorne. A drop of rain spattered on the cement. While Grace stepped in and settled herself, Brandy hurried around to the passenger's side. The older woman waited, stiffly erect, her hands fumbling with the catch on her knitting bag. Deep in the clouds to the west lightning flared. Across the hedge Brandy heard a car door slam. She paused and peered through the fluttering leaves. Under a parking lot lamp shone the sleek body of the Cadillac. Blackthorne had talked his way in.

As Brandy snatched open the door, she heard heavy footsteps echo beyond the screen plantings. Blackthorne? She slipped into her seat, pulled the door closed, groped in the sudden dimness for the lock. She felt a movement beside her. Grace gave a thin cry, raised a shaking white glove above the steering wheel and pointed toward the passenger window. "Isn't that someone you know?"

Brandy jerked her head up, fingers still on the door sill, eyes straining. Through the rain she could see no one. "Where?"

A handle clicked, from nearby came a strange, exultant cry, then a crashing pain flamed in the back of Brandy's head. She slumped forward, barely conscious of footsteps splashing outside, of a beam of light sweeping over them. A man shouted, and the door was flung open.

Brandy's arm dropped. She felt rain, felt herself crumpling downward through open space, saw the wet pavement rise toward her, tasted salt. She thought in slow motion: she would hit the concrete, would never know the answer. Her eyes closed and she gave herself up to pain.

But she did not smash against the pavement. Instead, she fell onto something with give. Arms turned her body so that she faced upward. Her eyes flicked open. Her vision blurred. With a fierce chill she thought of Blackthorne. Then through the rain above her, she saw another face, one with high cheekbones, brown eyes, and a dripping mustache.

Far in the distance she heard a voice say, "Most unpredictable woman I ever met."

She thought vaguely, Steve must have brought John for back-up. Couldn't have asked another deputy. Not a Sheriff's Office operation.

Behind them a man's voice boomed, as if from miles away, "What the hell happened? Her head's all bloody!" It sounded like the guard.

"Call EMS! Hurry!" John, once again. The man retreated, running. Cradling her head, he gently lowered her onto the damp pavement.

"Relax. You're going to be all right. You took a nasty blow." He turned away and spoke to someone else. "Let me have that rain slicker."

From the other side of the car, as in a dream, she heard Steve's sharp voice, "Don't touch that hammer!"

Hearing's the last of the senses to go, Brandy thought, drifting, and hoped water would not ruin Steve's equipment.

She remembered stepping into her car, the footsteps, Grace telling her to look out the window, the click of a handle, and then the blow. John still knelt, spreading a rain cape over her. Running down her arm she could see pinkish water——maybe she was bleeding——then a riverlet of dark gray. The temporary rinse.

"You do try a man's patience," John said. Unlike the perfect, cautious Sharon, she thought, bitter in spite of the pain. Sharon would be waiting somewhere in warmth and comfort with Captain Able and his helpful wife. John added, "Lucky Steve kept track of you after you came through the gate."

"Never saw him," she whispered.

"You weren't supposed to."

As John tucked something soft under her head and pulled up the rain slicker, his dark eyes widened. "What in God's name? Eva Stone's dress!" She wanted to tell him about the all–important red dress with the white collar, about the belt buckle and the buttons, but she was too tired and her head ached. The strand of blue beads had broken and, one by one, rolled down her bodice and hit the pavement with tiny plinks. She lay close to John, rain cooling her face, and closed her eyes.

Fuzzily, she floated over the scene, saw the boat house, saw John and the snake, saw Sharon. Wondered if she had fallen against his sore arm. "Did I hurt you?"

"Not badly." A siren shrilled nearby. Tires screeched on wet concrete. Another ambulance, she thought, weary from the throbbing. Getting to be a habit.

Steve again, distant. "You have the right to remain silent..."

Grace's voice cut, pearl–like, through the din. "She came back. I knew her immediately. Ghost indeed! She never leaves me alone."

Brandy's eyelids fluttered. A numbness crept over her like the closing of a shutter. But she had proved her theory. Thinking of

Grace roused her. A line of Lady Macbeth's wafted through her head. "Look like the innocent flower," she whispered to John, "but be the serpent under it."

Twenty–Five

Rain spattered the window, and in the twilight the glistening fronds of a cabbage palm bobbed against the glass. Brandy lay propped on a pillow, aware of a sharp, medicinal odor, her aching head swathed in bandages. A nurse was shining a small bright light into her eyes, and behind her, others were waiting. Among the faces she could not find John's.

The nurse looked up at Brandy's mother, hovering at the other side of the bed. "No sign of irregularity," the nurse said. "The doctor's still checking for a subdural hematoma." Mrs. O'Bannon's forehead was deeply furrowed——maybe with worry, maybe with disapproval. Probably both. Her worst fears about newspaper reporting had come to pass.

"You have a lot of guests. Too many. They mustn't stay long," the nurse said and swept out of the room.

Around the walls ranged a variety of faces. Brandy was surprised to see Sylvania and Blackthorne, Mr. Tyler looking quizzical behind his horn–rimmed glasses, and Steve in uniform. Even Ace Langdon lounged in the doorway. She was not surprised to see Detective Morris draw up a chair beside her, his lips turned down tight, but the corners of his eyes crinkling. She felt like the prime exhibit in a museum.

The detective poised his ballpoint pen over a spiral note pad. "I think you've recovered enough to explain what you were doing at Grace Able's place."

Brandy savored the moment. "Only one scenario fit all the facts in the murder," she said, unrepentant but careful not to move her head. "I was sure I knew how Eva Stone was killed, but I couldn't prove it. My memory's woozy about what happened just before I was hit and afterward, but I know what I planned to do, and I guess I did it."

From the back of the room Steve shot her a wry grin. "You sure did," he said.

"I reasoned out the method first. Lily Mae Brown saw Eva Stone walk into the lake and disappear. Her shouts raised a search, so in the beginning I couldn't figure out how Eva's skeleton turned up later buried near the same spot. I thought maybe a strong swimmer had dragged her under the water, struck her several times, and hidden her body in the shrubbery.

"But how could all those searchers fail to see what was going on? And how could the murderer place the tire iron where it was needed, drag Eva out of the water, hit her repeatedly, and then conceal the body where all those searchers couldn't find it? There wasn't time. Lily Mae was pretty fast getting down those four flights of stairs." Brandy paused and looked around her.

"And then people kept saying I reminded them of Eva Stone. That gave me an idea. From the back, almost any young woman the right size might look like Eva, especially dressed like her. Maybe Eva was killed earlier, and someone took her place for that walk into the water. The only women still on the premises near Eva's age were Sylvania and Grace. Because of her height, Sylvania couldn't be mistaken for Eva. But Grace could be. That fact was the key.

"The whole process came to me after we learned about the tire iron and Eva's clothes. If Ace was telling the truth—— and he was——he'd put the tire iron in Grace's car behind the front seat."

From the doorway Ace nodded vigorously.

"Ace told us Grace was there after the tire was changed. Think about that scene. Blackthorne said Brookfield was coming back to the house early for an appointment, but the tire was changed before Brookfield got back. We know Eva came to the party for the sole purpose of telling Brookfield about the baby. She must've asked to see him. When she learned about his engagement to Grace, she must've believed he'd call the wedding off and marry her instead."

Sylvania dropped her head and looked at her large hands in silence.

Brandy glanced at Brookfield's devoted sister. "And he probably would have. But Eva never got the chance to tell him. She hadn't seen him alone all weekend, so she asked him to meet her. Said it was important. Then she made a fatal mistake. She decided it would only be fair to tell Grace. After all, Grace was in for a terrible shock.

"Eva didn't know Grace well. She'd didn't know Grace has a tendency to feel persecuted. She always sees herself as a victim. Even now I've seen the symptoms. When Eva followed Grace out to the car and told her about the baby, Eva explained she was going to tell Brookfield. Grace's greatest desire in life——to marry Brookfield——was not only threatened, but ended. She saw herself, not Eva, as the victim."

Sylvania put one hand on Blackthorne's arm, her angular face a study in concentration.

"It didn't take Grace long to choose a plan of action," Brandy went on. "She would've asked Eva to sit in her car, so they could talk. Then she seized the tire iron behind Eva—— probably used some trick to get her to turn around, just like she did me——maybe said she saw Brookfield coming——and then she struck Eva several times so quickly and so hard that Eva had no time to defend herself or even cry out.

"Grace knew that she had to make it look like Eva drowned. When the deputies found those buttons, the belt buckle, and the beads buried near the tire iron and not with the skeleton, I knew I was on the right track. It meant that Eva's dress had been removed from the body."

Morris's eyes darted toward Ace Langdon. "I'll admit I suspected a different kind of crime."

"But it was Grace who stripped off Eva's dress," Brandy continued. "It wouldn't have been easy, but the dress buttoned all the way down the front. She might've pulled it down over Eva's feet, then thrown sheets over the body to hide it. Remember, those sheets and towels had been stored in her trunk. No one would have thought anything of Grace opening her trunk, even if they'd seen her. And no one else was in the area. Then she slipped into the dress herself."

When Brandy began her explanation, Mr. Tyler had been standing with arms crossed and eyebrows raised. Now he was also taking notes.

"About that time Brookfield returned," Brandy said. "Lily Mae heard him say he was looking for Eva. Meanwhile, as soon as Grace concealed the body, she headed for the water. She may have been paranoid, but she was shrewd. Her plan wouldn't work unless someone saw a girl they thought was Eva go into the lake, so she rang that bell loudly, waded out, and waited until she heard Lily Mae call out to her from the upstairs window. Then Lily Mae and Henry Washington saw her go under.

"I puzzled about the bell from the beginning. It was unlikely that it rang by accident. More likely it rang on purpose. That didn't make sense if Eva was committing suicide. But it made sense if an imposter faked a drowning."

Sylvania exhaled, her face no longer as tense. "After all these years,"she said, "Lily Mae will be glad to learn she couldn't have prevented Eva Stone's death."

"I plan to tell her myself," Brandy said. "To Grace, Lily Mae was just a tool. When Grace heard Lily Mae call out, she walked quickly out into the water. She was a good swimmer and Mabel says she still is. She sank down and swam under water around that spit of land. She would've climbed out on the other side of the bougainvillea hedge, while Lily Mae was still hurrying down those four flights of stairs. Grace was blocked from view by the hedge when she ran to her car, jumped in, and took off. Everyone remembered that she was gone before the search was well underway. Mr. Blackthorne saw her pass him on the road."

"Cold–blooded bitch," the developer said, then glanced at Sylvania and added more quietly, "You mean she drove into town with Eva's body on the seat beside her?"

"She must have. Once we knew Eva didn't drown, I was puzzled because the body wasn't found during the search. I figured somebody spirited it away somehow."

Fully interested now, Ace eased farther into the room. "How was the body buried, then, back on the property?"

"There's just one explanation. I imagine Aunt Sylvania knows. Grace couldn't have managed the job by herself. After the search failed, Brookfield drove into town to tell the Stones that their daughter had apparently drowned. He also told Grace. That's when she must have confessed the crime to him.

"Probably she told him she had panicked when Eva threatened to take him away from her. Eva was a beauty, remember? Grace knew that Brookfield once had a hot romance going with Eva. Grace would've said Eva claimed he was still in love with her, that he was marrying Grace for her money. I'm sure she told him she lost all control at the thought of losing him and struck Eva with what was handy, the tire iron. She may even have claimed that Eva attacked her first, out of jealousy. Grace would certainly have said that she never meant to kill her.

"But what about the baby?" It was Sylvania, her voice unusually soft.

"Grace couldn't risk telling him about the baby," Brandy said. "If she had, she knew Brookfield would bite the bullet and turn her in. But he believed it was a terrible accident, the result of a fight between the two women. He probably felt responsible because he'd had the affair with Eva the previous year. So he loaded the body in his trunk and agreed to bury it on the Ables' property. He could conceal it there more easily than anywhere else, especially since all those grounds had already been searched.

"The police never had any reason to check Grace's car for evidence. No one suspected a murder. Grace had plenty of time to clean up the car and the towels and sheets she'd wrapped the body in. No one but the Stones would understand the motive, and they weren't talking because they wanted the baby. Anyhow, they thought Eva had killed herself because of Brookfield."

Sylvania raised her head. She was wearing her usual loose smock–dress and black oxfords, but even in those clothes she had dignity. "Miss O'Bannon's right, I'm afraid. I admit that she's lifted a burden I've carried for years." Her long fingers gripped Blackthorne's arm. "I do know now how it was done, but I didn't understand until a few days ago.

"My burden was heaviest last week, when I found out about Weston Stone." For the first time she bestowed on Brandy a fleeting smile. "I heard Brookfield out by the bougainvillea hedge the night after Eva Stone disappeared. He'd brought Grace back to the house with him." Her voice took on an ironic edge. "He said to help his mother cope with the Stones.

"We'd searched all along the lake already, but Brookfield said he wanted to look again. He was gone so long, I thought maybe he'd found something. In about an hour, I followed him. When I got near the hedge, I heard him digging." She looked down briefly. "I don't know what I thought, but I was worried. I called out to him. He said he was digging all along the shore, trying to uncover some sign of the body. I believed him."

Brandy spoke softly. "Brookfield didn't dare hire a carpenter when he built the boat house over the grave, afraid they'd uncover the body. John spotted an amateur's hand. I wondered then why a man of his wealth would do the job himself."

Grimly, Sylvania nodded.

Brandy probed Sylvania's response in the same quiet tone. "Later he must have told you something nearer the truth."

Sylvania clasped her hands before her. "When he knew he didn't have long to live, he told me he was leaving me the house. He asked me to promise never to sell it to anyone to live in. When I questioned him about it, he put his hand in mine and promised on his immortal soul that he'd never hurt anyone himself nor done anything truly wrong. He said his request was for the good of the family."

She paused. "He also made me promise that if anything ever happened to Mabel, I'd see that Grace was taken care of. I didn't make any connection between the two requests at the time. I loved my brother and I believed him. Now I think he protected her from herself all her life. That's why he employed Mabel."

She folded her hands together. "I wonder now if Grace's mental condition kept them from having children. Maybe when she didn't get her way, she was still violent. That would explain some odd, nervous spells he said she had. Maybe he was afraid the tendency was hereditary. I know there were rumors that she was unstable."

Brandy nodded, remembering Mack's remark about the Able women. "And when you learned that he had a son by Eva Stone?"

"I was devastated. I thought Brookfield had abandoned his child. I remembered his digging that night. I thought he'd lied to me. He'd murdered Eva and buried her body. I thought that was why he didn't want anyone else living there ——because they might discover the body."

"And did you tell Mr. Blackthorne about your fears?"

Sylvania twisted her big hands together and looked at the portly man beside her. "I had to confide in someone, even before I learned about Weston. I finally told him about my promise to Brookfield, and he agreed to help me. I'd wanted to move for years. That house gave me a terrible feeling all the time I lived there." She shuddered. "I've never talked about it to anyone. But there was something there. Something on that fourth floor. Something on the lawn at night. I felt like a prisoner in my own house. There were places in it I didn't dare go. When Brookfield and Grace lived there, they had the same feeling." Her tone grew harsh. "Grace must have been especially frightened."

Steve spoke up again. "She said Eva never left her alone."

Sylvania sighed. "So Axel offered to buy it, tear down every plank, and the boat house, too, and build over it. He said at last I'd be free of my promise to Brookfield, and get some money out of it, too."

Sylvania looked at the heavy face of Axel Blackthorne with a gaze both reproving and tender. "He blundered around trying to help me, trying to frighten off your investigation.

First, so John wouldn't save the house. Then when you found the skeleton, he tried even harder. He had you followed by the security guard who worked at the new development. He just wanted to find out what you were up to and discourage you."

Brandy tried to sit up straight, then winced and sank slowly back. Her mother, who had been unnaturally silent, frowned.

"But it must've been Grace who tried to do me in at the garage," Brandy said. "She was researching something at the library the day I interviewed her at her apartment. I expect the subject was carbon monoxide poisoning. She also used a computer at her condominium."

Morris stopped writing. "We think she cased your place Friday afternoon, while you were both at work, and left the note. The neighbor heard a car. A clever plan. It might have worked, except for your dog."

Meg should be here, Brandy thought. Meg and someone else.

Blackthorne avoided Brandy's eyes. "Today I was on my way to see Grace myself when I spotted you," he said. "By then Syl and I both believed Brookfield had killed Eva. I thought Grace must know the truth, and you were going to worm it out of her. I wanted to convince her not to talk to you——or else convince you to give up the investigation. By then, I was desperate. It would break Syl's heart if the whole town learned Brookfield had murdered that girl." He dropped his head. "I called a friend from the guard shack and got in just in time to call the ambulance." Sylvania smiled again. "The first thing he did right, I'm afraid." She patted him on the arm. "But he did it all for me, mistaken though we both were. And that's the end of it."

A deep voice spoke from the rear. "So my father didn't murder my mother, after all." Weston Stone had appeared in the doorway and signaled to Steve. Steve must've called him, Brandy realized. He had more right to know the whole story than anyone else.

"The worst your father did was try to protect the girl he was engaged to," Brandy said. "Lots of men protect the women they love." Even women they don't, she thought sadly, remembering John. "Your father never knew you existed."

Ace Langdon cleared his throat. "I can confirm some details. When Miss O'Bannon didn't show up at the cocktail hour today, I phoned the *Beacon* office. Mr. Tyler told me what had happened, and I thought, 'No problem. I'll just go over to the hospital to see her.' I'd remembered something that might clear me. I called the Sheriff's Office, too." He paused and ran well–manicured fingers through his gray mane. "After I put the tire iron behind the front seat, I saw Eva walking toward Grace's car. That's the last time I saw her. That's why I didn't talk to her, and why I went back to the house and played billiards instead." When his eyes caught Sylvania's gaze, he looked away.

"That puts the two of them together at the crucial moment," Brandy said.

"I ought to get a medal for living in that house at all," Ace muttered. "I dare anyone else to stay very long in my room on the third floor, let alone on the fourth. I bolted my door, I can tell you that."

Morris ignored Ace's last complaint and turned to Brandy. "Why did you make appointments this afternoon with Mr. Langdon and Mr. Blackthorne? And why did you wind up at Grace's getting your head bashed?"

She lifted her chin and winced again. "I meant to tape Grace's reaction to my costume and to what I said. I was going to share the recording with everyone involved—— including Detective Morris.

"After I got to know Grace a little, I decided she tended to be paranoid. She was suspicious and watchful. I noticed it at the flower show, the condominium, and the funeral. She thought people picked on her. A psychologist told me that people like Grace can function perfectly well most of the time, but they have unstable spells. That explained the frequent trips with Mabel to Canada. And the fact that Brookfield had hired Mabel for so many years as Grace's companion. The psychologist also told me that paranoid patients can mistake someone in the present for a supposed enemy in their past."

Steve spoke up again. "Therefore the dress."

"If I was going to force a confession, I had to trigger that paranoia. Grace was already beginning to see me as her persecutor. Perhaps I could become Eva Stone and meet Grace in a place like the one where she last saw Eva. The lake shore was perfect. I wanted to phrase every word carefully, so she could associate it with Eva Stone as well as with me. I told her I had bad news about Brookfield. I imagine Eva said about the same thing.

"I liked the irony of disguising myself as Eva. Grace had pretended to be Eva, too. I thought Grace would give herself away when she saw me, and I'd get her on tape."

She grinned and motioned to her bandages. "But I didn't intend to sit in a car with her, like Eva did. When it began to rain, I hadn't much choice. My memory of what happened next is still awfully dim. I didn't expect her to have a hammer in that wretched knitting bag." She looked back at Steve. "I hope your equipment wasn't smashed."

"It's okay, but we didn't need the recording. I heard Grace say you were Eva and so did John and Mr. Blackthorne, and even the guard at the gate. He came running over when he saw there was trouble. She kept babbling about how she'd finally finished the job. Said Eva wouldn't be bothering her anymore. I expect she meant to throw that big raincoat over your body and drive out the way she did before."

There was a movement by the door, and suddenly the room grew more crowded. Ace looked up, murmured, "No problem" in an irritated tone and moved aside. Brandy looked up eagerly, but the tall figure muscling his way across the room was not John.

"What kinda job you got, kid? Like they say in sports, you're snakebit. Ever time I see you, you're in the damn hospital. We got to talk."

Brandy gave him a feeble wave. Coping with a psycho was hard enough. Now she had to cope with Mack.

TWENTY–SIX

Brandy reached for Mack's hand. "Wait until we can talk privately," she said.

Mrs. O'Bannon rose to give Mack her chair and turned on Brandy her severe look. "I'd better get home and feed Meg. You rest now, hear? The doctor says you'll be in the hospital about twenty–four hours. I'll be back in the morning." At least the garage escapade had earned Meg her mother's affection. His father's lucrative car agency made her feel the same about Mack.

All but Detective Morris took the cue. Weston left, quietly talking to his newly discovered aunt. Brandy heard him say he would meet John and Mr. Greene at the Lake Dora house tomorrow afternoon. Sylvania agreed to be there. Brandy wished she could join them. Ace paused in the doorway, winked, and gave her his dimpled smile, while Mr. Tyler stretched and put his note pad back in his breast pocket.

"Tonight's the deadline for my story," Brandy said to him in a voice grown hoarse. "I've got the lead in my head. I hope it's not too late for this week's edition."

Tyler lifted out the pad again. "Shoot."

Brandy dictated slowly with only a few pauses. "A murder of forty–five years ago was re–enacted by the killer at the Lakeview condominiums on Lake Harris Monday afternoon. Grace Southerland Able's attack on *Beacon* reporter Brandy O'Bannon brought to a successful close the investigation into the murder of Eva Stone, daughter of Anne and the late Richard Stone of Tavares. Miss Stone's skeleton was found recently on the Lake Dora property of Mrs. Able's deceased husband.

"O'Bannon's costume, which duplicated the dress and jewelry the victim wore the night of the killing, apparently triggered a latent paranoia in the murderer, according to a prominent Gainesville psychologist. Before witnesses Mrs. Able struck the reporter with a hammer in the same way that she is alleged to have struck Miss Stone with a tire iron. Sheriff's authorities confirmed that Grace Able later confessed to the earlier crime."

"My final notes," she added, "are on my desk at the *Beacon*."

Brandy stopped and took a deep breath. The painkiller was beginning to wear off. "I guess you'll have to finish the story yourself. My original notes are in a notebook in my bedroom at home. The first draft with the history of the house is on the office laptop and the photos beside it."

She had made her deadline, but John had not. He still had no buyer for Sylvania's house.

Mr. Tyler thrust the note pad and pen into his pocket again. "The *Beacon's* going to press," he said, grinning, and strode out the door.

"An editor right out of *Front Page*," Brandy said fondly, then shifted her attention to the detective. "Our paper's distributed Wednesday morning. I hope the Sheriff's Office won't release all the details until then. That would give Mr. Tyler a day to print. It'd be nice if he could scoop the big dailies just once."

"I'd as soon check some things out before the briefing," Morris said.

"What do you think will happen to Grace?"

He stroked his bristly mustache. "She's a Signal 20, all right. A real psycho. She also took things from other apartments at the condominium. We've had complaints from the manager." Brandy remembered Grace's maid saying she had to return something that belonged to another resident. "I expect she'll be committed to a psychiatric hospital."

"I feel sorry for Mabel."

"Her companion may be able to help her there. She'll probably want to. She's worked for Grace so long she's a little addled herself."

"Grace told me there was something evil in the house. There was. It was Grace herself."

A buzzer sounded on the hospital intercom, and the nurse reappeared in the doorway. "Visiting hours are over," she said. Morris nodded and followed Tyler.

Brandy sank back on the pillow, suddenly weary.

"Finally." Mack gazed up at the nurse. "I need a few minutes more." The woman looked at the blond wavy hair, the earnest blue eyes, and melted. "Just a few, now, really."

Brandy took his hand again when they were alone. "It's no use, Mack," she said in a quiet voice. "I'm not being fair to you. We're going in different directions."

Mack's jaw went hard. "It's that half–assed architect, right?"

"No, Mack," she said truthfully. "You and I——we've got nothing in common. We couldn't make a life together. You deserve the kind of woman who'll appreciate all you have to offer. I'm not that girl."

He pulled his arm away and dropped his head. "That's pretty tough to take——after all the years we've dated, all the laughs we've had."

"I promised you an answer when this case went down. This is it." She felt her eyes grow damp. "I'm so sorry, Mack."

He rose to his full height then, big hands on his hips. "Sorry, like hell," he said.

Sighing, Brandy lay back and closed her eyes.

        *   *   *

She sat in the back of a small boat with her father, Lake Dora glinting around them in the sunlight. He reached into the bait can. "Now you wouldn't fish for a fresh water bass with a salt water rig," he said, threading a worm onto her hook. "You've got to use the right bait for the right fish."

She flung her line out into the water and waited for the bobber to sink.

The boat and the lake faded. With a sucking sound, Brandy sank. She was standing alone on an outcropping at the bottom of a deep well. In the darkness she clawed at the slick, narrow walls, struggling for breath. Around her feet gurgled rising water. She thought she could hear a cottonmouth's fat body slither along the rock. Far above at the opening shone a distant patch of light. She tried to call out, but no sound would come. Footsteps echoed near the light. Then a face looked down, one with high cheekbones, dark eyes, a mustache. She tried to cry out again. Still no sound.

"Don't come in, please," a familiar voice said. "I've tried to explain. I'm sorry, but I'm afraid it's over between us." Then the face withdrew.

When Brandy stifled a groan, the well slipped way. She raised her hand and felt bandages, saw a square of light from the corridor and a woman in the doorway. Brandy could make out the blonde, tousled hair, the slim figure in tight jeans. "I want to see her," the woman said. "Just talk to her."

Now the man moved again into the light. "Sharon, please go home. She can't see you. She's been hurt. We can talk later." Heels spun around, clacked on the terrazzo floor, receded.

John moved silently into the room, leaned across her bed, and switched off the overhead lamp. "When I was in the hospital after the snake bite, I tried to tell you how I felt about you, but you kept blabbing on about Sharon and your boyfriend. I saw him leave a little while ago. He looked bent out of shape. As for me, I didn't want to be here with all the others." She moved her head and watched him place a tape player on the bedside table. "The only thing that seems right for you now," he said, "is Copland's 'Fanfare for the Common Man.'" Brandy remembered its soaring heroics.

She opened her lips, but still no sound came. John kissed the one spot on her forehead that was not swathed in a circular bandage. "Life would be forever dull without you."

She closed her eyes, warm and tingly down to her toes. Maybe she had used the right bait, after all. Then her lids flipped open. "You're forgetting," she murmured. "We're not finished yet. There's still the house, and what about the ghost?"

*　　　　　*　　　　　*

The following summer, as John and Brandy stepped out of the pontoon boat onto the pier, bromiliads sent scarlet heads shooting up under the live oaks around the Able mansion. Behind them, a crimson band marked the passage of the setting sun. In a thicket of wax myrtle at the water's edge, a cloud of cattle egrets had settled for the evening. A black and white sign nailed to a post on the dock read HISTORIC ABLE INN AND RESTAURANT.

"I miss the 'gator," Brandy said.

"Probably gone farther up the shore like the ospreys, where there won't be any more building."

Within the curved lines of the tiny harbor bobbed two pontoons, a small cabin cruiser, and several motorboats.

"No story tonight," John said. "No more sleuthing."

On a flagstone terrace beneath the high windows of the second floor, guests were seated at wrought iron tables, sampling an appetizer buffet.

Weston Stone advanced toward them across the lawn, his hand extended. "We have a nice room ready," he said, "on the fourth floor. I'll have your bags carried up."

Brandy glanced up at a dormer window, remembering the shadow that had once moved behind the glass.

"I offered her a honeymoon in a fancy Orlando hotel," John said, shaking hands. "But she insisted on coming to your grand opening instead."

Brandy noticed that Blackthorne's manufactured homes were concealed by a thick bougainvillea, ablaze with lavender, where one had stood almost fifty years ago. "You've got a clever landscaper," she said.

They followed Weston up a flight of stairs above the cement bays, now entrances into a kitchen, laundry, and work area, to a second floor deck, crowded with chattering couples, and entered what had been the parlor, now the dining area. Its focal point was the fireplace portrait of Brookfield Able, his stern gaze a sharp contrast to the broadly smiling face of his son. They admired the shining cypress woodwork, the re-furbished floors, the delicate egret wallpaper, the restored mantle, the Tiffany lamps.

Rising above the other diners, Brandy saw Sylvania's tall form. She sat at a table near the staircase, beaming at Weston's elder son, beside her the bulky figure of Axel Blackthorne.

"Curt Greene's been generous with your time," Weston said to John, showing them to a table below the stained glass fanlight. "Greene's lucky to have you on his staff. I couldn't have done the restoration without your research. As it was, it took months for crews working night and day to get this place ready for the anniversary."

John leaned across the table as Weston moved away to greet other guests. "Aunt Sylvania says Brookfield would've wanted his son to have the house, but restoring it as an inn and restaurant was Weston's idea."

Brandy looked out at the dark rim of the opposite shore, and her voice dropped. "It's ironic that I owe my new job to reports of Eva Stone's ghost."

With one hand John opened his menu. With the other he rubbed his forehead in that familiar gesture. "Let that go, Brandy," he said. "Forget it. You got your story a year ago."

She smiled then, and ordered, and tried not to look at the growing shadows on the terrace. After dinner they carried their cordial glasses downstairs to a cocktail table. A few low density lamps glowed around the outer flagstones. From speakers hidden in the cypress came the plaintive Irish melody —— *"it was a moment when I sensed a miss in the beat of time..."*

Inside the crowd had thinned, a murmur of voices drifted from the parking lot. The deck and terrace were deserted. Weston Stone stood on the pier under a moonless sky, helping the last boat customer cast off.

"It was just about this time of night," Brandy said. "Remember? When we found the skeleton. When I left you here." To herself she added, when I saw the form in the window, and later on the lawn.

"Not a night I like to recall."

The lighted boat pulled away and was lost beyond the palmet-toes and cabbage palms to the east. The only movement came from the lank silhouette of Weston Stone, coiling a line around a post on the pier. A chill passed through her. She pulled her light jacket around her shoulders and took a sip from her glass, her eyes on the bougainvillea. "I thought everyone out here had gone," she said, touching John's arm. "There's someone over there alone."

"I don't see anyone."

"Over there..." A slender form wavered in the shadow of the hedge, dark hair stirring in the slight wind, and looked toward Weston Stone.

Brandy's eyes widened. "My God," she whispered. "I can see a white border below the head and a smudge of red fabric. Can't you see it?"

The pale face lifted and turned for a moment in the terrace lights, its soft lines blurred, and then it began to fade, like the petals of a flower closing.

John's hand folded over hers. "Nothing there. The power of suggestion."

Brandy's own fingers trembled and then quieted. All that remained before her were the lavender blooms of the bougainvil-lea.

"Get real," he said. "You think hatred for Grace held Eva Stone here all these years?"

Brandy lifted his hand to her lips. "Not hate. Eva Stone was here because of something much stronger. Don't you know who she's been waiting for?" Surely, Brandy thought, she had seen a mother with her child at last.

She reached up and smoothed away the frown gathering on his forehead. "Not long ago who would've believed in neutrinos and quarks? But think what you like. We're certainly alone now."

"No more ghost talk," he said, drawing her close. "I've got something more substantial in mind."

As he slipped his arm around her waist and they turned toward the stairs, Brandy cast a last long look at the night sky. Undefiled by lights from the town, it rose above the tall house——black, serene, and splendid with stars.

Afterword

Tavares and Mount Dora are charming small towns that cluster near the Harris Chain of five large lakes in Central Florida. The Dora Canal, although usually packed these days with sight-seeing boaters, is one of the most beautiful short stretches of natural river in the state.

The lyrics of the Irish ballads in the book are actually from poems in *Prose and Verse Anthology of Modern Irish Writing*, edited by Grattan Freyer, Irish Humanities Center, Dublin, published in 1979.

> "It was a moment when I sensed
> A miss in the beat of time..."
> "On a frosty night
> and a bashful star
> Stood above a hill
> Frozen in the sky ..."
> from "That Moment" by S.E. O'Cearbhail, p. 3, 4

> "O you are not lying in the wet clay,
> For it is a harvest evening now and we
> Are piling up the ricks against the moonlight
> And you smile up at us —— eternally.
> *from "In Memory of My Mother"*
> *by Patrick Kavanagh, p.98*

About the Author

Ann Turner Cook began life as the model for the Gerber Products trademark, and her works emphasize the bond between mother and child. A member of Mystery Writers of America, the retired English teacher and her husband research her novels among the rivers, lakes, and small towns of Central Florida. The couple lives in Tampa.